Her Unsuitable Match

Her Unsuitable Match

SALLY BRITTON

PINK
CITRUS
BOOKS

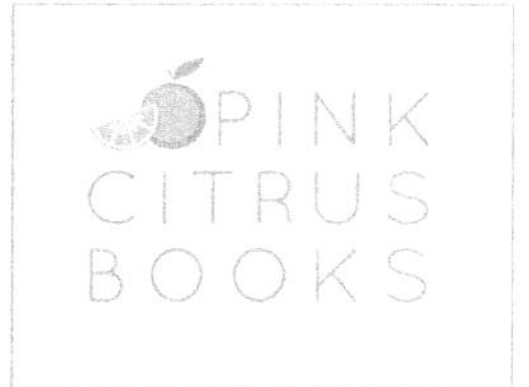

Published by Pink Citrus Books
Edited by Jenny Proctor of Midnight Owl Editors
Cover design by Ashtyn Newbold
Cover photo licensed through Arcangel

Sally Britton
www.authorsallybritton.com

First Printing: October 2021

For the Broken in Heart or Spirit,
May this Story of Love Offer a Small Respite

One

The stifling heat of the ballroom combined with a heavy fog of perfume pressed in around Philippa until her head ached and her vision swam. Three hours. She had danced, deflected flirtatious comments, and feigned interest in the small talk of her partners for three incessant hours.

All the while, her mother—Fredericka, Countess of Montecliff—stood near an open window, fanning herself. Her unrelenting gaze kept Philippa where she belonged, in the center of the room with no hope for escape.

"You are the epitome of grace, my lady," Philippa's partner simpered, bowing as the second dance in their set at last came to an end. Though Philippa knew it wasn't his fault, his voice had a distinctly nasal quality to it, and she had to fight a wince every time he spoke to her. "I do hope you will favor me with your partnership again, my lady. It has been a great honor."

"You are too kind, my lord." She forced a smile as her temples pulsed, as though twin miners had taken up residence in her head and pounded her skull with their pickaxes in perfect sync.

He frowned when her polite words did not offer a ready agreement to his proposal, though he still offered her escort to her mother's side.

Perhaps he would take Philippa's disinterest as a hint and not bother calling on her the next day. That might upset her mother, given the man held a title and estates in both England and Jamaica. The dowager countess would certainly blame Philippa for not encouraging him to call the next day. But then, Mother blamed many things on Philippa of late.

Especially Philippa's unmarried state.

The inducement to wed that most unmarried daughters of the *ton* felt with keenness eluded Lady Philippa Gillensford. As the daughter and now sister of an earl, she made a tempting target for many gentlemen and nobles. They saw her for her position and the connections it would give to *them*, not as a person. Thus she had shocked several of her formerly enthusiastic callers when she proved she had a functioning mind and strong opinions that differed from theirs.

Yes, Mother had reason for frustration.

But so did Philippa.

When it was just the two of them standing near the window, Philippa flicked open her fan and did her best to cool her face and neck with the inadequate bursts of air the lace-and-paper accessory afforded her.

"The duke's grandson did not appear happy," Mother said from behind her own fan. "You did not share your opinions on the sugar tariffs again, did you?"

Philippa beat the air faster with her fan. "No, Mother. You made it very clear that I cannot discuss political topics at balls."

"Then why did he look so cross?"

"Perhaps he always looks that way," Philippa ventured. She looked to the window near them, cracked open only a few inches. "Do you think we might step out for a moment, Mother? A little fresh air might be just the thing to perk both of us up."

"I am not a flower in need of *perking up*." The dowager snorted. "And Baron Bramber is approaching. You will dance with him, but do not encourage his attentions overmuch, dear. He is only a baron, after all." Her nose wrinkled as though dancing with barons was as distasteful as stepping in horse droppings.

Philippa smiled politely when the baron asked her to dance, and she treated him with the same distant respect that she had all her other partners that evening. While her feet took her through the motions, and her face remained a mask of appropriate enthusiasm, her mind dwelled on the ball she would attend the next evening. A much happier affair, and something she had looked forward to for more than a month.

Her brother, Adam, and his wife, Elaine, were hosting a charity ball at one of London's newest and most luxurious hotels.

Nothing delighted Philippa as much as the memory of her mother's face when she received the invitation. Everyone in London wanted to see the inside of the hotel's ballroom, the foyer, and the gardens rumored to be as fine as those at Kensington Palace. That Adam and Elaine had secured the hotel to host a charitable event had made Mother turn the unbecoming shade of puce.

"Is something amusing, Lady Philippa?"

When the baron's question interrupted her thoughts, Philippa swiftly schooled her features into an indifferently pleasant expression once more. "Do forgive me, my lord. I am afraid my thoughts were already on tomorrow evening. Perhaps you have heard that my brother and his wife, Mr. Gillensford and Mrs. Gillensford, are hosting a ball at Bell's Hotel?"

"Ah, yes. From what I understand, it is to be one of the finest events of the Season." That the baron said such made her more kindly disposed toward him. Until he added, "If one can even classify a charity event as such a thing. Given that they sent invitations out to common soldiers, it lacks the exclusivity of the private balls and assemblies."

Nothing made her so cross as people in Society disparaging what her brother and sister-in-law sought to do with their time and money. Thanks to an inheritance left to them by Philippa's late great-uncle, Adam and Elaine had the ability to dedicate their lives and much of their fortune to helping others. The *ton* ought to have admired their decision to solicit funds for a hospital—a hospital meant to help soldiers recover from battle in a quiet, safe place. And meant to see to

the needs of the soldiers' families while the men were away fighting for their country.

With her chin raised, Philippa briefly joined hands with her dance partner as the steps called for and spoke with a haughty tone she had learned from her mother. "I have heard that Lord Nelson himself will be in attendance."

The baron shrugged, unimpressed, and Philippa avoided speaking another word more than necessary for the remainder of their set.

Again and again, the situation repeated itself. Smiling, curtsying, dancing with strangers. Her mother whispered instructions before each dance, between sets, and while they walked around the humid, hot room.

"You cannot avoid marriage forever," Mother said when the evening drew to a close. Her frustration rose to the surface, her whispers becoming hisses. "It is ungrateful to your brother, and to me, to withhold your hand from a prosperous match. You have a duty to our family to lift Society's eyes to us—to strengthen our place amidst our peers."

Philippa remained silent, though her mother's words hurt. The dowager countess wanted things that her daughter had never wanted.

"You're behaving selfishly," her mother added. "It is a daughter's duty to wed and wed well. Georgiana understood this responsibility—why don't you?"

Much later that night—truly, in the early hours of the next day—Philippa collapsed into her bed with a weary groan. Her feet hurt. Her head ached. And in a few hours, she had to rise and dress to receive callers. More posturing. More pretending. She hated it.

During the carriage ride home, her mother had ceased talking but had commenced glaring. Despite Philippa knowing her own mind, her mother's censure was no less irritating. Mothers were supposed to be sympathetic to their children, weren't they?

Her sister-in-law, Elaine, was kind and compassionate with her two adopted children, and would certainly be so with the babe she had born a few short months before.

But then, Mother railed against Elaine's place in the family every

chance she had. Despite Elaine's kindness. Despite the grandchild Elaine had provided. The dowager countess acted as though Elaine's marriage into the family had created a scandal too great to live down. When, in fact, Society openly welcomed Elaine everywhere she went. Perhaps because of her money, initially, and her eye for fashion. But once people came to know Philippa's sister-in-law, they couldn't help but love her. No one kinder existed anywhere on earth.

Although happy for Adam and Elaine, there were moments when Philippa wished there *had* been a scandal. At least enough of one to keep their family in the country for a single Season. Hiding away from spiteful gossips and scheming bachelors.

Philippa loved the Season. But she hated the marriage mart. She had heard from friends that—once married—the time spent in London held many delights. No one had to stay at a ball longer than they wished. They could come and go from other events without worrying overmuch about what the gossips observed and spoke about later. Married women were protected from snobbery and criticism in a way no single lady was ever afforded.

It might be worth it—to marry someone—if only to end the constant speculation of others.

Philippa laughed quietly to herself and pressed a cool cloth to her forehead.

At three and twenty, she no longer felt the eagerness of a girl fresh from the schoolroom. She had no desire to marry in order to please her family or anyone else. When she married, it would be to please herself.

The dark shadows of her room painted swaths of gray forests upon her ceiling. Her eyes traced the imaginary branches, despite how heavy with fatigue they remained. She blinked, then gave in and closed them.

According to her father's will, upon her most recent birthday, she had won access to her full inheritance. Every pound meant as a dowry to tempt bachelors belonged to her, even if she never married. But her horrid eldest brother, Richard, kept finding reasons to delay the transfer of her funds into her name. More than once, she had thought about finding a solicitor to force the issue. But her family had already

undergone a painful fracture with Adam's marriage to Elaine, a former seamstress-turned-heiress.

Philippa didn't particularly want to begin a new war with her mother, brothers, sisters-in-law, and sister. What harm did it do for her to spend one more Season doing her mother's bidding? The money would still be there come summer, and then she would make Richard give it over to her.

And she would finally do as she pleased.

That thought made Philippa smile and think markedly happier thoughts as she finally slipped into peaceful slumber.

Two

The quiet hung heavily in the night air, thick as a fog. The lack of moonlight meant Myles couldn't see much farther than the tip of his nose. He heard the shifting of the men around him, their whispered complaints, and someone snored despite the mounting anxiety felt by his fellows.

Myles gripped the butt of his pistol tighter and attempted to force back a rising sense of wrongness. He could practically smell it, like acrid smoke and gunpowder. He'd been ordered to keep his men here. Yet an itching sensation in his heart made him want to move. Did he dare go against orders?

He struggled with instinct, wary of trusting himself when those ranked above him could make his life more a misery than it was at present. Surely his men deserved more from him, though.

He hesitated too long.

From far away, he heard the boom of what he knew, despite his hopes, was not thunder. A cannon had fired. But where? From their side, or the enemy's? And how? The enemy had to be as blind as Myles and his men.

Everyone woke. Flashes in the distance, coupled with the sound of rifle-rounds shot, brought everyone first to their feet and then their knees as they tried to duck down.

Who was foolish enough to begin a battle in the dead of night? Dawn was still hours away. Myles shouted for order, demanded his men pay attention to him—and then he fell forward, propelled by a force he couldn't see. He put his hand out to catch himself, and another flash of light revealed why it hurt when his palm made contact with the ground. He crumpled, gasping and uncertain of what he'd seen. He heard a loud ringing in his ear, until sound came roaring back to him.

Confusion reigned as his men shouted and scrambled to fall back, and someone took his arm to help. A pain in his shoulder and the fire in his left arm nearly brought him down. More gunfire, scattered from behind and on all sides, made him stumble. But he kept moving. Kept trying to get to safety and make sense—

An explosion of air knocked him backward, a tree he hadn't known was there shattered, and the pain was too much—too great. Then there was more screaming...

Myles sat up in bed, drenched in sweat, the screams still echoing in his head. He didn't shout, though. He kept his lips pressed shut, as he had that night, too. That night so many years ago—he hated to think on it. Never did, if he could help it. And he had thought himself winning at last when it came to repressing the memories of battle.

He covered his face with both hands and took several deep, measured breaths. Then he reached for the curtains surrounding his bed and ripped them open, desperate for sunlight. He was in luck. He hadn't woken from his nightmare in the dark hours; the faint yellow light of London's morning sun came whisper-soft through the windows of his small, rented room.

He knew why he'd had the dream.

Myles strode with purpose to the small desk near the window and sat in the chair, not caring that he'd left his robe behind on a hook by the bed. No one was around to see him, half-unclothed, or to remark upon the twists of skin on shoulder and chest where a Frenchman's round had passed through his body.

He picked up the letter, and its accompanying invitation, from one of his oldest friends. Truthfully, one of the only friends he had left. It wasn't that he hadn't wanted to maintain the relationships that had

been his before he went to war—merely that it had become too difficult.

The letter was brief. Written in Joshua Moreton's usual cheery style. The letter encouraged Myles to accept an invitation from Mr. and Mrs. Gillensford to their ball, as one of their honored guests, held that very evening. Moreton had sent his letter to Myles the week previous. Moreton had promised that Myles would enjoy himself. That the ball would be full of beautiful ladies. He insisted the host and hostess would need men like Myles present if they were to achieve their goal of raising funds for a veteran's hospital. "A most worthy cause," his friend had said.

"I am not a cause," Myles muttered to his friend's letter, narrowing his good eye at the paper. There wasn't enough light yet to read the faintly inked words, but Myles knew every bit of it by now.

He also knew what Moreton would say. *You aren't a cause, but you can help with one that benefits men like you.*

The truth of that thought, imagined as it was in his friend's voice, had kept Myles from tossing the invitation into the fire.

How different might things have been for him if there had been some place, and people, dedicated to helping men like him? Men so scarred, physically and mentally, from war that they hardly knew how to exist in a world of peace.

Myles dropped the letter and pushed both hands through his wild hair. He put his elbows on the desk—and it tilted. Again.

Muttering to himself about poor accommodations, Myles lifted the piece of furniture and felt around with one foot until he found the slim volume of sonnets he kept beneath the short leg to even out the plane of the desk. He pushed it back to where it belonged, and the desk settled evenly again.

What right did a man like him have to attend balls? Even charitable ones. He couldn't even afford a desk with even legs.

He left the invitation and letter both where they were and went about his preparations for the day. He scrubbed himself clean with the pitcher and basin of water in his room, grateful for the cool water that brought him more fully awake. He rubbed at the whiskers on his face

and sighed. He needed to find a barber, or risk looking like a madman let loose upon London's streets.

Myles dressed with military-efficiency, the missing fingers on his left hand not slowing him at all. Then he found his eyepatch on top of the small bureau that held all his worldly possessions. He covered his left eye and completely avoided his reflection in the mirror above that same chest of drawers.

He put a hat on his head—an unfashionable tricorn that had seen better days—and took himself out the door.

London's streets were already alive with people. He made his way northward to the more fashionable streets and addresses in search of breakfast. Along the way, he dropped pennies into cups and the dirty hands of orphans, never making eye contact with any of them. He had precious little to give, but the thought that the children begging or the women with the hollow cheeks and dark eyes might have lost their breadwinner to battle kept him generous.

And wasn't that why Moreton wanted him to attend the Gillensfords' ball?

Halfway through breakfast at a small tea shop on Fenchurch Street, Moreton himself appeared, standing beside Myles's table. "Knew I'd find you here," Moreton said in his confoundedly cheerful tones.

Myles squinted up at his friend. "That doesn't say much for your intellect or powers of deduction, given that I always take my breakfast here." Then he gestured to the single chair across the small table from his. "Sit. Have something to drink."

"Don't mind if I do." Moreton dropped into the chair with little grace. His wide grin nearly brought an answering smile from Myles, but the last threads of his nightmare still had hold of his mind. And he still blamed Moreton for that. At least partially.

"What are you wearing to the ball this evening?" Moreton asked immediately after giving his order to the kitchen boy. "And please tell me you're going to get a haircut. You look like one of those woodsmen from America. As covered in hair as a bear."

"Bears are covered in fur." Not the cleverest response, but Myles

didn't have it in him to match wits with his friend. Not today. "I haven't decided if I'm going or not."

"Oh, you're going. I am hiring a carriage for me, the missus, and you. All three of us will make a delightful party." Moreton shook a finger at Myles. "You would disappoint Emmeline if you didn't come, you know. She worries about you."

Emmeline Moreton, his friend's wife, was an angel in disguise. Nothing else could explain how easily she welcomed Myles into her life after her wedding, and despite the mess he had been at the time, so newly home from war. She had adopted him, the way one might adopt a growling mongrel from the street, and plied him with cake and kindness until he'd given up his growling. At least around her.

"She worries because you tell her to worry." Myles took the last bite of his toast, then tried to decide if his sausages were worth finishing. They were slightly burnt. "If she knew how much I loathed the idea of being trotted about as an example of the *poor wounded soldier*, she wouldn't want me to go."

Moreton chuckled. "That isn't your role in this at all. Believe me, if Gillensford wanted specimens of that sort, I never would have mentioned you to him."

"How do you know this Gillensford fellow, anyway?" Myles speared one of the sausages and waved it at his friend. "I understand he's from nobility and money."

"He is. But his wife is from trade, and *she* is the one with the money. Or so I hear." Moreton shrugged. "That's neither here nor there. I met him November last, when he needed more lawyers to look over the paperwork for the orphanage on Basing Lane. My firm represented their interests, and I was fortunate enough to be invited to dinner a time or two."

"So Gillensford is a social reformer?" Myles hadn't heard as much. But then, he ran in vastly different circles than someone with that much wealth and power.

"They both are—Mr. and Mrs. You'd like Mrs. Gillensford, too. Emmeline adores her. Mrs. Gillensford invited Emmeline to join a sewing circle. But again, beside the point." Moreton's tea arrived, and

he spent the next several seconds blowing across its surface before daring a small sip. "Ahem. Where was I?"

"Social reform." The response came out sounding more like a grumble than words.

Though his friend's antics might have amused some, Myles knew well enough that Moreton had a sharp mind. He used his good humor on occasion to make people see things his way.

Moreton narrowed his eyes and put down his tea. "Listen, Cobbett. I know you're wrapped up in pretending to be a calloused old codger, but I also know you want to help men in your situation to have a better chance at survival once the war is over. Did you even read the newspaper article I sent you three days ago?"

"I did." He had read it with a sinking heart. The newspaper had reported on yet another soldier returned from war, found lifeless in an alleyway, done in by drink, and all alone. Some of the men under his command, wounded at the same time and from the same cannon fire that had left Myles scarred and half-blind, had met similar fates. Because they had nowhere else to go.

"This hospital the Gillensfords want to build—it isn't merely to treat wounds. They mean it to be a place for recovery, where soldiers with similar experiences can speak with one another. Where they can prepare to reenter society again. Mrs. Gillensford hopes to partner with different trade guilds to offer work to men who need it. Truly, it sounds like a remarkable endeavor."

Myles put his half-eaten sausage on the plate and took a drink of his long-cooled tea. The scope of the Gillensfords' plans amazed him. Could such help for men like him be feasible? Parliament hadn't managed to do more than approve the payment of pensions. The only government hospital for returning soldiers was overcrowded.

"If I am not invited to the ball in order to garner pity and open pocketbooks, why would I need to be present at all?" He still had no desire to be trotted out as an example—yet he couldn't be selfish. If even the smallest sacrifice of his comfort played a part of offering hope to boys and men coming back with wounds too deep for most to see…? It was his duty to attend.

For the first time since he sat down, Moreton wore an expression of complete seriousness. There was no coaxing, no false-cheer in his voice when he spoke. “You would be present to answer questions, if anyone is brave enough to ask. To have conversations in which you are honest about what life was like for you when you returned to England. You are an eloquent man, when you wish to be, and none can doubt your sincerity given how openly you wear your scars.”

Myles lowered his gaze to the table, a lump forming in his throat. If only Moreton knew how difficult it was, every single day, for Myles to step out into the sunshine and bear the stares of others. But he had mastered himself, and his emotions, to a point where few could even guess at what strength it took for him to put on his eyepatch and coat as though both were perfectly normal to wear.

“I had better find a barber.”

Moreton blinked at him. “Pardon me?”

Myles gestured with his fully-intact hand to his face. “I wouldn’t want to scare away any of the ladies by looking like a bear.”

When Moreton rose to clap Myles on the back, he forced a smile. In a few hours, he’d be dressed in his finest clothing, moving about in a room filled with the wealthiest members of Society, and revealing much more than he wished about his past difficulties.

He hoped it would be worth it.

Three

Philippa and Elaine were the only two in the retiring room the hotel had set aside for ladies attending the Gillensford ball. The guests would begin arriving shortly, and Elaine needed a moment to herself. Philippa, dressed in soft rose-colored silks, sat on the padded bench next to her sister-in-law, admiring the older woman's subtle beauty while Elaine stared into the gilded mirror on the wall, smoothing her ivory-and-gold skirts.

Red hair hadn't been admired in Society for some time, if ever, but Elaine wore her natural color with grace. Her maid had piled the red hair loosely atop Elaine's head, held everything in place with pearl-tipped pins and golden thread, and finished off the whole with a broad satin ribbon that looked like liquid gold.

Sometimes, when Philippa saw Elaine looking like that, she wished to exchange her own dark-brown locks for something more unique. Something more auburn. Or gold. Many a man said they admired women with yellow-gold hair. Dark hair wasn't quite the fashion, though it was certainly a widespread hue among the *ton*.

"I am terrified." Elaine's abrupt statement, coupled with her meeting Philippa's gaze in the mirror, broke through the younger

woman's thoughts. "This affair is so much grander than the dinner we hosted to raise money for the orphanage."

Covering her sister-in-law's hand with her own, Philippa gazed back into her eyes with an upward tilt of her chin. "You are doing something incredible, Elaine. Of course you are nervous. But Adam will be by your side, and so will I. Everyone who attends here this evening is doing so because they want to make a difference, too. They merely lack the imagination to do so on their own. You are pointing them in the right direction and allowing them to dance while they learn how to do and be better."

Elaine's cheeks pinked beneath her freckles, and she released a wavering laugh. "You have a lot of faith in me."

"Of course I do. I know you have a good heart." Philippa squeezed Elaine's hand, then turned to look at her directly. Elaine did the same. "And what is the worst thing that could happen? Last week, the Earl of Coventry fell into a bowl of dark red punch at Baroness Gower's private ball. Everyone laughed about it for a few days, and then it was forgotten."

That brought a truer grin to Elaine's face, though she tempered it with a shake of her head. "The poor earl. And baroness."

"And last Season," Philippa went on with perhaps too much glee, "everyone was scandalized when Lord Dudley's mistress arrived at a ball, on the arm of her husband, and *still* flirted with Lord Dudley all evening. That made the papers, but everyone thought that particular ball a success."

Elaine wrinkled her nose and gave Philippa a gentle shove with her shoulder. "I think you ought not to enjoy such stories so much. Do you read anything in papers and magazines other than gossip?"

"I find people interesting." Philippa rose from her seat and tugged a bit at the slight wrinkles in her dress. "It isn't that I delight in the unfortunate things that happen, but that I'd rather read about my peers bumbling through life as I do than about less pleasant things—like tariffs and trade proposals." She shuddered dramatically, knowing full well that Elaine and Adam both pored over those articles in order to manage their funds and stocks.

Elaine did not rise to Philippa's bait. Instead, she rose from the cushioned seat and put her arms around her sister-in-law. "Thank you for being here this evening, Pippa. I know I can trust you to tell me when I don't behave correctly."

At this, Philippa snorted. "You are twice as polite as people who are born to the upper classes and peerage. You do not need *me* to help you at all."

"Except to remind me whom people are sometimes." Elaine winced. "I still don't think that baroness has forgiven me for confusing her as a baronetess."

"A minor mistake." Philippa looked Elaine over carefully once more. "At least she wasn't a duchess. That may have been awkward."

The former seamstress, now dressed finer than any of her clients had ever been, took both of Philippa's hands in hers. "Will you look after the soldiers coming this evening? It cannot be easy for them to be here, to speak of their needs to strangers. Adam thought it would be a good idea to have them, but I worry it might be insulting in some way."

"They wouldn't have agreed to attend if it bothered them." Philippa narrowed her eyes at Elaine. "How many said they would come?"

"A dozen, nearly right away. The last one agreed to be here only a few hours ago."

"Thirteen." Philippa raised her eyebrows and affected a concerned expression. She dropped her voice an octave. "An unlucky number."

Elaine tossed her head with a dramatic sniff. "I am not the least bit superstitious. And one might argue those who bring wives with them negate that, anyway."

Philippa nodded sagely. "I quite agree. I've heard that some people think thirteen is quite lucky. The French, for example."

With that, her sister-in-law gave a merry laugh. "There you have it. I am emulating the French, as any seamstress must know how to do."

After they checked each other's hair and gowns, Elaine and Philippa linked arms and went out the door to the main hall. Philippa had offered to stand in the receiving line with Elaine, but her sister-in-

law proclaimed that she needed Philippa to keep an eye on things in the ballroom once guests began arriving.

Adam waited at the top of the steps above the grand foyer. He gave Philippa the briefest greeting before taking his wife's hand in his and kissing her, right there where anyone might see, with a brief press of his lips to hers. Had a man ever been so besotted by his wife?

"Are you ready, my darling?" he asked, his blue eyes focused upon Elaine. "The hotel manager said there are carriages lining up in the street."

Elaine turned a little pale. "Is it too late for me to run back home to the nursery?" Her voice sounded strained, but Adam put his arm around her shoulders and Philippa saw her sister-in-law relax.

"Nancy and the nursemaid are quite happy looking after little Isabelle together. I promise they are well. You are needed here."

Elaine tipped her chin up. "I am, aren't I? You certainly couldn't manage a ball yourself, could you?"

He chuckled and pressed another kiss to her temple. "I couldn't manage anything without you, Elaine."

Philippa stepped back as they spoke, watching as her brother helped Elaine find her courage once more. As the third son of an earl, Adam had been born to privilege, wealth, and the games of the *ton*. As husband to Elaine, he stood as her defender and partner in all things. Between the two of them, Society had no chance of ignoring the amount of good they would do.

If someone promised such a match to Philippa, she'd happily do as her mother insisted and wed. But she'd seen too many marriages, up close and from a distance, that lacked such care and respect.

As Philippa stepped into the ballroom, she put her shoulders back and offered a nod to the orchestra on the balcony above the dancefloor. They took that as their cue and played music meant for listening rather than dancing. The ballroom of the hotel was twice as long as it was wide, with white-marble columns and an array of chandeliers above—lit by the gasworks across the river. Quite modern, in many respects.

The room was grander than Almack's ballroom, but no one would dare say it. The building still sparkled with fresh paint, and one could

almost smell the new lumber used in its construction. A ball at a hotel, while not a new concept altogether, was certainly unique. And everyone wanted a glimpse of this particular ballroom.

The evening would be a success for Elaine and Adam. Their dream of a veteran's hospital would come to fruition. Philippa had no doubt of that.

The doors to the ballroom opened, and the first of the guests came in, the hum of their conversation providing a gentle undertone to the music. Philippa glided toward the doors, ready with her most charming expression and words of welcome.

~

The dancing was well underway when Myles entered the ballroom a few steps behind Moreton and his wife. Emmeline cooed over the fine decor, the dresses, and everything else as though the whole spectacle had been created for her enjoyment alone. Moreton's affection for his wife was evident in the way he introduced her to the first knot of people they came to.

"I have the honor of introducing this enchanting woman on my arm as my wife, Mrs. Moreton." Moreton kept his eyes upon her through every word, his expression filled with adoration.

If the couple were not the closest friends Myles possessed, their display of affection would garner a cynical response rather than his reluctant admiration. Few men were as fortunate in their choice of a wife as Moreton. Then his friend introduced Myles, and the conversations became more focused.

"And this is my good friend, Mr. Myles Cobbett, a former captain in His Majesty's army."

Myles flexed his left hand within its glove, questioning again if it had been practicality or vanity that made him stuff the two empty fingers of the glove with scraps of fabric. He couldn't hide his left cheek as easily, the scars from the shrapnel as apparent as the (mostly unharmed) nose on his face. Then there was the eyepatch.

"A captain in the army, were you?" A gentleman with a self-impor-

tant tilt to his chin made a point of staring at the left side of Myles's face. "Then you must have some idea of what the Gillensfords are trying to achieve, and an opinion on the matter. Tell me, do you think it really necessary that the men returning home from battle—hardened soldiers who have seen death and dealt it for king and country—need a place such as this hospital will be? A facility where they will be coddled?"

Myles hadn't ever particularly enjoyed mingling in Society, and in less than five minutes, he deeply regretted being moved by Moreton's pleas to step out into the world again. Myles narrowed his eye at the man in front of him, noting the softness of his chin, the puffiness beneath his eyes, and the expensive material of his clothing.

"I think you ask the wrong question, sir." Myles couldn't be bothered to remember the man's name. "Here is what you should consider. Men without fortune, rather than remain home in London taking up positions in respectable places of employment, decide to place themselves in the line of fire between England's citizens and their enemies. With little pay, less gratitude, and the genuine chance of dying a slow death alone on a battle field, bleeding from wounds too painful to describe, these men do indeed see death. They deal it in order to delay their own." Myles took no pleasure in the way the man turned pale, or how he swallowed. "So the question you ought to ask, sir, is this: What are the people of England willing to do to show these men that their sacrifices are valued? How will England prove it doesn't hold the lives of its sons upon the battlefield as cheap?"

The question hung in the air; the people encircling Myles and the man he spoke to were absolutely silent, and he realized how impassioned his speech likely seemed. Emotion—strong emotion—was not permitted in Society. He didn't care. Much. He'd answered honestly enough.

A new voice spoke from Myles's blind side—a woman's voice, cultured and low. "Is establishing a hospital for the men to recover an appropriate answer to that question?"

Myles turned, drawing himself up and collecting his thoughts. The crowd around them had grown while he spoke, and this woman had

not stood among them when he first arrived with Moreton and Emmeline. She stood with a regal tilt to her head, dark curls sparkling like the night sky, with jewels tucked into their folds.

He gave a slight bow to the woman, the only concession to their lack of proper introduction he could give in the midst of a conversation. "I think it is a step in the right direction."

The blue of her eyes reminded him of indigo ink, swirling and dark. Those eyes glittered with interest, but her lips remained pressed closed as she considered him and his non-answer.

A gentleman appeared at her elbow, oblivious to the fact he interrupted the silent stare between Myles and the woman. "Lady Philippa, this is our dance. Do come quickly."

Lady Philippa.

She turned away from Myles and the conversation, allowing her partner to lead her to the row of dancers already assembling.

"Mr. Cobbett, what more do you think we could do for our fighting men?" one of the matronly women asked, drawing his attention back to the people he'd already been introduced to. The woman had more pearls around her neck than a single oyster bed could produce in a decade, but her expression indicated her question was in earnest.

The man who had been smug only minutes before had stepped back, his shoulder tucked just behind the lady who now addressed Myles.

"Many a man returns from war to uncertainty, madam. They do not know where to go to gain new employment. Even if they find a place to work, the adjustment from the life of a soldier to a civilian is difficult. I think what we might need most is more compassion from those who have remained at home. More patience and understanding."

Nearly an hour later, after fervent conversations with men and women introduced by Moreton, Myles needed a moment away. Desperately. Though he maintained a composed expression, his head pounded as though a gunner resided within, firing shots off at a steady pace. Myles wanted nothing more than to slip out a door at the back of the ballroom and make his way to the gardens. The cool night air might

clear his head sufficiently, making it possible to last another hour among the perfumed upper classes.

A deep voice intercepted Myles before he took more than two steps in the direction of his escape. "Ah, Mr. Cobbett. Here you are."

Myles turned to greet this new social assault—but immediately relaxed. The host and hostess of the evening had found him. They'd only had a brief introduction in the hotel's entry, and in those few seconds, Myles had felt they were earnest in their cause.

"Mr. and Mrs. Gillensford." He bowed. "I hope the evening is proving successful for you both."

"Thank you, Mr. Cobbett. I do think we are headed in the direction of success." Mrs. Gillensford's gentle smile turned more enthusiastic as she spoke. "The conversations we have heard are most encouraging. Several of our guests are thinking on the fates of our nation's soldiers for the first time. I am exceedingly pleased."

Her husband watched her speak with open admiration before adding, "We are receiving promises and pledges of patronage for our hospital from a few surprising sources, too. With members of Society finally addressing this issue, we hope to help many former soldiers find their way."

The lady stepped closer to Myles, clasping her hands before her. "Thank you for coming tonight, Mr. Cobbett. I know that speaking to you, and our other former soldiers present, has made all the difference."

"It is an honor to be of service, madam." His headache abated somewhat under the praise. If his presence had helped even the slightest, the evening's discomfort had been worth it.

"Mr. Cobbett, would you ever consider taking a more active role in an endeavor such as ours?" Mr. Gillensford asked the question with raised eyebrows and a thoughtful glint in his eye. "We are, of course, looking for people with experience as well as interest in what we hope to accomplish."

Mrs. Gillensford nodded along with her husband's words, then added her soft entreaty. "Yes, it's true. We need all manner of advisors, committees, and eventually a full staff for the hospital once it's built."

Myles shifted his weight from one foot to the other. His mind

swam with doubts too numerous to name. "That is a most interesting prospect, madam. I am not sure what help I could be."

"Think on it," Mr. Gillensford urged him. "And if you ever wish to discuss the possibility, come and speak to me. Our London house is always open to those who support such causes."

Nothing need be decided, or discussed further, at present. Myles relaxed somewhat. "Thank you, Mr. Gillensford. I will take that under consideration."

The music changed, and couples drifted away from the center of the ballroom. Myles noted Mrs. Gillensford's gaze dart in that direction, and he suddenly wondered if anyone had asked the hostess of the evening to dance.

Her husband could not, of course, in such a public setting.

"Mrs. Gillensford, do you dance this evening?" He gestured toward the orchestra. "I would be honored to stand up for a set with you." The woman had done much for his fellow soldiers. He could happily escort her down a row of couples.

Her lovely features showed surprise, but then immediately changed to express pleasure. "I would like that, if my husband will excuse me."

"Of course, my dear. Perhaps I'll find a lady in want of some exercise and join you." Mr. Gillensford bowed and swept away in search of his own partner.

Myles took Mrs. Gillensford by the hand and led her to the head of the dancers. The handsome lady he had seen earlier that evening, Lady Philippa, was in the principal location and had already called out the next dance. His gaze lingered upon her for a moment, though she did not glance in his direction. Despite the lateness of the hour, she appeared as vibrant and energetic as when he'd first cast his eye upon her.

"Have you met my sister-in-law?" his dance partner asked.

Myles turned his attention back to Mrs. Gillensford. "The lady in pink?"

Mrs. Gillensford nodded.

"I heard her name in passing. We have not been formally introduced."

"I will remedy that after our dance, if you like." Mrs. Gillensford arched her strawberry-colored eyebrows at him, and a gleam of speculation came into her eyes.

Any desire she had toward matchmaking would die the moment she knew how little his life was worth. Myles forced himself to sound neutral. Uninterested. "You needn't go to the trouble, madam. I am certain your evening is taken up with a great deal of work already. Would you tell me, Mrs. Gillensford, where you propose to place the hospital?"

She allowed him to switch topics, though a small tilt to her smile told Myles that Mrs. Gillensford was well aware of the abrupt change. She spoke at length of their plans, whenever the steps of the dance allowed them near enough to converse.

When the first of the set ended, a few of the couples left the floor to make room for others to join in the entertainment. On Myles's right, Mr. Gillensford appeared with a woman Myles hadn't met. On his left came another gentleman. Lady Philippa Gillensford partnered the stranger for the dance.

Mrs. Gillensford's eyes sparkled at Myles. "Perhaps we'll have time for that introduction after all."

He winced, and then he hoped the lady hadn't noticed. Though he had met over a dozen new acquaintances that evening, he sensed a proper introduction to Lady Philippa would be different. Young, beautiful, and noble. She could want nothing to do with him. He'd already subjected himself to the curious and disgusted stares of too many people that night, and every day since his return from battle.

Young women stared at him from behind their fans, taking in the half of his face covered in scars with mingled disgust and pity. They whispered about him. About what was behind the eyepatch, or beneath the crisp folds of his cravat. He hated it.

He'd stopped moving about in Society ages ago for precisely that reason.

The steps of the dance required him to come face to face with Lady Philippa before Mrs. Gillensford could introduce them. The young woman's dark blue eyes met his, and Myles nearly stumbled at the colli-

sion. Her gaze, bright and cold, was as the sun reflected upon ice. What had Myles done to merit such a sharp glare?

She cut her glance away from him and to her partner, and only then did Myles realize her frosty anger was directed at another.

The gentleman wasn't anyone Myles knew, which was unsurprising, but he immediately took the fellow under dislike. The man couldn't be older than five and twenty, but he wore an absurd smirk filled with all the arrogance of an emperor. His clothing marked him as a man of fortune and living at the height of fashion. The size of the emerald stickpin in the man's cravat was obscene—something more suitable to the former French court than an English charity ball. Then the man's hair—bright as burnished gold and likely curled with hot-tongs—fell about his ears and eyes like a sheepdog's.

Good manners meant Myles could not address Lady Philippa or her partner, having not been formally introduced, but nothing kept him from overhearing their conversation.

"You needn't rage at me, my lady." The golden-haired man spoke with the purr of a large cat. "Everyone knows your eldest brother wants you to marry, and he will not release your purse strings until you do. He's made no secret of your dowry's size, either. I merely suggest that if you would like your freedom—"

"That is quite enough," the lady protested, her voice almost too soft for Myles to hear. "This is not the time nor the place to discuss such things. Truly, I'd rather not speak to you on the topic ever again."

"Temper, temper." The man chuckled as he brushed by Myles to take a turn bowing and stepping about with Mrs. Gillensford, leaving Myles to take the lead with Lady Philippa, whose cheeks burned a bright shade of pink.

Myles fixed his expression to give away nothing of his thoughts. The conversation he'd overheard had nothing to do with him. Yet, seeing a woman distressed—angry, of course, but certainly also distressed—pulled at a latent piece of his character. The desire to set her at ease, if not set things to right, prompted his words.

"If you need to escape that popinjay after this dance, you might use me as excuse, my lady."

She blinked at him, confusion replacing displeasure. "Mr. Cobbett." That she remembered his name didn't surprise him. He didn't have a face one was likely to forget.

"Your servant, my lady." He bowed his head, the most courteous signal he could give in the midst of a dance.

The steps took them apart again, restoring him to Mrs. Gillensford, who didn't appear as upset by her time in the arrogant man's company as her sister-in-law had. It seemed the fellow didn't make everyone immediately dislike him. Though Myles kept his attention on his partner well enough to exchange the occasional pleasant comment, he made certain to look Lady Philippa's way from time to time, too.

No woman deserved to have her evening spoiled by a pretentious lout.

~

Slipping away from the ballroom and attempting to avoid Lord Walter Ruthersby at the same time proved difficult. Philippa kept glancing over her shoulder as she made her way behind columns and potted ferns, then out the large doors to the hotel's expansive gardens. The steps leading from the veranda to the ground were well lit, as were the pathways through elaborately shaped hedges.

There were others walking along the gravel footpaths, mostly in twos and threes, enjoying the night air. Ballrooms, even in the spring, were stifling places. Elaine had partly chosen the hotel for her ball due to its promise of gardens filled with fountains and night breezes. "Guests shouldn't be expected to brave the heat and still be generous," she had said during one of their many planning sessions for the evening.

Philippa nodded greetings to the people she passed, ignoring the few who raised eyebrows at her unchaperoned state. Doubtless, someone would tell her mother they had spied her walking through the gardens alone. Mother would lecture Philippa on decorum later.

Philippa passed two women near her mothers' age, noting the way they bent their heads together and whispered the moment her back was

to them. She glowered upward at the night sky, too filled with clouds and light from London for the stars to appear, and muttered to herself.

"Oh, Pippa, how dare you take five minutes for yourself? How *could* you go walking through public gardens all alone? Especially when those gardens are *full* of people who will notice just how *alone* you are." She snorted, then grinned. Her mother couldn't abide Philippa's unladylike noises. Everything from a burst of laughter to a sneeze was deemed "most unladylike."

The path turned as it neared an outer wall, and Philippa turned with it.

"Drat Lord Walter," she said, kicking a pebble somewhat viciously with her slippered foot. "And all second sons who think I owe them my hand." A common enough practice among noble sons not poised to inherit titles and estates was to find a woman such as herself, of similar lineage, with money of her own so her husband could keep the lifestyle to which he'd grown accustomed.

Just see if she didn't convince Richard to give over her inheritance the next time she saw him. Then she'd hire a companion and declare her intention to remain a spinster. Then she'd finally have freedom to do as she pleased, when she pleased. No more asking Mother to see the newest play or attend art exhibitions—she would never ask anyone permission for anything again.

Drat Society, too. She wouldn't care a penny's worth for what anyone said about her. She'd gallop through Hyde Park if she wished and visit Adam and Elaine as often as they would have her.

Philippa didn't realize she'd started to cry until the shadows she walked through blurred. At the edges of the garden, trees hung overhead, and most of the light filtered through hedges. She stopped walking and looked about her, through her irritating tears.

Somehow, she'd left the main paths meant for the guests. This little track, hardly wide enough for a wheelbarrow, had to be one used by the gardeners to come and go with their tools, or a way for servants to cut through from one side of the property to another without being seen.

A scuffle nearby caused Philippa to jerk her head up.

Several yards ahead of her, Philippa spied a small break in the hedge. Not a true path, but enough of a gap—given the amount of light streaming through the branches—that she could slip through and find herself in a brighter, safer portion of the garden.

Picking up her skirts to allow for a longer stride, Philippa hurried to the gap without looking back. But she heard a step behind her, matching her speed.

Gaining speed.

Philippa slid sideways through the small gap, spying one of those infamous fountains in a square-shaped courtyard surrounded on all sides by rose bushes. She realized too late that she had tried to slip through the very same plants—thorns caught at the back of her gown.

Then a hand caught at her arm and pulled her sharply back into the shadows before she could cry out or even see anyone who might help her.

"There now, Lady Philippa," a well-greased voice whispered in her ear. "Why rush off when we are finally alone?"

Anger burned in her chest, and Philippa whirled around to shove both hands into her captor's chest. "Unhand me, Lord Walter! This very instant!"

Her shove made him stumble back a step, but his grip on her arm tightened. "Now, now. Calm down, my lady. I only wish to talk." She could see the gleam of his cold eyes in the darkness, and she practically heard the calculations likely going through his head.

"You needn't detain me in such a way if all you wish is to *talk*," she hissed, jerking her arm away from him.

He released his hold but continued looming over her. "There is that temper I so enjoy." His teeth flashed in the dim light, his grin predatory. "I think you and I can come to an understanding, my lady. You have something I desperately want—a fortune. And your brother, Montecliff, has already said he'd consent to our engagement."

That Richard, her brother the earl, approved of someone like Lord Walter did not surprise Philippa, though it still struck her as sad.

"It is a pity I have more taste than my brother does," she said aloud,

stepping back to that break in the hedge. "While he might consent, I certainly never will."

Lord Walter's eyes narrowed. "Do reconsider, my dear. After all, several people saw you come into the gardens alone. More saw me follow, as I made certain to ask after you as I passed each one. The dowager countess, Lady Mary Fenchurch, certainly made note of it."

Her chin came up, and the first prickle of concern ran along her spine. "Are you threatening my reputation?"

The man laughed, the sound somehow more threatening than words. "Making promises, more like. You see, my lady—"

A new hand closed around her arm, this time from the other side of the rose-bushes, and Philippa found herself pulled through leaves and thorns again. This time, into the light. She heard Lord Walter curse, and the sound of cloth ripping at least several inches, before she stumbled into the arms of her new captor.

Trying to catch her balance, she had no choice but to take hold of the man's coat, and still her nose hit a horribly solid chin. Her eyes welled up with tears again, her nose stung terribly, as she looked up to see what new ogre had her in his clutches.

The sight that met her eyes might have made a lesser woman scream.

The man's head turned, leaving her only the left side of his face to see while he glared back the way she had come—at Lord Walter?—and what a face it was. Scars had rippled the man's face, puckering the skin along his cheek and jaw. A black leather patch covered his eye.

"Mr. Cobbett," she gasped, and he looked down at her. Though his right side remained in shadow, she saw the handsome, unmarred shape of cheekbones and jaw, the long dark lashes of his single brown eye. She hadn't taken such careful measure of him before, certain that staring at the juxtaposition of his uninjured face to the other side would be rude and perhaps hurtful if he noticed.

But now, as close as she was, she could not help but see all the details of both sides. Natural, masculine beauty on the one, and a terrible, frightening visage of war on the other.

He released her, and Philippa stumbled sideways.

"One moment, my lady." His voice wasn't gruff, but pleasant and deep. She'd noticed his voice before anything else about him, when she'd heard him addressing a group of peers on the matter of the hospital. It had made her turn from her own conversation to see who spoke with such unwavering certainty about the plight of returned soldiers.

Mr. Cobbett bent down, and she felt him take hold of the edge of her skirt. "The fabric is caught."

Philippa stared down in the weak light, noting that his left hand held her gown while the right carefully untwisted fabric from thorn. When her dress came loose, it fluttered out of his grasp. A long, jagged tear of the fabric from hem to her knee made her gasp. Thankfully, the layers of underclothes beneath the chemise were intact.

"I am sorry about the dress."

She shook her head, then looked to the gap. "Lord Walter...?"

"The popinjay is gone, my lady. He disappeared the moment he saw me." He sounded supremely confident. How nice for him.

Philippa rubbed at her temple, then delicately touched her nose. Everything except her dress seemed intact.

"I know we have not been properly introduced," Mr. Cobbett said, bringing her attention to the solemn expression upon his face. "But I think it best we re-enter the ballroom together. I am happy to return you to your brother or sister-in-law."

He was right. If the old cats of the *ton* had seen one man pursue her out into the night, another must take her inside again to cancel out that bit of gossip. How tired she grew of the games.

"Thank you, Mr. Cobbett." Her shoulders relaxed, and she released a heavy sigh. "You are truly a gentleman to trouble yourself with a stranger like this."

He bowed, then offered his right arm, putting her on his uninjured side. Philippa took it, and together they left the quietly burbling fountain for the main path—and nearly ran in to Lady Mary Fenchurch, Dowager Countess of Tinniswood. Arm-in-arm with her sister and another gossip, Mrs. Ufford.

Philippa composed herself with haste and bowed her head to both matrons. She exclaimed, with forced good cheer, "Lady Mary, Mrs.

Ufford. How wonderful to see you both. Are you enjoying your evening?"

The women exchanged a knowing glance, then eyed Mr. Cobbett.

"A lovely evening, yes," Lady Mary said.

"Absolutely marveling," Mrs. Ufford agreed. "So many people to see."

"People will be talking of nothing else for weeks." Lady Mary snapped her fan open and raised her gray eyebrows all the way to the edge of her turban. "Your sister-in-law has outdone herself, Lady Philippa. Do pass on our compliments to her."

"I will, of course. Thank you. Oh—forgive me. Ladies, might I present Mr. Cobbett? He is one of our special guests this evening, a former soldier in His Majesty's army." She met Mr. Cobbett's eye, pleading with him to say nothing that might launch them both into trouble.

"A pleasure, Lady Mary. Mrs. Ufford." He bowed as much as he could while keeping Philippa on his arm. "I find myself impressed with the evening, too. As well as the hotel itself. What think you of the gardens, my lady? I would venture to guess your opinion on such a subject is expert."

Philippa blinked. She'd never heard that about Lady Mary in her life—and her mother was friends with the woman.

The compliment, though unearned, made Lady Mary preen. "It is delightful, to be sure, though the walks are a trifle too dark for my taste. More light is wanted for evening strolls, lest young people find themselves lost in the shadows." She raised her eyebrows at Philippa, and Mrs. Ufford smirked.

"I quite agree," Mr. Cobbett said. "Atmospheric it may be, but I am in want of light and company once more. Excuse us, please. I must return Lady Philippa to her brother."

They were barely a dozen steps away when Philippa released a quiet groan. "Wait and see, those two are going directly to my mother tomorrow morning." She shivered and looked up at her escort, whose face had returned to an unreadable mask of solemnity. "They will paint me as a hoyden in twenty different ways."

"Your mother will certainly take your word over theirs," he said, confidence in his tone. Obviously, he knew nothing about her family.

"Unlikely," she muttered. They climbed the steps to the hotel, and in the brighter light of the ballroom, she examined her damaged dress again. "This will never do. I must away to the retiring room before I see Elaine, or she'll fret." She released Mr. Cobbett's arm. "Thank you again, sir, for your valiant efforts on my behalf."

He hesitated, and his lips parted as though he had something he wished to say, but then he tightened them in a smile and bowed to her instead. "I wish you the best, Lady Philippa. Good evening."

As he walked away, Philippa watched him go. She admired the square set of his shoulders, the way he held his head high without appearing arrogant or prideful. Did all soldiers walk that way?

His clothing might not have been the best quality, or the latest fashion, but it had fit him perfectly. It looked sensible, though entirely appropriate for evening wear. And he had been kind—doing her a favor without seeking any reward in return. Philippa couldn't think of many men who wouldn't at least tease her about owing them a dance or introduction or some such thing the sister of an earl could provide.

Only when she had found a maid in the retiring room to help her, putting the concern over her ordeal out of the forefront of her mind, did it occur to her to be disappointed. Because Mr. Cobbett, her rescuer, hadn't even asked her to dance.

Four

Three days after the Gillensfords' ball, Myles went through the motions of his usual routine, though his mind didn't dwell upon any of his actions. Indeed, as he walked from breakfast through the crowded streets of his neighborhood, his mind wandered far afield.

Moreton and Emmeline insisted that he get some semblance of fresh air from one of the pockets of green amidst the buildings of London. It was a request he honored without reluctance. His daily walk took him to different parks, affording him the only exercise he took outside of what he managed in the confines of his rented rooms.

He purchased a newspaper, then continued on to one of the larger parks in a more fashionable neighborhood than his. Keeping to the side streets and walking so his left side was to the shops rather than the other people passing by, Myles avoided meeting with anyone he knew.

He arrived in Green Park in between the two most fashionable times for people to ride about in the nearby, larger, more popular Hyde Park. Thus he found the place with few people wandering its paths. Mostly nursemaids and young mothers, leading children about and fussing when those children attempted any activity which might soil their fine clothes.

Green Park, adjacent to St. James's Park, was a wild patch of green with only a few paths, including the old Queen's Walk to the water reservoir that had served the royal palace for years.

Something about the neglected royal grounds appealed to Myles. The greenery was hardly tended, and in the past century had been a most popular place for duels, bandits, and the launching of hot air balloons. With such a varied history and bearing neither beauteous flowers nor elegant fountains or water features, Green Park reminded Myles of himself.

Myles found a patch of shade beneath an old oak tree, the likes of which might have stood in that place since the time of King James. He opened his newspaper, laying the wide sheet out across his lap to begin his study of contemporary history. Enough time had passed that the paper would report on the charity ball, at last, and likely hold information about how much of a donation the Gillensfords received for their hospital.

The first article he found on the subject, wedged between columns with news pertaining to Parliament, wasn't complimentary. He scowled as he read the opening paragraph.

Despite the Royal Hospital Chelsea, patronized by the ruling families of England, being open to any veteran of wars past or present, the Gillensfords would have us believe our nation does not provide for our soldiers after they have done their sworn duty.

Myles gave the paper a shake, wishing he could do the same to whoever wrote the article. The Royal Hospital Chelsea, an institution over a century old, might have suited the nation during peacetime—but after decades of war such as the kingdom had experienced?

When Myles had returned home, wounded and recovering slowly, he'd fallen beneath that hospital's supervision. The officer charged with informing Myles of his future—that of an invalid with a sum of money to be paid annually for the rest of his life—told him that the hospital itself housed just under five-hundred veterans of war. But over thirty-thousand pensioners lived outside of its walls, drawing their pensions

from the government based on what their rank had been when they left the battlefield for the last time.

"And the hospital doesn't care for the invisible hurts, or getting a man back upon his feet," Myles muttered, glaring at the newsprint.

He kept going through the newspaper, and he found the first promising words about that evening much deeper in its pages. The writer here praised the Gillensfords for bringing the needs of young men cast adrift after war spent their health and left them without the means to provide for themselves as they had previous to taking up arms.

"More like it." Then he found another bit of news listing himself and twelve other veterans who had been present, and he scowled at that. What did it matter that they had been there? Two of the men were titled, a handful more were third sons of important people, and the others were like him—barely even considered worthy of interacting with the gentry. Never mind that he'd been born a gentleman's son. He lived in tiny, rented rooms and took income from a pension and the occasional prize money when he deigned to take part in bouts of fisticuffs.

Though Myles did not classify himself as a pugilist, he found the occasional friendly match kept his mind and body sharp. The activity saved him from complete boredom.

As had taking part in the Gillensfords' scheme.

He snatched up the paper again and folded it into a small rectangle. He'd read what he most wanted to, and there wasn't much else of interest to him. Except he felt a sudden desire, a thing which surprised him, to call upon Mr. Gillensford.

To get to the Gillensfords' address, a house at Berkley Square, he need not walk far. He could at least leave one of his calling cards—one of his very few calling cards. He didn't have much occasion to use them, thankfully. He hadn't wanted to print them in the first place—a foolish expense, he thought, for one living in such reduced circumstances.

Starting on his way from the park, Myles rehearsed to himself *why*

he found himself motivated to do something that mattered. The Gillensfords would surely ask.

If he could do more than idle his days away, and do something that mattered, he ought to take a step in that direction. Myles hadn't trained for anything outside of the military. His birth position in his family, a third son with a healthy father and elder brothers, had meant choosing his occupation with care.

He'd no interest in the law. He had even less interest in joining the clergy. His family had scraped together enough money to purchase a commission in the military for him—and that was that. He couldn't ask anything more of his father, mother, brothers, and three younger sisters. Two of those sisters were still unmarried, without suitable dowries to tempt bachelors.

If a position for one of his experience existed within the framework of the Gillensfords' plans, if he could offer his help in even a limited way, Myles had to try.

With the newspaper under his arm, he made his way to Berkeley Square, ignoring when others on the walkways peered too long at his scarred visage. Let them stare if they wished. For the first time in months, he had a purpose beyond making it through the day.

Though Philippa and her mother normally stayed at the family's Town house, Elaine had prevailed upon the dowager countess to stay at her fashionable address in Berkley Square. "Just for a few days," Elaine had said. "I intend to host a tea, and your experience would be of great benefit to me, my lady."

Lady Fredericka had given in to the appeal to her vanity, while Philippa and Elaine had exchanged a knowing glance. Elaine had wanted to make peace with her mother-in-law for some time, in part to smooth the way for her children, and also to give Philippa more time in Adam and Elaine's home.

Three days after the successful veteran's ball, Philippa sat in Elaine's

morning room holding her little niece, Isabelle. Elaine and Adam's adopted daughter, Nancy, sat next to Elaine, learning a complicated embroidery stitch. Nancy's governess sat near the window, reading.

The peace and felicity in the room laid upon Philippa's heart like a warm quilt on a winter night. These were the moments she craved when she was away from her brother's family. There had never been any moment in her childhood home as calm and happy. Philippa's family always seemed at odds with each other, and never let an opportunity to sniff disdainfully at the misfortunes of others go by. Which was why Philippa had often sneaked away to visit her great-uncle, the man who had left Elaine and Adam his entire fortune. Her uncle had been unfailingly kind, like Elaine.

"You are such a fortunate little girl, Isabelle," she crooned to the little darling in her arms. The baby smiled and cooed, making it necessary for Philippa to coo back at her. "How wonderful it is to have such a handsome papa, sweet mama, and an older brother and sister to look after you."

"When will William visit again?" Nancy asked, looking up from her work at Elaine.

Elaine sighed and shared a commiserating glance with Philippa before she answered. "Your brother will come home with us to Tertium Park when we leave London. School is very important for young gentlemen."

Nancy jabbed her needle into her embroidery hoop with more force than necessary. "I still don't see why he cannot have a governess, like me. Miss Wilson could teach both of us. Couldn't you, Miss Wilson?"

The governess, obviously at ease with her place in the home, turned a page in her book as she answered. "I should be happy to teach the young master how to play the pianoforte, paint water color portraits, and serve tea. Though I do not think he will find any of those skills of much use should he pursue the law, as he has said he wishes to do."

Philippa had to bite her bottom lip to keep from giggling at the dark frown Nancy wore as she took another stab at her needlework.

"Nancy, it isn't so terrible. I missed Adam dreadfully when he went away to school. And look at us now. Still quite good friends."

Elaine nodded her agreement. "Absolutely. William's time away from us will only make the time he spends with us all the sweeter. You'll see—"

A bang elsewhere in the house made everyone in the room jump. It sounded as though a door had been practically flung off its hinges, and then the shouting in the corridor began. "Ruined! My daughter is ruined!"

"Oh, dear," Elaine breathed, gathering the sewing and putting it into a basket near her feet. "Nancy, be a dear and take Isabelle back to the nursery. I do not want her upset by your grandmother. Miss Wilson, if you'd take the children up the servants' stair?" She kicked the basket under her chair.

Nancy huffed but came to take her baby sister with a smile. "Come along, Belle. We mustn't let you see Grandmama's fits."

"Lest you think you're permitted to throw one of your own," Philippa added with a grin. "Thank you, Nancy."

The governess led Nancy and the baby through a door to another room, and the moment that door shut behind them the door to the corridor opened. In came the dowager, as puffed up as an angry hen, and squawking almost as horribly.

"Philippa, I warned you to cease behaving in a scandalous manner. Now we must all pay the consequences for your rebellious ways."

Adam's deep voice echoed down the hall. "Mother? What in blazes are you shouting about?"

The dowager came into the room, holding a folded-up newssheet. "Right there, in the gossip columns, a report on the nature of your *tête-à-tête* with that horrid Lord Walter. If you'd just said yes to his suit, we wouldn't be in this terrible mess."

"What terrible fix?" Adam demanded as he entered the room. "Mother, you cannot gallop through the house declaring Philippa's ruin. At least not until we have met to discuss it in private." He shared a sardonic glance with Philippa. "Unless you don't object to such proclamations."

"I object most strenuously." Philippa kept her expression calm. "Especially when Mother thinks saying yes to a man she admits is horrid would have prevented whatever dire circumstance we now find ourselves in."

Lady Fredericka drew herself up to her impressive height, then growled like a bear. "You may have come of age, Philippa, but you will not speak to me that way so long as I am your mother and responsible for your well-being. If this disrespect is what comes of spending time in your brother's company—"

"My lady," Elaine said, rising to her feet and floating closer to her irate mother-in-law. "I think we are merely all confused. Let me order tea for you—or would you prefer something stronger? You are most distressed."

Trust Elaine to treat the dowager countess with kindness, despite the fact the matron hadn't ever wanted the seamstress as part of the family.

"Tea. Of course." Lady Fredericka collapsed into a chair at the center of the arranged furnishings. Then she put a hand over her eyes and groaned. "What is to become of our family's reputation?"

Elaine rang for tea, then sat on a couch and gave it a pat so her husband would come sit next to her. Philippa watched them with unconcealed fondness. She'd seen Adam grow into a more patient man since his marriage. The security he found in his wife's affection had given him permission to be true to his heart, at last, and gave him the ability to slip loose of their conniving family's reins.

If only Philippa could be so lucky. First, she had to get Richard to release her funds to her.

She really ought to speak to a solicitor or lawyer of some sort about that.

"What is all this about Lord Walter?" Elaine asked in a careful way, her expression serious and her tone quite gentle.

Lady Fredericka groaned again but lifted her folded paper and waved it above her head like a baton. "It is all in the papers. How any of you missed it this morning, I shall never guess."

Adam and Elaine only read the papers when they had some invest-

ment in play, Philippa knew, or when they were paying particular attention to what went on in Parliament. Adam claimed papers did nothing but sensationalize nonsense. Elaine had too many other things keeping her busy.

Philippa read the gossiping bits and pieces, as well as socially important announcements, only after her mother finished with her copy of the *Times*. "None of us have had a chance to read the newssheets today, Mother."

Thrusting the paper out toward Philippa, her mother raised an imperious eyebrow. Her wide-eyed-distress markedly changed to a superior lift of her chin. "I have already marked it." Then she dropped the paper on a table, and the dowager countess swept out of the room without another word.

Dramatic exits were a specialty for her ladyship.

After glancing at Adam, whose furrowed brow and confused expression likely matched her own, Philippa rose and took the paper from the table. She unfolded it and swept the black ink until she found where her mother had meticulously drawn a box of blue ink around an article. The corners of that box were so sharp, Philippa briefly wondered how her mother achieved such exactness.

It seemed she had taken plenty of time to mark the words that had supposedly sent her careening through the house in a panic.

Which made everything about the circumstances most suspect.

"What does it say, Pippa?" Adam asked.

Though tempted to clear her throat in exaggerated theatrics, Philippa opted instead to read as though she found the entire thing one long joke. Horrid as it was.

Interested parties must want to know: according to a most reliable source, Lady P., sister to a well-known member of the House of Lords, was found in a most compromising position at another brother's so-called 'Event of the Season.'

We must confess to not being surprised, seeing as how Lady P.'s other brother made a similarly disappointing marriage last year. But how will her dear mother, a peeress so long at the forefront of fashion, ever hold her head up in Society again?

The young Lord W., a bachelor, is expected to defend the honor of said Lady P. by offering to marry her. Rumor is that her lordly brother is already in negotiations for this very outcome.

We do not think it will be long before Lady P. regrets her actions and flees London in hopes Society will forget all about her brazen behavior. Only an honorable marriage will see this tale to a happy conclusion.

By the time Philippa finished reading, she was grinding her teeth together over the last words.

"Who would publish such a thing?" Elaine whispered, her delicate features awash in shock. "And who would want to gossip about Pippa? She is the very definition of a proper English lady." Though her sister-in-law's defense warmed Philippa's heart, her anger yet mounted.

"I know exactly who." Philippa flung the paper down onto the table. "Lord W. himself! That disgusting toad has been trying to make me an offer all Season. When I turned him down at the ball—"

"Our ball?" Adam interrupted, a scowl appearing on his face. "He approached you there? While you were alone?" Had he been a protective hound, his hackles would've gone up. As it was, he certainly bared his teeth as though preparing to let out a growl.

Philippa briefly considered calming her brother's ire, but she rather liked him taking her side. Richard and Mother never did. "And made quite a spectacle of himself, coming to look for me in the gardens." Rising from the chair, she went to the window, glaring out at Berkeley Square. "If it was not he who saw to the publication of that loathsome article, it was one of the matrons he made a point of speaking to when he sought me out."

"Why is he such a persistent suitor?" Elaine asked, putting a hand on her husband's arm as though to temper his response.

"He is a younger son," Philippa answered with a shoulder shrug. "He feels it the duty of our lines to bolster one another. He wants my fortune and my bloodline."

Adam huffed and sat back, tilting his chin up so as to better glare at the ceiling. "A crony of Richard's, it sounds like." He took Elaine's hand in his and released a put-upon sigh. "It might not be all that terrible, Pippa. Perhaps if we ignore the gossip it will go away?"

“You know as well as I do how much a matter of chance that is.” Philippa turned from the window and massaged her temples with both hands. “If something scandalous happens in the next week, people will forget what they’ve read in the paper today. But if a popular, gossipy cat sinks her teeth into the story, I might as well withdraw from London in disgrace. And come back in a year or two.”

“Surely there are other options.” Elaine, for all her intelligence, still gave London Society far more credit toward kindness than it deserved. The former seamstress was undoubtedly blessed that she did not grow up amid the conniving, scheming crowds of the upper nobility.

Adam chuckled, the sound lacking genuine mirth. “She could marry someone other than Lord Toad.”

A tingle went down Philippa’s spine. She had no intention of marrying. And yet. That solution would also force Richard to release her inheritance to her. Without a battle in court, as she suspected it must come to since he refused to release her inheritance. But who would she marry? A woman gave up much when she took a man’s name. She needed someone honorable, a man without expectation of controlling her or the use of her fortune. A man of which Adam and Elaine approved, but without other important connections in Society. Then he would be less likely to get the unsavory ideas people like her mother and Richard often entertained.

Where was one to find such a man?

The butler entered the room. “Mr. and Mrs. Gillensford, a Mr. Cobbett is here, seeking an audience with you both.”

Philippa went still. Mr. Cobbett. Her garden rescuer? She met Elaine’s eye and nodded, not objecting to the interruption of the conversation. Adam said nothing, merely continued his upward glare.

“Lovely. A distraction.” Elaine sent a soft smile to Philippa, her eyes full of sympathy. “Send him in, Hopkins.”

Adam rolled his head forward again, his eyebrows drawn together. “The military gentleman from the ball. You danced with him, didn’t you?”

Elaine gathered up the paper from where it sat on the table in the center of the room. “I did. I found him most amiable. Where

should we hide this horrid thing?" She held the newsprint between two fingers, as though it was a dead rodent rather than ink and paper.

"Troublesome newsprint." Adam took it from his wife and stuffed it behind a cushion on the couch. He caught Philippa's eye and scowled. "We're going to have to talk about it eventually, Pippa. I have the feeling Richard and our mother will not let the subject rest, even should the rest of Society forget about it."

"It is a problem for another day." Philippa came to stand before her favored chair, adopting a properly welcoming pose. "For now, I am interested to see why Mr. Cobbett has called." Did she dare tell Adam the near-stranger had rescued her from Lord Walter? The former soldier was a witness to the innocence of her garden stroll.

The door opened again, and the butler announced, "Mr. Cobbett to see you, Mr. and Mrs. Gillensford."

Adam and Elaine both rose, and everyone performed the proper bows and curtsies. Philippa kept her eyes up as much as she could, taking in the appearance of the man once more. He dressed well, though his clothing was cut for practicality rather than fashion. And looked a little worn. His black leather eyepatch covered his left eye, and his scars were as she remembered. The left side of his face looked as though a giant cat had raked its claws across him, leaving jagged scars behind.

Standing upright again, as stiff and proper as any soldier, Mr. Cobbett did not smile. His countenance was quite solemn. "Thank you for admitting me into your home today, Mr. Gillensford. Mrs. Gillensford. It is a pleasure to see you both. I have no wish to take up your valuable time." He cut a quick glance at Philippa, and for the briefest moment his brow creased, as though he had not seen her there before. "I beg your pardon, Lady Philippa. I hope you are well." His expression seemed to communicate a question, and she had to smile at his lingering concern over their last interaction.

"I am quite well, all things considered. Thank you."

He nodded his acceptance of that response, then turned back to Adam and Elaine. He reached into his coat, withdrawing a folded

rectangle of newsprint. Philippa's heart jolted. He'd read the gossip and known at once what it alluded to!

He brandished the paper before him like a saber, his solemn frown unwavering. "After reading the paper this morning, I knew I had to come and offer your family my services in whatever way will help most."

With a groan, Philippa lowered herself into her chair and dropped her face into her hands. Through her fingers she saw Adam's eyes go round as a clockface, and just as white.

Mr. Cobbett looked from Adam to Philippa, his frown turning to one of perplexity. "I am completely at your service," he continued, sounding entirely uncertain of himself.

A strange sense of relief flooded her at his earnestness. Did he mean to provide a rebuttal to the newspaper's statements? Or had he come—her heart sped at the very idea—to offer another sort of fix altogether?

"Mr. Cobbett," Elaine said quickly, stepping forward with hand outstretched to his newspaper. "Might I ask to what you refer? None of us have read the paper this morning." Ah, ever practical, Elaine wasn't about to jump to conclusions. Philippa blinked. It hadn't even occurred to her there might be something else in the paper worthy of a visit from Mr. Cobbett.

The visitor focused on Elaine, his frown lessening somewhat. "There are several descriptions of the ball. Remarks about your proposed hospital, too. I had hoped I might prove useful. In regard to the hospital project." He glanced again at Philippa, the confusion resurfacing. "But if I have called at an inappropriate time, I will happily return later."

Adam found his voice again. "Not at all. This is an ideal time. But perhaps we had better go into the study." He gave Philippa a worrisome look, then held his arm out to Elaine. "My wife will join us, of course, as she is at the heart of this work. Pippa, you will excuse us."

"Of course." Philippa rose unsteadily to her feet. Why had her mind immediately jumped to her own plight as it had? And why, when Mr. Cobbett had offered his help when she thought it applied to her, had she experienced such a hopeful moment of ease? "It is good to see

you again, Mr. Cobbett." She curtsied as he took his leave, following behind Adam and Elaine, though she noted a brief glint of curiosity in his eye before he turned away.

Crossing the room, Philippa reached beneath the cushion to the hidden newspaper. She drew it out and sat down, her eyes sweeping across the pages until she found what had brought Mr. Cobbett to their door. Then she settled in to read about Adam and Elaine's hospital for soldiers, trying to push her own difficulty from her mind.

Mr. Cobbett's character interested her. First, he had spoken passionately about what England owed her sons returned from war. Second, he saved her, a stranger, from the advances of another man. Without thought or word of a possible reward for his kindness. Third, he came in person to offer his services to her brother and sister-in-law for their cause. Not once revealing the situation in which he had found Philippa.

By the time Philippa closed the paper, she had several seedlings of ideas in her mind. One of which included the noble former soldier.

"But first," she murmured to herself, "I need to find a solicitor."

Five

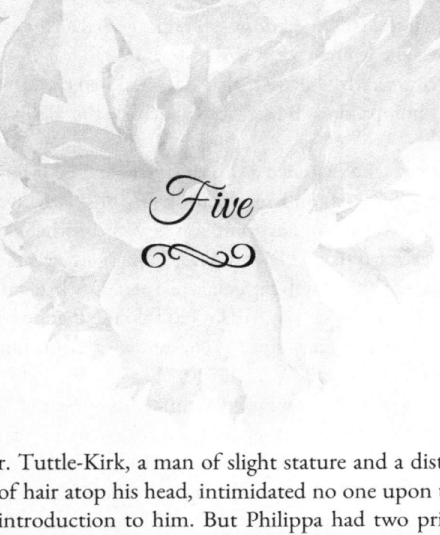

Mr. Tuttle-Kirk, a man of slight stature and a distinct lack of hair atop his head, intimidated no one upon their first introduction to him. But Philippa had two prior meetings with the solicitor and given the way his mustache twitched upward with a smile, he had a favorable enough impression of her. She was glad she had worn a walking suit of dark blue, hopefully giving her the air of someone much older and mature. Not everyone took young ladies seriously.

"Lady Philippa." He bowed as she and her maid entered his office, then gestured to one of the more comfortable chairs across the desk from him. "And Miss...?" He met the maid's eyes with a kindly expression.

"This is Bessie Lambert, my maid." And the only servant she trusted not to tattle to her mother, brothers, or sister-in-law. Two days had passed since the newspaper published its ugly piece of gossip about her. She'd undergone two days of her mother's worries and her brother's frustration before daring to sneak out of Adam's house on her own.

"Miss Lambert, won't you please sit here, next to your mistress? Ah, wonderful. I trust my secretary will know to bring tea." He looked

up through the still open doorway and nodded at the young man who had shown the women in. “Carver?”

“Of course, Mr. Tuttle-Kirk.” Carver closed the door behind them, leaving Philippa and Bessie seated across the desk from the wiry solicitor.

His mustache twitched as he sat down, and he lifted a pair of spectacles from his desk and fit them on his nose. “Lady Philippa. It is lovely to see you again. Last time was at your brother’s wedding, was it not? A beautiful day.” He chuckled, looking every bit as pleased as if he’d arranged their match himself. He’d certainly had a part in it.

“Yes, it was a lovely day. Adam has told me that he has worked with you on a few contracts since then, and he has nothing but positive things to say about you.”

Tuttle-Kirk’s eyes twinkled behind his glasses. “Not always the case, was it? Yes. Your brother is a fine gentleman, just as his great-uncle hoped. I have heard marvelous things about what he and his wife get up to these days. Opening orphanages and hospitals. They are veritable saints.” He sighed happily and joined his hands together on the table. “But none of this explains your presence in my office today, my lady. Which makes me most curious, indeed.”

A knock on the door forestalled Philippa’s answer, and the young man came in pushing a cart with a plain, dark blue tea service into the room. The cups were all gold-rimmed, but otherwise the set was most unremarkable. The assistant withdrew again, and Mr. Tuttle-Kirk offered to pour out for all of them once the door had shut.

“Here you are, my lady. You did say cream, did you not? Ah, and this is for you, Miss Lambert. Don’t be shy. Help yourself to the biscuits, or else Mr. Carver will eat them all and have a terrible stomachache.”

Bessie hid her smile behind her tea cup but did take a biscuit. The maid likely hadn’t ever been treated so well by anyone other than Philippa and Elaine. Philippa made certain to give an approving nod to her maid before she turned back to business.

“Mr. Tuttle-Kirk, allow me to satisfy your curiosity.” She rested her teacup in its saucer. “You see, I have found myself in something of a

muddle with my elder brother, Lord Montecliff. You do remember Richard, do you not?"

"I have many a memory of your brother to draw from." Mr. Tuttle-Kirk's eyes darkened. "I battled wits with his solicitor for some time, over the matter of the inheritances."

"And you came out victorious," Philippa noted with a quickness she hoped didn't sound overeager. "For which I am most grateful. And that is why I am here. I need someone to draw swords, figurately of course, and champion my cause in the Court of Chancery. If it goes that far." Philippa met Bessie's eyes and nodded. Her maid put down her tea and drew out the leather portfolio she'd carried in her basket.

Mr. Tuttle-Kirk accepted the portfolio, the wrinkles of his forehead deepening. "Are you having financial misunderstandings with your eldest brother, Lady Philippa?"

"Of a sort." Philippa pointed to the top paper when the solicitor opened the fold of leather. "That is a copy of my father's will, which I obtained from my brother Adam's records. I have been unable to get my own copy from my eldest brother and his solicitor. But I've always known what that will entitled me to, as you will see in the fifth paragraph."

The gentlemen wrinkled his nose as he read, his spectacles reflecting the words as he spoke them aloud. "'...And to each of my daughters, I leave the sum of twenty-one thousand pounds. Should they marry before reaching majority, the sum will be their portion in marriage as part of the dowry agreement. Should either daughter reach the year of their majority unmarried, the executor of my estate will transfer twenty-thousand pounds into that daughter's stewardship, that she may live in a manner befitting a lady of the household. The one thousand pounds remaining will return to the executor for his trouble.' A handsome sum for the mere act of signing a few banknotes," Mr. Tuttle-Kirk mused. "This seems very straightforward."

"Yes, it does." Philippa started to relax and managed to take up her tea without her hands so much as trembling with excitement. "Except

my brother, Lord Montecliff, is refusing to adhere to the terms of the will. I turned three and twenty just above two months ago."

Eyebrows shooting up, the solicitor bent to examine the paper again. "Ah. Your brother has not released your funds to you, I take it?"

"No. Despite the fact that I have asked, several times. In person as well as in writing. I included copies of my letters to him, and his replies, beneath the will."

With a purse of his lips, Mr. Tuttle-Kirk turned through the pages and read over each. "Yes, I see. Here he simply puts you off and reminds you to enjoy the Season. And here he tells you that you have no business with the funds that a husband should control. Yes. Ah. And here it is—as I thought. He claims he has a year from the day you turned three and twenty in which to render you that which is already yours." He looked up at her.

Philippa nodded. "Precisely. Because of how it's worded. "'Should either daughter reach the year of their majority,' is what it says. Can he be correct in his interpretations?"

"That depends. One could argue this means when you turned two and twenty, as that completed your twenty-second year and began your twenty-third." His mustache rustled above his deep frown. "Or we could read it as your brother wishes. Though I think any sane person—which not all who sit in judgement are, I should warn you—would interpret it as both you and I have interpreted it. That the money is yours as of the day you reached three and twenty."

Her heart thudded heavily in her chest, and Philippa leaned forward in her seat. "What can be done, Mr. Tuttle-Kirk? I should like my independence from my brother and my mother, but until those funds are released, my brother is legally keeping me bound to him and his wishes."

"And what are his wishes, Lady Philippa?" Mr. Tuttle-Kirk leaned forward, too, his gaze searching hers. "I should think he would have no reason to, if you'll pardon the phrase, lord over you as he does. Unless he has a purpose for your future which you do not share."

"He wants me to marry." Philippa sat back again, looking away from the kind solicitor's puzzled frown. "Specifically, he would like me

to marry one of his cronies. The younger son of another lord. To keep our bloodline unsullied. Someone who will be pliable to my brother's will, no doubt."

"A nefarious plan, indeed. And I suppose your brother means to make you more desperate for the release of your funds as time goes on."

That brought Philippa's attention back to the solicitor. "What do you mean?"

Mr. Tuttle-Kirk rose from his place behind the desk and paced to the large window overlooking the busy street below. Lawyers and solicitors made up the tenancies of the entire row. "I must ask, my lady, if you have noticed any strange behavior by your brother—or any of the family members who agree with his way of thinking—that would seem to push you toward a particular match?"

"I know my brother approves of a certain man, who has been most persistent in seeking an attachment." Philippa raised her eyebrows. "I know he has spoken to my brother, and he does seem to show up everywhere I am invited."

"Ah." Mr. Tuttle-Kirk turned around. He went to a drawer in his desk and opened it, then pulled out a copy of the newspaper. A newspaper she had seen far too often of late. "You speak of the mysterious Lord W."

Her jaw dropped open, and she looked up at him in shock. "You have read about that?"

"Of course. I had to know everything about your brother's charity ball. And this was in the same paper." He dropped it to his desk, his frown returning. "I am not usually one for gossip, Lady Philippa, but as several days have passed, I must ask if this piece of rumor has died down or become inflamed."

Her mother had spent all of the afternoon before writing letters to her friends in Society. Philippa had thought little of it until that moment. But if Richard and her mother worked together, as they so often did, perhaps her mother meant to stir the rumors about rather than let them be laid to rest. That she suspected her own mother of such a thing caused a sharp pain in her breast. "I have not been out much in Society this week. Yet I have the sudden feeling that you are

right in thinking...in thinking that this will not be the last Lord Walter's name and mine are bandied about together."

Bessie appeared sympathetic as she lowered her gaze to the plate of biscuits in her lap. The maid surprised her further by speaking, her words soft in the large office. "Beggin' your pardon, my lady, but I don't think the gossip has died down. The servants below stairs are saying it's only a matter of time before his lordship makes you agree to a contracted marriage."

"Thank you for speaking up, Miss Lambert." Mr. Tuttle-Kirk paced back to his chair and sat, meeting Philippa's gaze with a hard look in his eyes. "As the servants think, so too does London. At least, in my experience, that's how it goes."

Philippa rubbed at her temples before remembering herself, adjusting her posture and affecting an air of calm that she certainly didn't feel. "I would like to remove myself from my brother's protection and have the financial security my father intended for me as soon as possible. What, in your expert opinion, ought I to do?"

Mr. Tuttle-Kirk looked down at the papers upon his desk, and Philippa appreciated the long moment's silence as he considered the situation. When he spoke, his voice was gentle even as his words were firm. "You send a legal notice to your brother, written by a man of law whom you trust, informing him to make the full payment of your inheritance to you or else you will take him to court for a very public trial."

"Would you please represent my interests, Mr. Tuttle-Kirk?"

His smile briefly appeared beneath his mustache. "Of course, Lady Philippa. I am honored that you've asked." Then he went back to his more serious mien. "That will begin the proceedings. Knowing your brother from my past interactions with him, I do not believe he will easily acquiesce to your request. So I must prepare you to do battle before the judgement bar, my lady."

A sickly, sinking feeling took hold in her stomach. "I understand."

"And then we are at the mercy of a judge, who might well side with your brother, meaning you will have no access to those funds until your twenty-fourth birthday."

Philippa wilted, her shoulders falling and her calm disintegrating a little more. "I see. All while the public watches, no doubt, as my brother tries to bend us all to his will." She closed her eyes and sat back in her chair, not caring about imperfect posture. "If this is the only way, then I am prepared to go forward. I am certain Adam and Elaine will let me stay with them until it's all over."

Her mother really had no say over what Philippa did, given that Philippa had come of age, but she had wanted to preserve that relationship as much as possible. Even if it meant letting her mother drag her from ballroom to ballroom, and salon to salon, questing after a social status Philippa didn't even care to possess.

Her hands trembled in her lap, and she hurriedly folded them on top of one another. She couldn't lose heart yet. Despite her realization that her mother and brother could both make her life quite miserable when they found out how determined she was to avoid marriage to Lord Walter—or anyone like him—and gain her freedom.

"There may be one other way," Mr. Tuttle-Kirk said, sounding most reluctant. When she lifted her eyes to peer at him, he was grimacing. "I am loathe to propose the idea to you, Lady Philippa, given that you are attempting to gain independence. But if, perhaps, there is a gentleman to whom you would not mind attaching yourself to through marriage, that would put an end to anyone else deciding your fate for you."

At once she remembered when Mr. Cobbett had appeared at the townhouse, paper in hand, visage serious. When she'd thought, for one absurd moment, that he'd come to propose marriage, to save her reputation like some hero from a gothic novel. Thank goodness Elaine had said something before Philippa answered him.

But what if that *had* been the case? Was there any gentleman of her acquaintance who might take her cause up as his own and marry her without expectation of gaining control over Philippa herself?

"You are thinking of someone," Mr. Tuttle-Kirk said, and Bessie inhaled sharply.

"Perhaps." Philippa glanced at her maid, then looked up at Mr.

Tuttle-Kirk. "I do not know the gentleman very well. Yet. And I am not certain how to make inquiries..."

Mr. Tuttle-Kirk withdrew a pencil and sheet of paper from his desk and slid both across to her. "Write down his name and anything else you know. I can have a full report ready for you on Monday. I'll also have a draft of the letter to send to your brother, and a draft of a marriage contract for you to look over to decide if that option is worth your pursuit."

Philippa's heart raced as she picked up the pencil. Was this at all wise? Could she not think of another man whom she might trust? Yet she wrote Mr. Cobbett's name, what she knew of his military career, and a brief description of him. Then she folded the paper and handed it back to Mr. Tuttle-Kirk, her hand no longer trembling.

His blue eyes met hers, an unexpected warmth and kindness within them. "Take heart, Lady Philippa. I will bend my mind to this issue, and I will not rest until you are happily settled. One way or another."

"Thank you, sir." She measured her breaths, regained control of her calm, and managed a smile. "I am glad I came to you."

"As am I."

She and Bessie left shortly after. If anyone asked where they had gone, Bessie knew to report that her ladyship had needed a walk in the park to clear her head. Philippa intended to plead a headache and hide in her room. But Monday was four days away, and she doubted she could hide away the whole time she waited for Mr. Tuttle-Kirk to gather his forces in preparation for battle.

Which meant she might have to get creative in her avoidance of her duties as a dowager countess's daughter.

Six

Mr. and Mrs. Moreton kept a handsome home above the law offices where Moreton worked. Myles had always admired the large rooms with their wide windows looking over a quiet street. He especially liked when the couple invited him to take dinner with them. It meant further preservation of his funds and a pleasant evening spent with people he held in high esteem and affection.

Emmeline Moreton kept a well-laid table. As it was only the three of them dining together, they were always informal, too. Which meant Myles didn't need to stuff the two smallest fingers of his left-hand glove. He could simply leave the gloves off, and not concern himself over who might stare at him.

"I'm quite pleased that you went to Mr. Gillensford," Moreton said. "It sounds as though you have found a productive distraction from your busy schedule." He chuckled.

Myles allowed his friend the jest, and he even smiled about it himself. "I cannot say I am overjoyed at the prospect of interacting with humanity again." He shrugged and put down his fork. "The Gillensfords make it more bearable. They have asked me to take charge of a medical advisory committee. My assignment is to bring together

doctors who have treated soldiers and compile their recommendations for continuing treatments in a hospital."

The enormity of the task weighed upon him. Nothing had induced him to seek any company, outside of the Moretons and occasionally his family, since his return from war. Yet for how daunting it seemed, the knowledge that he worked to better the situations of men injured for their country kept him hopeful.

"That is marvelous, Myles." Emmeline gave the signal for a waiting manservant to take away the meal. "I am pleased that you have become so deeply involved. I am on Mrs. Gillensford's committee, soliciting donations for the interior of the hospital. Bedding, linens, even artwork. We believe a pleasant environment is necessary for the speedy recovery of the mind and the body."

His throat tightened as Myles nodded his agreement with her.

Myles had spent hours a day staring at a blank wall after he'd moved into his rented rooms in London. He had lacked motivation to do much more than exist. Then Moreton and Emmeline had come to visit for the first time. Myles had been embarrassed at the poverty in which he lived. They had seen his bare walls and floors. And though they hadn't commented upon the state of things, Myles had made up his mind that he was unworthy of their notice. He'd sunk into a deep melancholy when they'd left that night.

The next morning, as he sat and stared once more at the blank wall, Emmeline had arrived with her servants, carrying two small carpets and three framed paintings. Where the things came from, she never said. But she put the largest painting on the bare wall. It depicted a scene in the country of a hillside dotted with sheep and a man walking with a rake slung over his shoulder.

That simple scene became something Myles studied every day. And somehow, the peace of the artwork transposed itself to his heart. Inexplicably, it made things better.

"I do hope the rest of London can get behind this hospital idea," Moreton said as they all rose from the table in the small dining room. "The Gillensfords' efforts haven't had as much attention of late, with all the fuss over Mr. Gillensford's sister."

"Lady Philippa?" Myles blurted with some surprise.

Emmeline looked over her shoulder as they went through to the modest and comfortable sitting room. "Yes, the poor dear. I don't suppose you would've heard, or read about her in the paper? You do not strike me as someone who reads the gossipy bits of the newssheets regularly."

They seated themselves, the couple on their usual couch where Moreton could put his arm around his wife's shoulder or easily hold her hand. Myles sat in the chair nearest the hearth, his left side to the fire and away from his hosts.

"A gentleman wouldn't interest himself in gossip, my dear." Moreton crossed his legs and leaned closer to his wife.

She tutted at him. "Gentlemen are the very worst gossips. I have heard what they put in those betting books of theirs at White's and Boodle's. Everyone has. I should think gambling over gossip is worse than merely gossiping."

Remembering the deep blue eyes of Lady Philippa, Myles recalled that the woman *had* seemed out of sorts when he called at the Gillensford home the week before. "What fuss has there been made over Lady Philippa?" he asked with genuine interest. He well remembered that when he asked after her health, she had said she was "Well enough, all things considered." He hadn't thought she referred to more than her unfortunate incident in the garden with the popinjay.

"Oh, that." Emmeline settled against her husband, apparently forgetting she had been lecturing him on the ills of gossiping men. "It's quite awful. There was that first article in the paper, of course, about her slipping into the garden with a lord."

Myles's breath hitched. He knew a great deal about that incident.

"Apparently, her mother's friends are spreading it abroad that she is a terrible flirt. Lady Darwimple was quite vocal at some ball or other last evening, saying that she had warned Lady Fredericka for ages about Lady Philippa's independent nature."

Moreton's eyebrows drew down sharply as he stared at his wife. "How do you know all of this?"

She barely turned her head to answer him, lowering her eyelashes

prettily. "My dear husband, how does one know anything in London? The papers and the servants."

His curiosity unsated, Myles drew the conversation back quickly before the married couple could use the opportunity to flirt with each other. Again. "Surely an independent nature isn't something to cause an uproar in Society."

"It certainly is for an unmarried young woman," Moreton said, settling more deeply into his cushions. "Though plenty of married men will tell you it's not at all uncommon among their wives."

Emmeline glared at her husband and snatched one of the cushions from behind his back, making him protest. "There is nothing wrong with a woman who is capable of making decisions on her own."

Sensing the precariousness of staying on topic, Myles hurried to speak before his friend could respond. "An article in the paper and a rude peeress despising independence in younger women don't seem like enough to cause an issue or take away from what the Gillensfords are trying to accomplish."

"One would think." Moreton glared mockingly at his wife. "Do tell us, my darling, how any of this puts plans for the hospital in shadow?"

"The article that appeared today would explain it best." She rose, making her husband's arm drop suddenly, and went to a table near the window. She opened a drawer and pulled out a folded pamphlet. "This appeared in one of those little things children sell on the corner. It's one of those satirical drawings. What does one call them, Joshua?"

"Comical caricature, or something." Moreton folded his arms and made eye contact with Myles. "I've heard people in the business are calling them *cartoons* now. That will never catch on. Made-up words never do."

"It's French, isn't it?" Emmeline muttered, then dismissed the comment with a wave of her hand. She turned the pages of the newspaper as she walked toward Myles. "Ah-ha. Here it is. Midway down the page, on the left." She handed the newssheet to Myles and tapped the spot.

Taking the paper, Myles rose and stood closer to the hearth and a

lamp upon the mantel. Having only one good eye, and standing in the semi-dark room, conditions were not favorable for reading. He stared hard at the paper until the words came into focus, then read aloud. "'Readers may find it interesting that Lady P. of last week's scandal is yet refusing the suit of the most eligible Lord W., though all know it is only a matter of time before she capitulates for the good of her reputation and her family's future endeavors.'" He folded the offending piece of writing in half. "They mean the hospital, surely."

"That is how I interpreted it." Emmeline reseated herself beside her husband and folded her hands in her lap. "The poor girl. The snobs of Society would love to see her capitulate, so they can congratulate themselves by saying 'I told you this is how it would end.' And if whomever is shaming Lady Philippa tries to use her supposed lack of virtue as a reason to withdraw support from the Gillensfords..."

"Her supposed disregard of honorable behavior will reflect badly upon her brother and sister-in-law." Myles cast the paper into another chair, glowering at it. "This is yet another example of why, by principle, I avoid people entirely. Surely this whole ridiculous drama will be forgotten in a week."

"Unlikely, given that Lady Fredericka and her friends are discussing little else." Emmeline looked up at her husband. "I wish I knew how to help. Mrs. Gillensford must be at her wit's end, with her horrid mother-in-law and Lady Philippa living beneath her roof at this moment. I imagine there isn't a great deal of peace in that household."

Myles said nothing, but retook his seat, and soon enough the couple across from him were speaking on other matters. And flirting rather outrageously, considering he was still present. But he settled in, content to remain in their company for an hour more before returning to his rented rooms.

When he turned in that evening, he thought more about Lady Philippa's predicament. The night of the ball, he'd left the hotel's grand halls for the cool air of the gardens. He'd had no thought of playing rescuer to anyone, let alone the sister of the host and hostess. Yet he had been there, near the fountain, in exactly the right place to hear the dishonorable Lord Walter threaten a woman. A woman whose identity

he did not even know until he had pulled her from the darkness between the hedges.

Lady Philippa had appeared shocked to see him. And exceedingly relieved. Was there more he could have done to help preserve her reputation? They had only encountered a few people on their way back into the ballroom, and Lady Philippa had made a point of gaining their attention. Someone had spread rumors they knew to be false, but why? To sully the good name of a woman and her family? Or, more likely, to find some way to turn the situation to their advantage.

Lord Walter himself became suspect.

Sleep did not come at once that night. When he finally drifted off into a fitful slumber, Myles was as disgusted with High Society as ever. The *haute ton* cared for nothing and no one, except when it came to climbing higher upon their pile of wealth and self-importance.

Upon waking the next morning, Myles prepared himself for the day as usual. He dressed, made a few notations in his diary, and then went out in search of breakfast at his usual spot. His mind never strayed far from Lady Philippa's dilemma, and he searched his paper with an eye for the small squares of ink devoted to sharing the *on-dits* of Society.

He grew hopeful until he found a new entry that had to have something to do with Lady Philippa. *It is rumored that a certain sought-after young lady will not appear at any more of this Season's events, marred as her reputation has become through unscrupulous flirtations.*

Who takes joy in writing such drivel? Myles glared at the paper and laid it down in an empty chair at his table. The sort of person delighting in Lady Philippa's circumstances, and trying to spin a story from whatever hardship the lady faced, belonged in polite Society no more than a rabid cur.

Myles went back to his breakfast, trying to enjoy the now-cold sausages and beans. Today, the cook had burned the toast rather than the sausage. An interesting change.

The bell over the door jangled, the sound familiar to him enough that he never bothered checking to see which regular had entered the cafe. Even if that did make it easier for Moreton to creep up on him.

When the chair directly across from him scraped against the floor, Myles didn't even look up.

"If Emmeline has sent you to spy upon me again, I beg you inform her that I am perfectly capable of looking after myself."

"One would hope, given your age."

The voice that answered was not at all the one he expected. He immediately stood up, nearly knocking his chair backward as it made a horrible screeching noise sliding across the floor. "Lady Philippa." He bowed, then realized he still held a fork in one hand. He dropped it on his plate. "I did not see you come inside."

Her dark brown eyes gleamed with good humor, and the curve of her lips softened. She wore a pale green gown and jacket with epaulets, and a small tricorn hat pinned atop her head at a jaunty angle. As though the military style were a fashion one could command rather than a necessary uniform. Of course, she certainly looked far better than most he had seen don such a style.

"I am sorry to have disturbed your meal. I thought I might join you, if you do not mind. There is something I should very much like to discuss with you." She looked over her shoulder and gestured. A young woman dressed in darker clothing and a modest straw bonnet curtsied, then withdrew to another corner of the cafe. "My maid will likely welcome a respite from following me all over Town."

Then Lady Philippa sat down, not waiting for him to get her chair or accept her offer of companionship. He looked to where the proprietor of the cafe stood, eyes wide and staring at the most finely dressed person who had ever entered his establishment.

"Would you, er, care for something to drink, my lady? Or eat?" Myles offered.

"Tea would be lovely, thank you." She daintily removed her gloves and laid them atop each other on the worn blue tablecloth.

Myles made eye contact with the proprietor again and mouthed the word *tea.* The aproned man nodded quickly and disappeared through the doors to his kitchen. The confused fellow likely didn't have any idea how to serve someone so obviously above his own class.

"Lady Philippa." Myles reached behind him to drag his chair

forward again, then sat down with some measure of decorum. "I cannot remember ever seeing you in this establishment before."

She folded her hands before her on the table. "I have never been here before." She glanced around the room, then to the large window near them. "I understand you frequent this cafe."

He stared at her, trying to take her measure and failing. Miserably. "I am here most mornings. Though not many people could have told you that."

"No. Not many." She turned to look at him again, and the pink in her cheeks darkened. "As I said, I have something important to discuss with you. And I do not imagine you are going to enjoy parts of this conversation. I think I must get the unpleasantness out of the way before anything else."

Myles narrowed his eye at her, utterly flummoxed. What could the woman mean, seeking him out? They were strangers to one another. Yet she knew where to find him and had some matter of business to discuss with him. It had to regard the evening of the ball. Did she perhaps wish him to refute the rumors in some way? Would that not only give them greater credence?

"If that is what you feel is best, my lady." Myles glanced again at the maid in the corner, noting she had taken out a book to read rather than spend her time gawking at her mistress. That either meant the maid knew what was going on or that she didn't care to know. Myles wagered on the former. "What unpleasant thing do you have to say to me?"

Lady Philippa's chin tipped upward, and he saw her defenses go up the way one might raise a shield. The merriment in her eyes faded, and her lovely face grew pale. "I requested that my solicitor investigate you so I could learn more about the sort of man you are and what kind of family you have come from."

Myles stared at her. "You did what?" He wasn't certain whether to be amused or affronted.

The proprietor arrived and sat a tea tray on the table with one pot, two cups, and the necessary containers of cream and sugar. Then he

vanished without a word, leaving Myles and Lady Philippa staring at one another in silence.

~

Philippa did not fidget. She had command enough of the moment to keep perfectly still. Mr. Tuttle-Kirk had insisted that she maintain a veneer of calm, even if she did not feel it, when she approached Mr. Cobbett. He hadn't liked that she wanted to do it alone. In a place where Cobbett was comfortable. But it had seemed cruel to invite him to her home or have Mr. Tuttle-Kirk try to explain the situation to the former soldier.

If she was desperate enough to approach Mr. Cobbett with her ridiculous scheme, she ought to be brave enough to present it to him by herself.

She poured herself a cup of tea, using the time it took to add a splash of cream to prepare her next words. "I know it is not the thing, to admit one dove into your life without your knowledge. But I would much rather begin this conversation with honesty. I have no wish to cloud the issue with politeness."

"The issue," he repeated, staring at her with a dumbfounded expression upon his face. "Which issue would that be, if it is not your delving into my privacy?"

He had every right to be upset, she reminded herself. Philippa stirred her tea with the small, slightly bent spoon from the tray. "I find myself in the midst of a dilemma, Mr. Cobbett."

Avoiding eye contact seemed wise for the moment. With such a fierce man glaring at her, she might never get her words out. Feigning bravery was easier when she needn't see his frowns.

"The night we met, and wherein you subsequently rescued me from the attentions of a man I did not wish to entertain—"

The gentleman interrupted her with a dark chuckle, and then he said, "You mean the night Lord Walter accosted you, and I pulled you through a bush."

She put the spoon down. "Yes. That is what I meant."

"If you are going to speak honestly, Lady Philippa, you might also speak plainly. I would prefer to get to the heart of the matter rather than listen to your pretty use of the King's English."

She darted a look up at him then, her eyes wide with surprise. She expected him to appear vexed, and instead she saw the glimmer of humor in his eye. And a slight smile upon his half-ravaged face. He looked most pleasant, actually.

"Very well." Philippa shifted her hands to her lap. She chewed her bottom lip a moment, reordering her explanation. How did she fully explain and use the fewest possible words? Her rehearsed speech had sounded impressive to her in the mirror that morning.

Perhaps brevity and bluntness would serve as her allies. "If I am to speak plainly, then here is the circumstance. My brother will force me into a marriage I do not want, to a man I cannot trust or abide. To save myself from this fate, I must find my own match, and quickly take a husband of my choosing."

Mr. Cobbett arched an eyebrow at her, but he said nothing. Perhaps he waited for her to do the unthinkable. What woman offered marriage to a man? Let alone to a man she barely knew. Yet she had considered the few options available to her, discussed them with Mr. Tuttle-Kirk, and had found this course best. Being missish now would serve no purpose.

Philippa held herself perfectly erect, the very model of a British noblewoman. "To take control of my situation, I need a man who will understand these circumstances and be as much a partner in business as in life. I have decided to ask you, Mr. Cobbett, if you would consider marrying me."

Seven

Desperation had driven many a man past the edge of reason. Now it had led the elegant, beautiful woman sitting before Myles to the brink of ruin. The earnest expression upon her face and her previous-to-that-moment calm kept him from immediately dismissing her words as a poorly timed jest.

She was serious.

And she waited for Myles to make an answer while her cheeks grew from pale to pink, then pink to red.

"My lady." Myles leaned closer and lowered his voice, though the old cafe was nearly empty of patrons. "Your proposition is...interesting. But even if marriage is the only way you can escape the predicament in which you find yourself, you cannot consider me as your partner in it. You do not know me."

She leaned closer, one elegant finger tapping the table between them. "I *do* know you. I know all about you. I know you have two older brothers and three younger sisters, and two of your sisters are not yet married." She kept eye contact with him as she rushed through her words. "You are a gentleman's son, and your family cannot support you. Yet you have maintained your dignity by living within the limited means of your pension. Sometimes you train other gentleman as a

pugilist, but only in private clubs. You are not liberal in your drink. You have no debts. You give pennies away to the poor nearly every morning. You keep to yourself. But you always, *always* help others when the opportunity arises."

He sat back, narrowing his eye as he took in the woman before him. Yes. She had said before that her solicitor had investigated him. It seemed the man had done a thorough job.

"Please, do not be offended." Lady Philippa's liquid blue eyes pled with him. "My brother and his wife think highly of you, too. They were impressed by your ideas about the hospital, and your willingness to help."

She knew the barest details of his life. She *didn't* know enough to propose marriage. They were complete strangers. "There must be other gentlemen more suitable," he said. "You are a beautiful woman, the sister of an earl. You must have other options."

Lady Philippa shook her head slowly. "I have met almost no one without my mother's approval. And beyond that, I need to marry someone like you. Someone honorable, who isn't looking to marry me for my connections or money. You are precisely that sort."

The notion was insane. He had no business speaking with her any further. He should stand up and walk out and never speak of this strange interlude to anyone. Yet Myles found himself curious, too. He leaned forward. "And what if I am not inclined to marry?"

"I will do my best to persuade you. You see, I am not inclined to marry, either." She picked up her gloves, but only to fiddle with them upon the table. "I have no wish to be under any man's thumb. We would negotiate terms as you would in a business merger, and I believe you would find my conditions favorable. Though you live modestly, would you not like to have a better income? If not for yourself, perhaps to contribute more to your younger sisters? Or to helping others?"

Myles quite forgot himself and raked his left hand through his hair. "You wish to bribe me into matrimony?" Could the conversation turn any stranger?

Her cheeks flared red again. "I should say not. This is a business negotiation, remember? There would be benefits to both parties." She

likely wanted to try to sound like she was laying out a contractual agreement, but Myles sensed the slight tremor in her voice. He could see the way her fingers shook as she played with the gloves. "If you marry me, I can go about in Society without fear for my reputation. Married women are given vastly more freedom than those who remain single all their lives. I will come into my inheritance. My eldest brother can no longer threaten me in any way, because I will be my husband's responsibility."

He arched his eyebrow at her. "Really. There goes your freedom again."

"Not at all, because how much say you have over me can be included in our contract." She glanced to the wall where her maid still sat, then back at him. "I have been away from home too long already. If you will at least consider my proposal, I would be greatly appreciative. Here." She opened the reticule that had rested in her lap since her arrival. "This is my solicitor's card. He's agreed to speak with you, and to show you the preliminary terms I have had him draw up. He's prepared to answer any questions you have, too."

Myles took the card in his right hand, but then fixed her in place with a hard stare. "You must understand how mad this sounds."

"I do." She tied up her purse strings again. "But people forge marriages every day where both parties stand to gain less and lose more. Please, Mr. Cobbett. At least speak with Mr. Tuttle-Kirk."

His gaze flicked to the card in his hand to confirm that absurd name belonged to her solicitor. Then he stood as she rose. He tried one more question. "What if my affections are engaged elsewhere?"

Lady Philippa's eyes widened somewhat. "I suppose...that is..." Her cheeks flushed as she began to stutter. "It would depend on the circumstances?" Her voice rose to make the statement a question. "If you cannot marry where your affections are engaged, then—if we married—and if you were discreet...?" She appeared mortified to even speak such a thing aloud.

Myles narrowed his good eye at her. "I was raised to believe in both honor and fidelity, my lady."

She visibly swallowed before nodding with a solemn expression.

"There are few men who are, it sometimes seems. I must leave now." She lowered her gaze from his and tugged on her gloves. He caught the bright glimmer in her eyes he had seen once already, before she started crying. "Won't you please speak to Mr. Tuttle-Kirk? Then if you remain against the idea, I will never trouble you again."

He picked up his handkerchief from the table and caught her hand in his, feeling the tremble in her fingers as he placed the cloth in their grasp. "My lady." He bent his head toward her, drawing her gaze up once more. "I will speak with him, if only to impress upon you that things cannot be this desperate."

"I am this desperate," she whispered. "And though they don't say it, I know my brother and his wife are already feeling the consequences of being linked so closely to me. I cannot see them hurt by the family's schemes for my future." She squeezed his hand once, then took the linen to wipe at her eyes again. "Thank you for speaking with me this morning, Mr. Cobbett. You have been very kind." She walked away quickly and out the door. The bell jangled above her, then rang out again as her maid rose and hurried after the young lady.

Myles looked down at the card he'd dropped on the table, then out the window in time to see Lady Philippa climb into a hired hack across the street. She looked out the window when she'd settled, the soft green of her dress and hat a bright spot of color in an otherwise dull view.

Myles worked his jaw, then withdrew the coins necessary to pay for his mostly uneaten breakfast and her untouched tea. He snatched up the card and left without a word or glance at anyone else.

Mr. Tuttle-Kirk's offices were on the same street as the Moretons' home and law practice. Without hiring a hack—Lady Philippa had been perfectly right in what she said of his economical nature—he made excellent time and arrived at the address upon the card the lady had left for him.

Upon entering the offices and giving his name to a young man behind a smallish desk, he soon found himself seated across the desk from a man with more hair in his substantial mustache than atop his head. Mr. Tuttle-Kirk looked more the part of a kindly grandfather, apt to sit before a fire with a pipe in his mouth, than a cunning solici-

tor. Yet the more Mr. Tuttle-Kirk spoke, the more Myles had to respect the man's sharp mind. Mr. Tuttle-Kirk spent a quarter of an hour laying before Myles drafted contracts and explaining the same situation Lady Philippa had described to him. But the solicitor used more dire terms than the young woman had uttered.

"The articles in the paper struck me as highly suspect," Mr. Tuttle-Kirk concluded, pacing to his large window. He held his spectacles behind his back, in his clasped hands. "Though Lady Philippa didn't request it, I went about the extra work to determine who submitted them to the *Times*. Thus far, I have traced them only to someone who delivered the article by courier along with a substantial payment to see that the words against our lady were featured prominently, and above any other of the kind."

Myles leaned back in his chair, not hiding his disgust. "That the *Times* editors would take part in the deliberate sabotage of a young woman's reputation isn't as shocking as it should be."

"Indeed." Mr. Tuttle-Kirk turned where he stood and nodded to the contracts upon the desk. "While I must admit that I believed Lady Philippa to be reacting more strongly than necessary to her situation, looking deeper into everything leads me to believe she is precisely on point. For some reason which I do not yet understand, Lord Montecliff and the dowager countess are forcing Lady Philippa's hand. The family's prominence in Society is not under any threat of which I am aware. This desperation to make a match with another noble family is inexplicable."

Myles picked up the marriage contract, glancing over the draft. His sympathy went to Lady Philippa. She faced a terrible situation. But did it necessarily fall to him to do anything about it? "Why me?" he asked, voice low in the office. "Surely there are other gentlemen who would happily help Lady Philippa. She must have suitors. Friends."

"I wondered the same thing." Mr. Tuttle-Kirk paced back to the chair behind his desk and put his hands upon its back, the wrinkles above his eyebrows deepening. "Yours was the first—and only—name spoken by the young woman. The first time she visited me."

"She barely even knows me." Myles looked down where his left,

altered hand rested upon his thigh. He wore a glove with stuffed fingers again. They never looked quite right, no matter what he did to them. "And one look at me shows well enough why I am unlikely to be a love match for her or anyone else."

Mr. Tuttle-Kirk's frown deepened. "I didn't take you as a vain gentleman, Mr. Cobbett. Surely, you do not believe affection is only granted to those of physical beauty? If that were true, none of us would be loved after reaching two and forty years." He patted the top of his bald head. "I had already lost all of this by that time, you know. And Mrs. Tuttle-Kirk never seemed to mind."

Myles laughed, then covered his mouth with his fist. "Pardon me, sir. I have never heard anyone speak so plainly of such a thing." And despite the humor, Myles didn't quite equate his bodily scars with a man whose hair loss did nothing to lessen the affection of a woman already his wife.

The solicitor took his seat behind the desk, waving away the apology. "You are a man of the military. Tell me, did the handsomest soldiers perform the best? With the most honor and dignity? Or did the wealthiest officers command with the greatest wisdom and foresight?"

Slowly, Myles shook his head. "The opposite of those things was often true."

"Consider that Lady Philippa, though not as experienced in battle tactics as you are, is quite experienced when it comes to weighing and measuring her peers." The solicitor affixed his spectacles above his nose as he spoke. "She knows well enough what the men of her more immediate acquaintance offer, and yet she chose you. Why do *you* think that is?"

Myles couldn't meet the older man's eyes. He lowered his gaze to the carpet instead, not seeing its whirls and flourishes as he tried to sort out his thoughts on the matter. Prior to their meeting that morning, Lady Philippa had only interacted with him twice. The first of those instances with the most substantial time. When he had saved her from a scoundrel. Had that act alone endeared him to her?

How could she possibly know, from such a short moment, the

truth of his character? Because Myles, incredulous though he was at her proposition, knew he would be precisely the sort of man she wanted as a husband. Because he would give his wife—should he ever have one—the freedom to enjoy her life. He would want her happiness above his own.

But he had never considered marriage. Because he couldn't support a family on his pension, and he refused to hunt down a woman just to force her to support them both. He detested the very idea of fortune hunters. Even though he could well have benefited from a greater income.

Then there was the matter of his scars, both physical and otherwise. He wasn't even sure what to call them. Spiritual scars, perhaps, given how often he prayed for the welfare of other veterans less fortunate than himself. Mental, for certain, given the way his past strained his mind both waking and sleeping.

What woman would willingly look at his face every day at her breakfast table, let alone every night in her bed? Should he find himself with such an angel, how would she tolerate his nightmares or his headaches? What about the myriad of times he startled at a sudden noise and flinched away from quick movements?

Yet he had to consider the offer before him, despite his misgivings.

With all that Lady Philippa had proposed, and the drafts upon Mr. Tuttle-Kirk's desk, she was freely giving him access to more money than he had ever dreamed of. He could invest funds, give to charitable causes, and see that his sisters had doweries that would give them a greater ability to find their own matches.

"I have been a solicitor for nearly fifty years. In my time, I have seen many things that you would not believe. I speak of legal cases, of course, but more than that. I have seen people find the most unlikely paths to happiness." The man's eyes twinkled, his expression relaxing into a smile. He looked more the part of a doting grandfather than a man of law once again. "Perhaps, Mr. Cobbett, this is your path. I am going to ask you a question, and I would like your instinctive response."

Curiosity brought Myles's gaze up again. He raised his eyebrows

and took hold of the arms of the chair. "Very well. What is your question?" He sat with the stiffness the military had drilled into him, his chin up and his bearing that of a man poised to lead others into battle. That past life seemed far less daunting than the possibility of what the day had presented to him.

"Do you want to marry Lady Philippa Gillensford?"

One word entered his mind and echoed loudly for him alone to hear. Even though he hadn't expected that question. He'd only had time to think it might be something to do with honor, or duty, or integrity. There were dozens of reasons, *logical* reasons, for him to answer the inquiry differently.

Myles frowned up at Mr. Tuttle-Kirk, no less confused when he uttered the answer out loud. "Yes."

The solicitor nodded slowly. "Are your instincts generally right?"

His left hand twitched. Had he followed his instinct the night he'd lost men, half his sight, several fingers, and more than he could put into words, things would have turned out much differently.

"Yes," he said again, closing both hands into fists. "Though I have not always trusted them as I should."

Mr. Tuttle-Kirk gave a solemn nod. "We often fight against our best judgement when it goes against what Society has told us is best. A common failing among men and women both." The solicitor pushed the drafts to the end of the desk. "Take this. Read them over. Consult a solicitor of your own, if you wish. But do not take long in deciding, Mr. Cobbett. Lady Philippa deserves my best effort to ensure her future happiness. If you will not be part of aiding her, I need to know soon so I might plan another course of action."

With the papers bound up in a protective folder, Myles left to speak to the only people he trusted to advise him. The Moretons. But while he walked the short distance to their home, he realized something that stopped him in his steps.

He had already answered Mr. Tuttle-Kirk as he intended to. He'd said yes to marrying Lady Philippa Gillensford. And he didn't mean to change his mind.

Heaven help them both.

Eight

Philippa had spent too much time with Mr. Cobbett. Her mother had regarded her with suspicion all day after her visit to the gentleman's preferred breakfast location. The next morning, to escape more pointed questions and lectures on familial duty, she snuck away again to go hat shopping.

A new hat might be just the thing she needed to cheer her up a bit.

Yet the whole while she visited her favorite hatmaker, Philippa's thoughts lingered over Mr. Cobbett. How startled he had been to see her, and how shocked at her proposal. She didn't blame him. Even while she tried to decide between a feathered cap that put her in mind of a medieval tapestry and a bonnet festooned with silk flowers, she easily recalled the look of him with one eye looking on in sympathy and the other covered with a leather patch.

He certainly cut a dashing figure, though she doubted he meant to do so. His dark hair, cut short in the way of many a military man, hung longer on the top and front, threatening to fall into his eye. And he was a lovely height, though not so tall as her brothers. The scars—they did mar one side of his face and were of such a nature that she could not doubt the pain his injuries had caused when they were new.

How had such a thing happened to him? She looked down at the

hats upon the table and realized she wanted neither. Despite the fashionable appeal, they were rather ridiculously overdone.

Instead, she chose a cunning blue hat with a silver ribbon and white roses along its brim. She loved roses. And the sky-hued hat appeared elegant in its simplicity.

Entering the carriage Adam and Elaine kept when they were in town, Philippa stared out the glass window and wondered why Mr. Tuttle-Kirk had yet to contact her. Had Mr. Cobbett not gone to see him after all? Had he turned down her solicitor, leaving the older man to prepare a doomed legal case for her instead?

The errand didn't take nearly long enough. When Philippa walked through the front door, her maid carrying the hatbox behind her, Hopkins appeared.

"You are wanted in the upstairs morning room, my lady." He appeared more stern-faced than usual. A sign she took as an immediate warning.

"How bad is it, Hopkins?" she dared to ask as she handed hat and gloves to her maid.

The butler glanced up the staircase. "The earl has come to pay a call."

Her heart fell clear to her toes, and she nearly turned and walked out the door again. What new mischief would Richard have in store for her? "My eldest brother?"

She doubted he had received any correspondence from Mr. Tuttle-Kirk yet. He could have no idea of the legal issues about to befall him. She hoped.

"Yes, my lady." Hopkins's dark eyebrows drew sharply together. "They know you went out, my lady, but not when." Hopkins had proven to be a most sympathetic person when it came to her situation. She had caught his eye one afternoon after her mother had railed at the butler for some small slight, and Philippa had said a kind word to him immediately after. Since then, he'd been exceedingly attentive to her.

"Are Adam and Elaine in the morning room?" she asked, shifting a step back in her nervousness. If only she could take flight through the front door and back into the street, she might spend all day away from

the house in hopes that Richard would eventually give up. But all the Gillensfords were rather stubborn. Richard would out wait her. Even if it meant spending the night under the roof of his younger brother.

"Yes, my lady."

Releasing an agitated sigh, Philippa went to the mirror to straighten the neckline of her gown. She fussed with her fichu. Then she lifted her chin and affected her most regal expression. Her brother would see any display of emotion as weakness. It was best to pretend indifference to whatever he wished to speak to her about.

She ascended the staircase, aware that Hopkins watched her go with the same expression one might watch a martyr trudge to her execution.

Philippa pulled in a deep, fortifying breath outside the doors to the room wherein her eldest brother laid in wait for her. Then she squared her shoulders and went inside, chin tipped upward and eyebrows raised superciliously.

Elaine's eyes fell upon her first, as she sat with her chair facing the door. "Ah, Pippa." She rose and widened her eyes enough to signal caution. "Here you are. You see, Montecliff, she is safe and sound." Adam rose from the chair next to his wife, his expression as closed as Philippa meant hers to be.

Her eldest brother stood at the hearth, his back to the room, and he didn't immediately turn upon Philippa's entry. "Safe and sound, after gallivanting about alone and unchaperoned in London."

Lady Fredericka sat in the most comfortable chair, as usual, and she took that opportunity to sniffle so loudly that the pug in her lap looked upward with confusion. Then sneezed. "Philippa, we were so worried about you."

"Worried, Mama?" Philippa came into the room and bent first to kiss her mother on the cheek, then gave the little pug dog a pat on the head. "Why ever were any of you worried? I took my maid, and the carriage with Adam's driver, and I am of an age when I might wander about without becoming lost." She turned on her heel to face her eldest brother. "Richard, how good it is of you to come visit."

"Visit?" he repeated with a snort. "I am here to bring you back to my home on Grosvenor Square."

A tremor of fear shook her heart, but she affected a confused expression. "Whatever for? I am quite comfortable here with Adam and Elaine. We have had the loveliest time, and I am quite content to remain here the rest of the Season."

Elaine spoke softly, meeting her husband's gaze. "She is quite welcome—"

"We do not wish to intrude a moment longer," Lady Fredericka interrupted somewhat shrilly. "Especially with all the horrid gossip."

"It is precisely because of the gossip that Philippa must come home with me, immediately." Richard held himself up to his full height, his nose in the air as he looked down upon Adam. "Given that what began as a rumor is now regarded as fact and bandied about in my very own gentleman's club, you are obviously not a good influence upon our sister."

Adam glowered and came to his feet. "You know as well as I do that the papers are circulating false rumors. Our sister has done nothing wrong. That disgusting acquaintance of yours—Lord Walter, the little rat—is to blame for all of this. How could you encourage the attentions of such a dishonorable man toward our sister?"

Philippa, sensing she would not be needed while the brothers sized each other up, sat down upon the footstool in front of Elaine's chair and prepared to watch. Her three brothers, all older than her by several years, had never been fond of one another. Richard had always been arrogant, vain, and domineering. Henry, her brother serving as a lieutenant in the army, saw the world as his playground. Then Adam, favored of their kindly great uncle, had set about doing all he could to annoy them both. Until recently.

"Lord Walter Ruthersby is perfectly respectable," Richard insisted. "His father is the Marquess of Bute."

"Having a marquess for a father doesn't make him an honorable or suitable match for our sister." Adam started pacing the room. "The man tried to corner her during our ball last week. He is bullying her."

The dowager countess tightened her grip on the arm of her chair. "And succeeded in compromising her, if the papers are to be believed."

"We already agreed we do not believe the papers," Adam said in clipped tones. "And if he had accosted her, would you really want to reward him by giving our sister into his care?"

"That is how things are done. He is offering to do the right thing by taking her as his bride." Richard drew back when Adam exploded in an angry snarl at that idea.

Philippa ignored their bickering for a moment and looked up at her sister-in-law. Elaine had gone dreadfully pale, so much so that her freckles stood out, like flecks of paint on a clean canvas. Given how kind Elaine had been toward Philippa, seeing her in distress made the younger woman's stomach knot in concern.

"Are you all right?" Philippa asked quietly, laying a hand on Elaine's arm.

Elaine's gaze flickered from her husband, where he had crossed the room to stand toe-to-toe with Richard as they argued, to Philippa, and back again. "I am worried for you, Pippa."

"As well you should be," Lady Fredericka snipped from her seat. "Philippa, I don't care what circumstances brought us to this point. I have already given instruction for our things to be packed. Richard is the head of this family, and we will remove to Grosvenor Square as he requests."

Adam spun on his heel. "Absolutely not. The moment you two have her there, you'll let that spineless eel into the house to go about a farce of a courtship. I'll not let you do that to my sister."

"Philippa is under my care," Richard said, puffing his chest out with self-importance. "If I say she removes to Grosvenor Square or to Bangkok, it will be done."

With her eyes still on Elaine, Philippa made her announcement. "I am going nowhere."

"Nonsense, child." The dowager took up her pug and began to stand. "Come along and do as you're told."

Philippa came to her feet, meeting Richard's eyes and mirroring his stance. "No, Mother. I don't think I will. Not anymore. It seems I

need to remind *all* of you that I came of age two months ago. I am three and twenty. By rights, I should have received my inheritance from Father and be well on my way to establishing my own household."

"Philippa," her mother gasped. "You are a child!"

Richard glowered at her. "A spoilt child." He stepped toward her, looking down his long nose—broken by Henry, and so somewhat crooked—into her eyes. Their eyes were a match for each other, though Richard's had never been particularly warm when he looked upon his sister. "Your inheritance remains with me for another year. My solicitor has made that case quite clear."

"Actually." Philippa resisted the urge to rise to her toes to bring them closer to eye level. "He hasn't made that case at all. He hasn't been to court. Yet."

Narrowing his eyes, Richard loomed closer. "Nor will he need do so. Because you will obey me."

For an instant, Philippa had to fight a smile. Richard had no idea that she had seen her own legal expert. Nor did he know that his sister had the intelligence to seek out counsel to thwart him. Keeping calm, Philippa played her first card against her brother. "No, I will not."

"I will support our sister in this." Adam peered around Richard's shoulder. "If you attempt to remove her from my home, I swear by all I hold dear that I will fight you before every court of law who will hear my case."

Casting a grateful look to Adam, Philippa hurried to shake her head. "That will not be necessary. You see, my dear brothers, I have already taken the first steps to gaining my independence." She raised her chin in the air.

Richard laughed. "I am a peer of the realm. Philippa comes with me if I say she does. If you attempt to stop me, Adam, I'll see you imprisoned and brought up on charges of assaulting a peer." He took hold of Philippa's arm. "I can see the sooner we get you away from this place, the better. You are a child under my care, at least until I can convince some poor fool to take you off my hands."

"Let me go." Philippa pulled as hard as she could, but Richard's

grip didn't loosen. He'd never laid a hand on her before. His blue eyes burned, his features appearing strained.

A thin, nasally voice spoke from the doorway. "I must insist you unhand that lady, Lord Montecliff, or we will need to take legal action against you for your assault of one of His Majesty's subjects."

"Mr. Tuttle-Kirk?" Elaine blurted at the same time as Richard choked out, "What is *he* doing here?"

"Not him again," added Lady Fredericka with marked disdain. "Who let that horrid little man in the house?"

Philippa, held fast as she was by her brother, couldn't turn to the doorway. But she felt a mix of hope and dismay. Her solicitor had come with news for her, no doubt. Grievous news, if he felt the need to arrive at her home rather than send her a note or wait for her promised visit the next day. Mr. Cobbett must have turned down the marriage proposal, which meant a longer, harder fight for her ahead.

Nevertheless, she squared her shoulders and lifted her chin. "I have retained Mr. Tuttle-Kirk as my legal counsel. We are even now preparing our case against your interpretation of our father's will."

Richard looked down into her eyes again as his face turned red. "You are taking me to court?"

"Indeed. And I intend to make it a most public case. I intend to write the papers myself about *all* the particulars of a British peer taking advantage of his younger sister."

He glared down at her. His words came out in a hiss. "I must warn you, little sister. You are making a mistake."

"As are you, Lord Montecliff."

Philippa's whole body grew still, her ears pricked, and her heart beat a new and more excitable rhythm. That wasn't Tuttle-Kirk or Adam speaking. It was Myles Cobbett.

"Take your hand off of Lady Philippa at once, or I will remove it myself." Despite the calm, even tones of the former soldier, Philippa sensed an undercurrent of danger in every word. Richard must have as well, as he released the bruising hold he'd taken of her arm and stepped back.

He wasn't finished posturing, however. "And who are you, who dares to speak threats to an earl?"

Philippa turned around, and there stood Mr. Cobbett in the doorway, half a step behind Mr. Tuttle-Kirk. The two had come together. Did that mean what she hoped it did?

Mr. Cobbett's gaze collided with Philippa's, and he gave her the barest nod. "Myles Cobbett. Former Lieutenant in the King's Army. A friend to the Gillensfords, and someone who does not take lightly to men of any rank accosting young women."

Richard glared at Mr. Cobbett, then Tuttle-Kirk. "You are making a mistake. I will see to it that you are never permitted to work in England again. Mark my words."

"I have withstood you in a courtroom once, Lord Montecliff." Mr. Tuttle-Kirk actually sounded bored as he spoke, his mustache not so much as twitching. "I dare say, I can successfully do so again."

"How dare you." Lady Fredericka rose to her feet. "Adam, I insist you eject this man from the premises."

Now appearing far more amused than alarmed, Adam folded his arms across his chest. "Mr. Tuttle-Kirk is a dear friend to my family, Mother. He is welcome in our home whenever he wishes." Though Philippa thought her brother stretched the truth with that statement, she appreciated it, nonetheless.

She stepped farther away from Richard, tucking her hands behind her back lest she give him too easy a target to take hold of again. "Adam, might I have the use of your study? I believe my solicitor has come on a matter of business."

"Of course, Pippa." Adam stepped between her and their eldest brother. "I will see our brother and mother out, of course."

Lady Fredericka started to sputter. "Are you throwing me out, you ungrateful boy?"

Philippa fled to the door in as unhurried a manner as possible. She slipped between Mr. Cobbett and Mr. Tuttle-Kirk as they each opened one side of the double door.

"Not at all, Mother. You are already packed, after all, and wanted

nothing more than to return to Richard's townhouse a few moments ago. I am only seeing to your wishes."

"But Philippa—"

The two doors closed behind Philippa, but she didn't turn to thank her rescuers. Not yet. Instead, she walked quickly to the front of the corridor. "This way, please." She went to another set of large, dark doors and pushed one of them open.

The men entered behind her, and she closed the door quickly, then slid the bolt into place. While not necessarily the most appropriate thing, Philippa had no intention of making it easy for Richard to intrude upon them should he wish to try it. She leaned against the closed door, turning to face the two men who had followed her inside.

Mr. Tuttle-Kirk walked to the desk, and she noted he held a leather portfolio under one arm. "Dashed ridiculous family," he was muttering to himself.

Mr. Cobbett remained only a few steps inside the room, facing her, his expression rather grim. "Are you hurt, my lady?"

A trembly laugh escaped her. "There will likely be a bruise in the shape of my brother's fingers, but it is of no consequence." She stepped away from the door and approached him slowly, aware of Mr. Tuttle-Kirk laying things out on the desk and muttering to himself. "I confess, I am most surprised to see you here, Mr. Cobbett."

One corner of his mouth went upward, the expression more of a grimace than a smile. His dark brown eye studied her with care. "I met with Mr. Tuttle-Kirk again this morning, with my additions to the contracts. He thought, once we finalized the papers, that we should present them to you with some speed."

Mr. Tuttle-Kirk spoke loudly from the desk. "It is always better to have both parties present when finalizing these sorts of things. It makes the process much easier."

Philippa looked up at Mr. Cobbett again. "Your additions? Does that mean you agree to—to—" Her cheeks warmed. Good heavens, she hadn't struggled to say the words to him before, had she?

"Marry you? Yes. I suppose so." His smile untwisted itself, appearing more natural and softening his features. "I hope you haven't

changed your mind. That would make my uninvited visit to your home most awkward."

"No, of course not." Philippa shook her head quickly. "Though I do wonder at what your proposed changes might be. I thought we made the terms quite generous in your favor."

"You did." He looked over his shoulder to where Tuttle-Kirk now prepared a pen he had found in Adam's desk. Then Mr. Cobbett took her hand and led her to the window. Once they stood in the light, he picked up her other hand, too. "The things most important to you, I did not touch. Your independence. The way in which your fortune will be invested and used. Your generosity toward my family—thank you for that—it is all there." He paused, and for a moment she thought she saw his unscarred cheek turn somewhat pink. But that was the side facing the window. Perhaps it was only a trick of the light.

"What did you find lacking in the agreement?" Philippa winced when she heard the breathiness of her question. One would think she hadn't initiated the agreement, given her tone. She cleared her throat and lifted her chin. "I want to be certain I understand the motivation behind your changes before I read them in Mr. Tuttle-Kirk's clever hand."

The gentleman looked over his shoulder at Tuttle-Kirk again, and Philippa had the distinct impression that he didn't like the idea of the solicitor listening in. Which was preposterous, since Mr. Tuttle-Kirk would have needed to know the particulars of whatever Mr. Cobbett wished to say in order to put it into the paperwork.

Finally, after smoothing his expression into something more stern and unreadable than she'd seen him wear thus far, Mr. Cobbett answered her question. "I never thought to marry, my lady. Not on a soldier's pay, and especially not on my pension. But now that the opportunity has arisen, I find that I am loathe to make this a business arrangement only. I would like to make our relationship into something more. Perhaps—if you are amenable to the idea in future—we might have children." That warm, dark brown eye of his searched her gaze, only the barest hint of hope appearing there.

Heat suffused Philippa from the tip of her nose through to her

fingertips and toes. His hands felt far too large upon hers, their gentle grip too warm, and his whole body too near. She stepped back, dropping her hands from his. "You added *children* to the contract?" Her voice went into a high register she doubted she had ever used before.

His eyebrows shot upward. "Of course not. How does one put such a thing in a legal document?"

Philippa looked to Mr. Tuttle-Kirk, who most certainly had been listening to the whole thing. He appeared amused, the horrid man. "Quite right," he said dryly. "Progeny? In a contract? It would never hold up in court."

Mr. Cobbett muttered something cross and shoved his hand through his hair. Then he faced her again. "I put in the stipulation that we must spend the first year of our marriage in each other's company. We live under the same roof. We attend the same social functions—only those you wish to attend, of course—all with the hope that we form an understanding for our shared future outside of what the contract stipulates."

Philippa's mouth opened, then closed. Then she looked at Mr. Tuttle-Kirk. "What do you think of Mr. Cobbett's adjustments?"

Mr. Tuttle-Kirk stood at attention, his eyes gleaming with what she didn't dare think of as *glee*. "I am in favor of them, and I rather wish I had thought to suggest such a thing myself. After all, you are still quite young, my lady. You may find you wish for more than a business partner, at some point. Life has many unexpected paths, and should you find yourself in a difficult position, it would be better to face it with someone to whom you are bound by things other than ink and paper. As to the matter of children—"

Philippa raised her hand. "I quite understand your point, Mr. Tuttle-Kirk. Thank you. I should like to look over the documents now."

A sudden shriek down the corridor made all of them jump. Philippa put a hand to her throat. "Oh dear. Mother must be leaving."

Mr. Cobbett's eyes widened. "That was your mother?"

"She can be quite theatrical." Philippa winced and walked to the desk. "We had better get started." Before Mr. Cobbett changed his

mind, leaving her to a legal muddle far more difficult to win than the one that marriage might solve.

~

AFTER MR. TUTTLE-KIRK HAD PUT AWAY THE SIGNED documents, Myles breathed a sigh of relief. It was done. Lady Philippa had accepted his conditions, which the solicitor had taken to calling "the relationship addendum." He would need to thank Moreton for his advice yet again. He'd spent the better part of yesterday afternoon convincing Moreton that he wasn't insane for considering Lady Philippa's proposal. Then he'd gone over what he wanted added to the document, and Moreton had written up suggestions for what he termed "unconventional nuptials."

It seemed everyone had a name for what Myles wanted except for him. Because he couldn't quite explain what drove him to add those things to the contract. He hadn't ever thought to have a conventional marriage of any kind. But now that a wedding lay within his future, he had to consider what such a thing meant. And what he wanted.

If he and Lady Philippa got along, they might provide each other companionship. Support. And if they found they suited well enough to have children—well. Myles had loved growing up in a large family of children. His family held a genuine affection for one another.

Perhaps he'd do well at fatherhood.

Not that such things bore thinking of yet. He grew warm around the neck and adjusted his cravat.

Mr. Tuttle-Kirk had all the documents in hand, tucked beneath his arm, and led the way to the door. "I must be on my way. With your permission, my lady, Mr. Cobbett, I will obtain a common marriage license and you can be married by Sunday next, so long as it is within one of your church parishes. I am assuming, since you live in London year-round, Mr. Cobbett, that yours might be the easier of the two options."

Lady Philippa followed them both, her hands tucked behind her back and her head lowered. She hadn't spoken much after they had

begun to sign things. Perhaps the reality of the situation began to sink in for her, too.

Married by Sunday. Myles cleared his throat. "That is acceptable. I attend at Chelsea Old Church. The vicar there went to school with my father."

"Excellent, excellent." Mr. Tuttle-Kirk slid the bolt open. "I will be in touch with you both when everything on my end is finalized."

He opened the door and standing in the hall was the same butler who had shown them up the stairs when Mr. Tuttle-Kirk claimed he had come to assist Lady Philippa with legal matters.

That butler appeared highly suspicious now, rather than relieved as he had before. "My lady."

Lady Philippa stepped between the two men, her bearing changing to something far more confident. "Hopkins. I understand I have you to thank for the timely arrival of these gentlemen."

He appeared suddenly concerned. "I thought they might help with the situation above stairs, my lady."

"And so you were right." Then Philippa surprised Myles, and the butler, given the way he reddened, by laying her hand upon his cheek. "You have always been kind to me, Hopkins. If there is ever anything I might do by way of thanks, do let me know."

"My lady." He bowed, as a knight before a queen. Then he rose and gestured down the corridor. "Mr. and Mrs. Gillensford hope you and your guests will join them for tea, if you have concluded your business."

Mr. Tuttle-Kirk chuckled before anyone else could answer. "I am afraid I must be off. Work to do. But do not let my absence hinder the two of you." His mustache twitched. "I can show myself out. Good day, my lady. Mr. Cobbett."

"Good day," Lady Philippa responded, sounding surprised.

Of course the old man would depart now, leaving Myles and Philippa to explain what had transpired to people he respected. Mr. Gillensford would likely throw him out on his good ear.

Slim fingers found his gloved left hand and twined with his. She had to feel the unnatural stillness of the smallest two fingers in his

glove, but Lady Philippa did not draw back or question him. Instead, she came up beside him, the length of their arms pressed together.

"Well, Mr. Cobbett. Here is our first test. Adam and Elaine mustn't think us desperate so much as practical."

Looking down into her lovely blue eyes, Myles forced himself to relax. Tentatively, he squeezed her hand with his. "I will follow as you lead, my lady."

Her soft pink lips turned upward in a soft smile. "Am I to play the general?"

"Field marshal, I should think." He untangled their fingers and offered her his arm instead. Though he wore his glove, having her bare hand in his was too much for him. Too soon. She didn't know the extent of his scars. She hadn't cared to ask about them. Maybe that meant she didn't mind them. Though he found that difficult to believe.

He suddenly wished he had offered her his right arm, and thus his right side to look upon.

They went to the same room they had abandoned with Mr. Tuttle-Kirk earlier, and this time when they entered together, only Mr. and Mrs. Gillensford waited inside. The two of them sat together on the sofa, and they moved as one to stand when Myles and Lady Philippa entered, arm-in-arm.

"Adam, Elaine. You both know Mr. Cobbett." Lady Philippa's arm tightened around his, and Myles looked down to see that—despite wearing a serene expression—her eyes were full of worry. "I have the honor of introducing him to you both anew, as my betrothed. We are to be married this Sunday, by common license."

Nine

Medieval churches were a common enough sight in Britain, and several dotted London's maps. Yet Chelsea Old Church had a special feeling to it when Myles stepped inside, Sunday after Sunday. It wasn't as large or elegant as its sisters in Westminster or near the Tower. In fact, it was quite small. Homely, even, with a distinct lack of marble and artwork. A few columns bore carved scrollwork, and the largest glass was many-paned and colorful. But that was all that adorned the space. Yet the simple arches and well-worn wooden benches always set Myles at ease.

No one of great importance attended any of the services. Simply members of the neighborhood who had a care for Sabbath worship. Myles hadn't had any trouble when he presented the vicar, Mr. Perry, with the common license and made his intentions known.

Thus, the Sunday morning after signing the contracts in Mr. Gillensford's study found Myles seated next to Mr. and Mrs. Moreton at a pew toward the front. Across from him, the distinguished Mr. and Mrs. Gillensford accompanied Lady Philippa. A little girl sat with them between the red-headed matron and Myles's almost-bride. She leaned forward several times to peer at him, which made Myles all the more

grateful that he sat on the left side of the church, so his scars wouldn't distress the child.

"I find it sweet you can't stop staring at her," Emmeline whispered from beside him. "She is lovely." When Emmeline had heard Myles and her husband arguing about the marriage contract, she surprised Myles by supporting his decision to wed Lady Philippa. She had continued with positive commentary on the arrangement from that time forward. "I think this will be quite good for you," she had said when they arrived together at the church.

Moreton, still unconvinced, had offered up a lament. "It isn't a summer abroad, Emmeline. It's marriage. A life-time commitment."

Lady Philippa, never once looking at him as she paid rapt attention to the sermon, appeared perfectly at ease. She did not appear nervous at all, even while Myles had to clench and unclench his hands into fists repeatedly to keep the rest of himself still.

Emmeline was right about one thing. Lady Philippa looked as lovely as the spring. She wore a gown of soft yellow, putting him in mind of a sunrise, and a bonnet with a white veil put back for the time being. She held a bouquet of roses, yellow tinted with pink, in her gloved hands.

Myles made the mistake of letting his gaze drift from Lady Philippa's profile to her brother's. The man's eyes narrowed, and he immediately cut Myles a glare. Mr. Gillensford hadn't been unsupportive, necessarily. But he'd taken the first opportunity he could to meet with Myles under the guise of business, then had spent an hour closely questioning Myles about his habits, former loves, family, and his future objectives.

Adam Gillensford's interview had left Myles exhausted, but strangely vindicated. He had been honest in all he said and answered everything to Mr. Gillensford's reluctant satisfaction.

Given his current glare, he remained as satisfied as an older brother could be to give away the hand of a younger, beloved sister. Myles thought of his own unmarried sisters and how he would react if either of them had arranged their marriage without consulting the family.

He'd likely behave just as Mr. Gillensford had. Likely even more

overbearing, given that his younger sisters lacked the natural confidence Lady Philippa exuded.

Mr. Perry finished the sermon, and then invited all to remain in their seats. "We will now partake of one of the most joyous occasions in this mortal world—the holy sacrament of marriage between one of our own, Mr. Myles Cobbett, and Lady Philippa Gillensford."

Myles stood with haste rather than grace, cracking his right knee into the hard wood in front of him. He bit the inside of his cheek to keep back a groan. Thankfully, the rustling and hums of conversation brought on by Mr. Perry's announcement meant no one noticed Myles's clumsy injury. He moved to his expected position near the front of the church.

A moment later, Lady Philippa stood beside him.

"Who brings this woman to be married to this man?" Mr. Perry asked loud enough for all to hear.

"I do, her brother." Mr. Gillensford took his sister's right hand and gave it to the minister, who then handed it into Myles's care.

Her slim hand was ungloved, and her skin against his was warm and soft. For the first time that day, Lady Philippa raised her gaze to meet his. Her deep blue eyes captured him in a way that made all of time stand still. Her eyes wrinkled at the corners, and then she whispered, "This is the last moment to change your mind."

His throat had gone tight, his mouth dry, but Myles shook his head. "I wouldn't dream of it, my lady." He squeezed her right hand in his, then faced the minister.

"First, I am required to ask anyone present who knows a reason why these two may not lawfully marry to declare it now." Mr. Perry made a show of peering about the congregants, and for one awful moment, Myles wondered if Lady Philippa's elder brother might burst into the room with some ridiculous objection. It wouldn't be legal in the slightest, of course. Lady Philippa was of age and could marry whomever she wished.

Then the vicar looked down at Myles and Lady Philippa with a congenial smile. "I must ask you both the same. The vows you soon make are made in the presence of God, who is the judge of all and

knows all the secrets of our hearts; therefore, if either of you knows a reason you may not lawfully marry, you must declare it now."

"There are no such reasons, sir," Lady Philippa answered, her voice calm and clear. Myles felt the nervous buzzing that had been in his heart and mind all day grow still as he regarded her, noting no sign of regret or hesitance.

"None," Myles added. He took strength from the smile she immediately bestowed upon him. Theirs might not be a love match, or even the strengthening of a relationship formed over time, but they had both come to this point with honorable intentions. He would make his vows, with Philippa beside him, and they would leave as husband and wife.

~

EVERY WORD THE MINISTER SAID RANG THROUGH Philippa's ears as she promised to love and obey the near-stranger standing next to her. He held her right hand, while in her left she grasped the flowers Elaine had procured for her. They were so similar to what grew at Tertium Park, Philippa could almost believe they came from those very gardens. She clung to the reminder of that safe, protected place so tightly, she worried the stems might snap and reveal her state of nervousness to everyone.

Myles Cobbett, for his part, stood straight and stiff as the soldier he had once been. In fact, he looked ready to face a line of cannons given the grim set of his mouth as they began repeating after the vicar. The brief smile he had given her before the ceremony started in earnest had been the sole pleasant expression upon his face that day.

With the last words of the vicar's benediction, Philippa finally allowed herself to take in a trembling breath of relief. Her eldest brother hadn't been informed of her marriage, and now he could not intervene. As the vicar said, what God hath joined, let no man part.

Myles tucked her right hand through the crook of his left arm and turned to walk out of the church with her. This part they had planned with precision. Together, they would climb into a carriage hired by

Adam. The carriage would take them to the Gillensford townhouse, where Myles's things waited in the bedroom adjoining her own. Formerly the room Lady Fredericka had occupied, before she left the house squawking like an indignant chicken.

They would remain in London with the Gillensfords. Long enough to post wedding announcements, appear together at select events in public, and finalize the contracts with Mr. Tuttle-Kirk's firm. Then they would lease their own lodgings in town and set up house.

As Myles handed her into the carriage, Philippa felt one last tremble of fear. She settled into the forward-facing seat and closed her eyes. What had she done? Marrying a complete stranger—to thwart her brother? How absurd! She had escaped an unwanted union with Lord Walter only to form her own with a man who appeared about as thrilled with his wedding as he would have been with a funeral.

He dropped into the seat across from her, then he removed his hat and placed it on the seat beside him. He stretched one leg forward and winced.

"Did you hit it very hard?" Philippa had caught sight of the blow he'd suffered as she had stood to make her way to the altar with Adam.

His hand stilled. "You noticed?" His expression softened into a cautious smile. "It will be purple for days, I should think."

"I suppose that is what you get for being over-eager." Philippa bit her lip after the words escaped and directed her next words more to the window than to her new husband. "I cannot thank you enough for all you have done for me."

From the corner of her eye, she watched as he settled more deeply into his seat. "You made a compelling argument regarding all the ways this arrangement will benefit me, too. If we're going to start expressing gratitude, you must know how greatly I appreciate your trust."

"We cannot have that. We will wind up talking ourselves in circles as I thank you, and you appreciate me, and we will both grow insipid and dull before the week is out." Philippa arched her eyebrows and gave him the slightest of smiles. "We best talk of something else."

"As long as it isn't the weather." His amiable smile made the whole of his face far more attractive. Not that she noticed such a

thing. But that smile quite made one forget about the scars lining one side of his face. "I detest drawing room conversation topics. They are far too..." His eye narrowed as he searched for the right word.

"Safe?" Philippa ventured.

He chuckled and took up his hat, brushing off the top of it with his left hand. The left never seemed to move as she expected. Perhaps the same mishap which left him without vision in one eye had harmed his hand, too. "I suppose I would say impersonal. But yes, they are far too safe. If I must converse, I would prefer to speak of topics that are of unique interest to the people around me. For example, your brother tells me that you are an accomplished rider."

"I suppose that might be said of many ladies." Philippa dipped her head in acknowledgement of the fact. "But yes. I do enjoy riding, excessively. At home, I have the most wonderful mare. I always miss her when I am in Town."

The scent of her roses drifted into the air between them, the perfume soft and gentle as a mild spring day. It reminded her of home. Not her elder brother's estate, of course. But of Tertium Park, where she had spent all her free time as a child with her great-aunt and great-uncle, until time stole them both away from her.

"Your brother assures me the two of you are quite a sight, riding across the meadows." His dark eye gleamed with interest. "What do you call her?"

"You will think me terribly silly. I named her ages ago." Though not as long as she would have people believe, given the name she had given the finely bred mare. "I call her Bunny."

Myles didn't even bother hiding his sudden laugh. "Bunny?"

Philippa allowed herself a grin. "She did a great deal of hopping about the field as a filly. And she has the loveliest white coat."

"Marvelous. I cannot wait to meet her."

"I suppose we ought to have her brought to our house in the country," Philippa said, the idea coming to her most suddenly. "I would love that. She cannot stay in Richard's stables now that I am not returning to his estate."

A frown appeared on her new husband's face. "Will he part with her, do you think?"

"He had better. She was a gift from my late great-uncle." Philippa ran a gloved finger over a flower in her bouquet. "I wish you could have met him. He never would have stood for what Richard and my mother tried to do to me." She shuddered and let the roses rest upon her lap. They were nearly at Adam's townhouse.

Rather than linger upon memories of her great-uncle, Philippa tried to put more cheer in her voice as she asked, "And what of you, my new husband? Do you have any particular interests for us to discuss?"

He looked down at his hat again, his expression turned solemn. "For a long time, no. Nothing in particular. But now—I think I must say my interest is deeply taken up in the hospital your family intends to create."

She arched her eyebrows. When the solicitor gave his report on the man seated before her, he'd not had many details of what Myles Cobbett did to amuse himself. She easily recalled the few things of note. "You teach gentlemen what you know of pugilism, don't you?"

"I used to. I cannot say it was with relish so much as a need." He turned to the left, leaving her only his unscarred profile to observe as he spoke. "I was often 'rewarded' handsomely for giving up my time to instruct others."

Because gentlemen didn't work, that would have been a difficult situation for him to navigate.

"And you spend a great deal of time with the friends I met today—Mr. and Mrs. Moreton." She had liked the look of them both. "We should invite them to a family dinner while we are at the Gillensford house. I would like to get to know them better."

He turned toward her, head tilted to one side. "You would?"

"Of course. They are important to you. I know ours is not a traditional arrangement, but we can certainly be cordial to one another's family and friends."

"Cordial. Yes." He turned away again, looking out the window. Dash it all—she hadn't phrased her response especially well. Knowing what he hoped for—an eventual understanding that would lead to chil-

dren, of all things—she shouldn't speak lightly about things that mattered to him.

"Mr. Cobbett?"

"Myles." He didn't turn as he corrected her. "I think being cordial extends to using my Christian name. It's Myles."

She knew that. But she hadn't spoken it once, that much was true. She tried at that moment. "Myles. You stipulated that we live under the same roof for a year and come to know one another better. I am not trying to discount the importance of meeting with your friends. I truly want to get to know them."

"Thank you." He reached for his hat, momentarily giving her the full view of his face again. "We are arrived."

And that was the end of the conversation. As soon as they entered the house, a footman led away Myles to show him to his room. They had forgone the tradition of a wedding breakfast, given the nature of their match, and no one else had returned home from church yet. Philippa trailed a step behind Myles, going to her own room to lay aside her flowers, veil, gloves, and prepare for the absolutely ordinary meal the family would have upon Adam and Elaine's return.

When they arrived in the short corridor with the family's bedchambers, Philippa hesitated at her door and watched as the footman opened her new husband's door to show him inside. Myles stopped on the threshold and glanced her way, the scarred side of his face dominant. He gave her a curt nod and the barest of smiles.

"Until we meet again, my lady." Then he stepped inside the room and was gone from her view.

Only then did Philippa realize she hadn't returned the courtesy of asking him to call her by her Christian name, without her title. She chewed her bottom lip and wondered how many missteps the two of them might take as they found their way toward friendship.

Ten

Two days after Myles became a husband, he sat in the same room he had entered to proclaim himself an advocate for the Gillensfords' hospital. He wore his second-best clothes, a tea service waited at his elbow should he need it, and he held the newspaper open before him. For the first time in the house, he wasn't wearing gloves, either. Leaving his left hand, and its missing fingers, bare to the world.

Thus far, he'd tried to avoid entering rooms already occupied by members of the family. Mr. Gillensford still regarded him with a cautionary cordiality that led Myles to believe that his wife's elder brother still questioned the wisdom of their arrangement. Mrs. Gillensford, on the other hand, treated him with such exceeding kindness that he grew uncomfortable by her desire to see to his every need.

Then there was his wife. Lady Philippa. She had spent a day closeted with Mr. Tuttle-Kirk, drafting newspaper announcements and letters of both personal and legal importance, and had retired to bed early with a headache, leaving Myles to make his own way in the house.

As a fully grown gentleman, it ought to have been easy. Instead, Myles found himself avoiding situations in which he might be alone with another member of the family. And he had very nearly left the

house that morning to walk all the way to the little cafe where he used to take his breakfast every day.

Except he recognized the absurdity of eating in that dingy little place when he had access to a fine cook and comfortable house for his morning meal. Only—the interruption in what he was used to had given him a strange feeling. It was as though a bur had entered his mind, prickling him and distracting him. He would grow used to his new circumstances in time, of course. Yet he couldn't get comfortable on the couch, or either of the chairs he had tried sitting in. He'd had the same issue with his bed, soft and fine as it was, and hadn't slept well.

The door to the sitting room opened just as he stood in preparation of moving across the room to another chair, and he froze.

Nancy, the adopted daughter of Mr. and Mrs. Gillensford, poked her head around the edge of the door. Her eyebrows raised when she saw him there. He waited for her reaction to finding him alone, as they hadn't seen each other except at tea with the family.

"Good morning," he greeted her in as gentle a voice as possible, bowing as he would to a lady. Though she hadn't shied away from him yet, Myles could only imagine that his visage—unpleasant to adults—would outright frighten a little girl.

She smiled and slipped inside the room, then curtsied prettily to him. "Good morning, Uncle Cobbett."

His eyebrows raised in surprise. Yes, he supposed he was an uncle to her now. "How do you do today, Miss Nancy?"

She came further into the room, her eyes on the pastries stacked atop one another near his teapot. "I am quite well. I've been searching for Mother. Have you seen her?"

Myles picked up a plate of pastries and held it toward her, a silent invitation for her to partake. "I cannot say that I have."

With the nimbleness of youth, she came forward to snatch a large strawberry pastry from the plate before skipping over to the window to look out over the garden. "Hm. I did not think she meant to leave the house today." She turned around and met Myles's gaze again, fixing him with a curious stare. "Do you know where

Aunt Pippa is?" She punctuated the question with a large bite of her tart.

Myles slowly lowered himself into the seat he had meant to vacate before. "I am afraid I have not seen her this morning, either."

"Oh." The little girl came closer to sit in a chair near his own. "Do you like being married, so far?" She pushed herself backward on the chair until her feet hung freely in the air, then she swung them while she chewed her food.

Though his experience with young children was markedly limited, Myles couldn't help being amused by the openness of the little girl's questions. "I suppose so. With two days of experience, I am not certain I am ready to judge such a thing."

"I suppose that is true." She finished the tart in another bite and looked at the plate again. Myles dutifully held it out to her. "Thank you." She took a biscuit this time. "Why did you get married to Aunt Pippa anyway? My mother and father married because they fell in love, but Mama says that isn't true for everyone."

Myles shifted with discomfort again. What was the correct response to give? He wasn't in a position to tell her the question was inappropriate, surely. And he had detested having questions adults wouldn't answer when he was young. He considered her a moment, watching her nibble at her biscuit.

"It isn't true for everyone. I married your Aunt Pippa because—well—we can help one another best by being married."

"Yes, I heard Papa say you'd keep her out of trouble with Grand-mama. But then he said you might cause more trouble, too." She brushed crumbs from her skirt, thankfully missing his likely stunned expression. "Did you know that I'm adopted?"

The sudden change in topic took a moment for him to think of what to say to that. "I think I heard something about that, yes. You have an older brother, adopted, too?"

She nodded, a serious little frown upon her lips. "I thought you should know. In case you aren't feeling like part of the family yet. My mama—Elaine—raised me as long as I can remember, and I always thought of her as my mama. But I didn't even know I could call her

that until she married Papa. Anyway. You should know that just because you haven't always been part of the family doesn't mean anything. If you married Aunt Pippa, we'll all love you now. Even if she doesn't yet." The child delivered each word with a solemnity more appropriate to a vicar, staring at him all the while, giving them even more weight.

Myles's heart stirred. Nancy rose before he said anything and made her way to the door. "I'm going to keep looking for my mother. If I see Aunt Pippa, I'll tell her you're looking for her."

That made him start and come to his feet. "But I'm not looking for—"

The door opened just before Nancy reached it, and there stood Lady Philippa in a light-blue morning gown that made her eyes seem brighter still. "Nancy, here you are. Your mother is in the dining room, and she needs your help to write invitations for your birthday tea."

"Oh, the *dining* room." Nancy aimed a grin over her shoulder at Myles. "I didn't look there. Aunt Pippa, Uncle Cobbett was looking for you." She skipped out the door without another word, tugging it closed behind her.

Myles remained standing, staring at the woman he'd wed and yet only seen less than a handful of mealtimes since their exchange of vows. Philippa came toward him with a curious tilt of her head, and a fondness in her expression.

"Nancy is such a dear, isn't she?" Ah. So the fondness wasn't for him. Of course not. Silly of him to think it could be, really.

"I enjoy her straightforward conversation," he admitted. "She seems a kind child." Then he looked about for something to distract him from his wife's lovely smile. "Would you care for some tea or a pastry?"

"No, thank you. Were you really looking for me?" She glanced pointedly at the folded newspaper on the arm of his chair.

The honest answer won out. "Not at the moment. Though I mentioned to Nancy that I hadn't seen you today."

Philippa hummed thoughtfully and went to the couch, lowering herself with the same grace with which she did everything. Perhaps

earl's daughters received special lessons in comportment, wherein they were taught how to walk as though they floated.

"I have been terribly remiss in seeing to your comfort." She spoke as she would to any house guest, which made a wave of disappointment surprise Myles when it struck his mind. He tried to ignore the offensive feeling as he returned to his chair. "Now that Mr. Tuttle-Kirk and I have things settled, I cannot think of any more demands on my time. Which is why I have accepted an invitation to a ball for tomorrow evening. It was sent to Adam, Elaine, and myself, but you, of course, must be included. The invitation came before anyone could have known of our marriage."

"A ball?" The only ball he'd been to in more than a year was the one where they had met, and he had ended the evening with a headache that pounded in his skull like a loose cannonball. "Are you certain you want my company? Many a married man sends his wife to such events alone."

The cheerful expression she had worn faltered. "It is the first since our marriage. Appearing together in public is important to my reputation—and to how our marriage is perceived by Society."

"No one even knows me." He tried to sound indifferent. He didn't enjoy balls. Yet if she asked it of him, he would go. Because the whole reason they had entered into a marriage was for her ability to move about in Society with freedom and without a scandalous reputation. Somehow, he had thought little on the fact that he must appear with her at such events. At least, not so soon.

"That is the point." Her smile returned, looking less natural than before. Her dark lashes fluttered prettily at him, and he suddenly had a vision of a much younger Lady Philippa getting her way with that clear-eyed, sweetened expression. "People must come to know you, especially given your newly elevated status. A ball such as this one is just the thing. It is one of my mother's friends, Lady Darwimple, hostessing the event."

"Ah. One of the suspected sources of the gossip surrounding you and Lord W." Myles considered another moment before he nodded. "Strategically, this is an important occasion. Very well. Tomorrow

night, you say?" He looked down at his left hand on the arm of the chair. Had she noticed it yet?

"Yes. There won't be time for you to have a new suit of clothes made," she continued brightly, oblivious to the wince he couldn't hold back. "What you wore before should do well enough. In the meantime, I thought you and I might go shopping today. Adam's tailor is quite excellent, and he will certainly expedite anything you order since Adam has been such a faithful patron for many years."

Though Myles could readily admit to enjoying the luxury of new clothing in the past, an ache started in his temples as he contemplated the necessity of going out. Yet one glance at Philippa's hopeful smile meant quelling his misgivings.

"If you wish, we can undertake that mission." He curled his left hand into a fist, and for the first time she glanced at his marred hand. Her body went still and rigid, her eyes first narrowing as she likely tried to puzzle out what she saw, then widened with realization.

Myles uncurled his thumb and remaining two fingers slowly. He looked down at his hand to avoid her gaze. "I normally stuff the fingers of my gloves." The quiet words laid between them for several long seconds. In a culture that valued physical beauty and noble blood, with Myles possessing neither, he had learned to keep as much of himself hidden as possible. There wasn't much to do about his face, except avoid humanity entirely. His bare hand, however, left him feeling vulnerable.

"Oh, Myles. How awful." Philippa didn't stir from where she sat, and when she spoke he wasn't certain what she meant. Awful that he was disfigured? For whom? For her, to be stuck with him?

His heart clenched, and his chest tightened along with it. "I've learned to live with it. Some men were less fortunate. Losing entire limbs. Or their very lives." He cleared his throat when his voice came out rougher than he meant.

"I cannot understand what it must be like," she said quietly, and Myles looked up at last when he heard the gentleness in her words. Her expression had softened, her eyebrows drawn together, and she leaned

toward him as she spoke. "Your eye, your hand. You gave up so much as a soldier. I am sorry for it."

She meant well, he knew, so he gave her a smile he hoped wasn't tinted with too much bitterness. "There are the things people can see, like the eyepatch and the scars." He gestured to the left side of his face as he spoke. "Yet there is more that no one will ever see. For some, their bodies are whole, but their minds and hearts are wounded. For others, both body and soul are forever changed. That is why I went to the ball that evening, my lady. In hopes that people like your brother and sister can make a difference and convince others to do the same."

For the barest moment, he thought he saw her eyes gleam with unshed tears. But then she blinked rapidly and stood. "Adam and Elaine are quite single-minded when it comes to their hospital. With your help, I am certain they will be a success. Now, if you will excuse me, I will prepare for our outing. Will you be ready to leave in a quarter of an hour?"

Myles rose slowly. "Of course, my lady."

She made an impatient gesture with her hand, shaking her head at the same time. "Myles, do call me Philippa. We are married, after all." Then she hurried from the room without looking back.

Standing where she left him, Myles put a hand to his forehead in an attempt to massage away the pain that threatened to bridge across it. Did he disgust her? Was that why she had rushed away? She had seemed kind. Nothing in her voice or expression had given away more of her emotions than her surprise and her sorrow. But then, what did it matter how she felt? One could have pity for someone and still have a friendship. Even a marriage.

But he hoped it wasn't pity she felt. Because for the first time in ages, he had begun to imagine a life other than the one into which he'd settled. The upheaval might be uncomfortable, at first, but if Philippa and he could come to some kind of understanding...

Myles picked up his paper and looked at the pastry tray, untouched by anyone except Nancy. His stomach turned over at the idea of eating anything. So he left it for the servants to clean up and went in search of a footman to help him dress for an outing with his wife.

~

As Philippa left her room, a thrill of excitement raced through her. For the first time in her life, she would leave the house without a maid or chaperone in attendance. Instead, her husband would accompany her, and she might stay out as long as she wished. True, she meant to spend her time accomplishing much-needed tasks. Myles simply *must* have clothing more suited to his new status as a well-connected husband and gentleman.

She started down the steps, pulling her wrist-length gloves into place as she did. As she wriggled the fingers of her hand to get the best fit, she paused and looked down, turning her hand palm-up. It had jolted her to see that her husband lacked two full fingers. Though she had suspected an injury, she hadn't realized the seriousness of it.

An eye, his fingers, scars on one side of his face—where else might the war have touched his body?

Her cheeks warmed and she hurried to shake loose that most inappropriate thought. It wasn't her business. Despite their marriage. And she wasn't about to ask to inspect the horrible marks made by an awful wartime injury. How awful for her to even think such a thing! Doubtless, Myles wanted his privacy when it came to that subject. He certainly hadn't ventured any explanations, and she didn't need them to know that he conducted himself with honor and integrity.

Shaking her head at herself, Philippa continued down the stairs. She had nearly gained the ground floor when the front door opened with a slam. Philippa froze, and a footman hurried from the next room where he remained stationed to let guests into the home.

"Adam," her brother Richard shouted, his voice bellowing through the house like an angry roll of thunder. Then his eyes caught sight of her, and Philippa very nearly turned to run back the way she had come.

"Phillipa." The anger glazing in her brother's eyes assaulted her, freezing her in place. He snarled as he strode forward, and the anxious footman shut the door to the street.

Despite the quaking in her knees, Philippa lifted her chin. "Richard. How good of you to call."

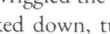

"How dare you." He came all the way to the steps before she realized he held a letter in his hand. He shoved it toward her, making her catch it. "This is a letter from your solicitor." He then swore most colorfully about Mr. Tuttle-Kirk's nature before continuing in only a slightly less frenzied tone. "You are coming with me, at once. The madman says you are married—"

"She is married." The voice came from behind Philippa, but she didn't dare turn her back to her brother. Even though she very much would have liked to see Myles descending the stairs, if only to determine how shaken he was by the earl's anger. His firm tone and deep voice rippled across her like a gentle wave. "To me, in fact."

"You? Who the devil are you? Cobbett—a nobody, and a cripple?" The venom in Richard's words made Philippa shrink where she stood.

"My lord." Myles sounded nearer now, and then she felt him descend to stand next to her. "There are better ways to vent your spleen than to shout in the face of my wife."

"A farce," Richard snapped, then glared at Philippa. "You married this cur rather than Lord Walter?" He jerked his head toward Myles. "Tell me it can be undone, Philippa. Now."

Though she went cold at her brother's tone, Philippa stiffened her resolve. Myles stood beside her, ready to support her. "No, Richard. It cannot."

"Of all the stupid things to do, you ungrateful chit—making an alliance with a nobody when you could've inherited a duchy." Richard threw his hands in the air. "Lord Walter's brother has nothing but daughters, has lost his wife—"

Though the news surprised her, Richard's determination to marry her off to a toad like Lord Walter suddenly made a great deal more sense. "I have no desire to be a duchess, nor to go about gloating because a man lost his wife."

Richard's hands balled into fists. "You selfish child. What that union would've done for our family—"

"You mean what it would do for *you* and your greed and arrogance! I won't sacrifice myself for you, Richard. Give me what is mine and leave me be."

He lunged forward, but what he meant to do she never learned. Because Myles was suddenly between them, his hand snatching up Richard's wrist and twisting it deftly behind his back, turning the earl about at the same moment. Myles shoved the earl forward while the lord gasped out an oath that made Philippa's mouth drop open.

"You will not threaten my wife," Myles said as he propelled Richard toward the door. The footman who had been hovering before now opened it, his face ashen. "Nor will you appear before her again until you have learned to keep hold of yourself. Good day, my lord." Myles gave one last push at the center of Richard's back, causing the earl to take a stumbling step outside. Then Myles gave a quick nod to the footman, who hastily slammed the large door behind the nobleman, then slid the bolt in place.

"Will there be anything else, sir?" the footman asked, still pale but wearing an expression of awe.

"That will be all for now." Myles waved a hand dismissively, and the servant bowed before hurrying away, likely making his way below stairs to spread news of the scene he had been privy to.

Myles stood still, his back to her. His shoulders were square and tense, and at that moment, Philippa's trembling knees gave way. She sat on the steps and dropped her face into her hands. "I am sorry, Myles."

"Sorry?" He sounded incredulous.

Philippa's eyes prickled with tears as she spoke to the floor. "Richard is dreadful when he loses his temper, but he has never acted quite like that before."

"Philippa." A scuff on the floor told her of Myles's approach, and then his fingers grazed her shoulder. "You have nothing to apologize for."

"But how he acted—what he said about you—" Philippa raised her head to look up at him. But the moment their eyes connected, Myles went down on one knee before her and made a handkerchief appear from his coat pocket. "Thank you." She sniffled as she took the linen from him, then managed a weak smile. "This is the second time I have ruined one of your handkerchiefs."

He shrugged, then released a deep sigh. "What your brother says or

does is no reflection on you, my dear. It is best you put him from your mind and let Mr. Tuttle-Kirk handle the details of your inheritance. For today, do you still wish to go out into the world on a shopping expedition?"

Philippa gave a hesitant nod. "If you are still willing, then yes. Perhaps after we visit the tailor, we could go to Gunter's for ices?" She felt a bit like a small child, looking to Myles as she did for comfort.

"I am completely at your command. First the tailor's, then ices." He stood and held his gloved hand out to her, which she took. He gave her fingers a gentle squeeze, then tucked it through his arm. "We will push past the unpleasant things and enjoy our day."

She leaned into him for a moment as they stood upon the top step in front of the house, but with no sign of the earl, she relaxed and smiled up at her husband. His gaze still swept the street, and she could feel the tense muscles in his forearm. She needn't fear any danger with Myles at her side. The comfort that thought gave surprised her, and as he handed her into Adam's waiting carriage, Philippa wondered how many benefits to her marriage she had yet to see.

Eleven

Walking up the stairs to enter Lady Darwimple's ballroom meant Myles and Philippa had to pause every few steps to wait for those ahead of them to move. Before the war, Myles had only attended one event that could be called a *crush*, but this was so much worse than that local assembly ball had been.

Despite the cool weather outside the massive townhouse, Myles already felt perspiration forming at the back of his neck, beneath the white silk cravat his wife had bought for him the day before when they had gone to the tailor's.

Philippa bounced on her toes and stretched her neck to peer upward. Her enthusiasm made him forget, at least for a moment, how much he despised crowds.

"I thought arriving a half hour late would mean avoiding the rush on the staircase." Philippa looked over her shoulder, down toward the entry hall. "I haven't seen Adam and Elaine arrive yet. Perhaps we all ought to have ridden together."

"Your sister-in-law urged you to go on ahead," Myles reminded her in a low voice. Elaine Gillensford had finished readying herself at the same time as his new bride, but then her infant had woken and cried

with such urgency that the nurse had felt obliged to inform the parents of the child's upset.

Philippa chewed her bottom lip as she nodded, a sight he found almost distracting enough to make him forget his growing headache. She stood on her toes again, this time peering upward, and the swell of music in the ballroom rushed down to meet them both.

The people around them on the stairs raised their voices over the music, and the mounting din momentarily sounded as the shouts of soldiers on the battlefield. The perfume stunk of ash and sweat, and the hot taste of iron filled his mouth.

Like a sudden and welcome breeze against his skin, Philippa's concerned whisper broke through the haze of memory. "Myles?"

He opened his one good eye, not having realized he had closed it. First he saw several empty steps ahead of them, and then the frown of his young and beautiful wife. She gripped his arm with surprising strength. Her fingers shifted, and he focused on the pressure releasing from her touch.

He forced a smile that likely looked more like a grimace. "I beg your pardon, my dear. I was lost in thought." He spoke more for the people behind him than the woman at his side. She raised her eyebrows, her only response, and he took her forward up the steps.

They gained the upper floor at last and found Lady Darwimple waiting a few steps inside the ballroom, an ostrich-feather fan in her white gloved grip. She waved them in languidly, as though the room didn't maintain an almost intolerable temperature.

"Ah, Lady Philippa. You have arrived at last. I wished particularly to greet you this evening." Lady Darwimple raised her time-softened chin to direct her diamond-hard gaze at Myles. "I am terribly sorry. I have already forgotten your married name. Though I believe I met your husband somewhere before."

Myles didn't need the upbringing of a titled man to recognize the snub, though he acted the part of a gentleman by ignoring it. He forced himself to chuckle as he looked to Philippa to provide a proper introduction.

His wife's expression surprised him. Philippa held her head in such a way as to look down her nose at the countess. Her eyes had gone hard, too, and her expression smoothed with what he would deem affront. "You are not mistaken, my lady. I believe you met Mr. Cobbett at the charity ball a fortnight before. Indeed, you glimpsed us shortly after a rather lovely interlude in the gardens that evening."

"Ah yes, of course. I had no thought on that night that we would soon learn of your engagement, let alone a wedding. Special license, was it?"

That comment had yet another barbed insult beneath her ladyship's feigned curiosity. Myles hadn't any hope of obtaining a special license, given that one had to hold either a high rank or more than a passing acquaintance with the archbishop.

Philippa proved perfectly adept at handling the countess's smug comments. "Oh, goodness, no. I have always thought that special licenses show a certain amount of vulgarity, given that one not only disturbs the archbishop's more holy work, but it also is such a mark of impatience. No. We had a lovely wedding at one of the oldest churches in England. The charm of marrying in a medieval church quite delighted me." She batted her eyelashes up at Myles, and he couldn't resist smiling at her in return.

His wife waged battle on Society's fields quite well. It made him wonder, yet again, why marriage to him had been the best answer she'd had to combat the rumors that had started to erode her reputation.

Lady Darwimple felt the sting. Her nose lowered, and her eyes narrowed. "Indeed." She cut her gaze toward Myles. "My felicitations to you both, Mr. Cobbett. Lady Philippa Cobbett." She folded her fan and pointedly turned to the person next in the receiving line.

Myles led his wife away, down one long wall behind the growing crowd. Her hand flexed against his, and her shoulders dropped such a slight amount that he almost missed the movement.

"Can you believe her?" Philippa bit the words out, and he watched her jaw stiffen so she spoke her next words through her teeth. "For her to offer such insult at an event to which she invited me!"

"You routed her well enough." It was a husband's place to offer such words, surely. "She retreated with speed."

His wife stopped her angry march along the wall, allowing him to pause, too. She looked up at him, a twinkle of mischief appearing in her eyes. "I did, didn't I? I recalled at the last moment that Lady Darwimple married by special license herself. My mother has many theories as to why and discusses them still with great relish." Philippa's smile faded, and she slowly shook her head. "Perhaps that was less than kind of me. Elaine wouldn't approve."

"I heartily do, if that counts for anything." Myles chuckled. "But then, I was trained to use every means I have against the enemy. And Lady Darwimple set herself as your enemy this evening."

"I certainly didn't expect such an attack, to use your war-like vocabulary." She tilted her head to the side as she regarded him. "She is a friend to my mother. One would think she would be a little more respectful, at least to our faces."

Myles didn't exactly care, except in regard to how her ladyship's barbs might have hurt Philippa. Since she had regained her good humor, he could easily forget the moment. In truth, it had proven a distraction from his inward disquiet. "I doubt you will have any further difficulty. Lady Darwimple's rank gave her the courage to speak in such a manner. Come. Enjoy your first ball as a married woman. Without chaperone. You may wander as you wish, dance as you wish, and converse with whomever you wish to converse."

Her expression brightened, and her gloved fingers gave his arm a gentle squeeze before she released him. "I did see a friend a few steps in. Will you be all right?"

He took up her hand only to release it, as one might cast off a line to set a boat adrift. "I have faced things far more dangerous than a ballroom, my dear. Enjoy your evening. Look for me if there is anything I might do for you."

She took one step backward, her eyes still upon him. "I will not dance the supper dance, so we may go in together."

What did it say about their relationship, that he had not expected that offer? "I look forward to the time in your company." He bowed,

the movement too slight for most to notice, but she granted him one last grateful smile before she turned and entered the crowd. He watched her go, keeping sight of her by the spray of white roses in her hair.

A snake emerged from the crowd, dressed in fine velvet and a white silk cravat. Lord Walter. The brazen fool met Myles's gaze with a smirk.

"Ah. If it isn't the fortunate bridegroom." Lord Walter approached with confidence, and Myles stiffened in response. His perceived rival didn't have the air of one defeated. Instead, the man had the audacity to position himself on Myles's blind side.

"Lord Walter." Myles snapped out the title without any enthusiasm in the greeting, grudging the respect he must show merely because the man was the son of a marquess.

"Mr. Cobbett. Congratulations on your nuptials." Lord Walter's overly smug tone made Myles grind his teeth. He couldn't abide officers who lorded their position over the men they ought to command with a sense of responsibility rather than one of entitlement. Lord Walter was the same sort of man as they.

Myles acknowledged the comment with a nod.

"It's quite interesting, isn't it?" The lordling didn't sound any less sure of himself as he spoke, amusement in his voice. "One would think when a woman's name appears alongside one man in the paper that she wouldn't even consider legally attaching herself to another. Especially when she is as notable a woman as Lady Philippa."

The music had increased in volume again, and the conversation in the ballroom matched. A faint buzz began in Myles's ears. "We are married, Lord Walter. Your business with my wife, though you never truly had any, is over. You needn't concern yourself with Lady Philippa's decisions."

"Yet as a friend of the family, I feel I am obligated to warn you." Now the serpent sounded positively giddy. "Lady Fredericka is on the other side of the room, along with her son the earl, and they are far from pleased with your inclusion in the family. In fact, I should not be surprised if their mood is infecting other guests."

That Lady Philippa's mother meant to punish her came as some-

thing of a surprise. Once Philippa and Myles exchanged wedding vows, and confronted her snarling eldest brother, things ought to have calmed. Whatever the upper echelons of Society thought about the matches made by its children, families always pulled together to save face and quell rumors. At least, that's what they had always done before.

Though he had a suspicion he played into the enemy's hand, Myles's good eye swept the room in search of his wife. She might have need of him yet. "If you will excuse me, Lord Walter. I find I grow—" Hang being polite. "—irritated by your conversation. Good evening." Myles offered the barest bow, barely more than a tip of his head, and walked forward into the throng of people, watching the dancers and those gossiping behind their fans.

The noise swirled around him, as did the scents of bodies and fabrics, and heady perfumes that repelled rather than refreshed him with their scents. He spied the white rosebuds woven through his wife's dark curls and focused only on getting to her. The narrowing of his thoughts sharpened his ears, and he picked out conversation he otherwise would not have heard as he angled through the press of bodies. His only thought was to provide reinforcement to whatever battle Philippa may find herself facing.

But what he heard made him scowl as he went.

"—married a commoner. There he is, there. Horrid—"

"Wouldn't want to wake to that—"

"Do you suppose she does? I would sleep in another wing—"

"—no reading of the banns. Do you suppose—?"

"Her mother must be ashamed."

"How dare they show their faces here?"

A snide giggle, then, "Especially *his* face."

Myles doubted storming up to his wife would quell any of the lashing tongues. He slowed his pace as he neared her and forced his expression into one of neutrality. His wife stood among women near her own age, and they formed a semi-circle before her. There were four of them, all dressed in fine clothing and dripping with pearls and amber.

Philippa wore the same face he had seen her put on before Lady Darwimple. Her battle mask, he dubbed it then. She caught sight of him from the corner of one eye and startled, as though surprised, then her lips curled into a smile as she turned to welcome him.

"My friends," she said, voice raised and light. "Allow me to introduce my husband. Perhaps this will ease your concern on my behalf. Mr. Cobbett, a servant to the crown and our country. Husband, these ladies came out the same year I made my debut. Of course, they married with greater haste than I did." He couldn't tell if that was another well-aimed thrust of her spear, but Myles stood next to his wife at attention. She gestured to each lady in turn. "Lady Bannfield, Lady Ian Crawford, and Mrs. Anthony Havenbrough."

~

THE WOMEN STANDING BEFORE PHILIPPA HAD ONCE INVITED her to their drawings rooms and salons to take tea. They had stood gossiping with her along crowded balconies, looking down into ballrooms like Lady Darwimple's. All three had laughed with her about her mother's ill-timed matchmaking efforts. But now, their eyes held a different sort of amusement.

They were laughing *at* Philippa rather than with her.

Philippa had no inclination of letting them win. After Myles bowed to the little group, she slid her arm through his and tipped her chin upward. Proudly. Her husband, though untitled and without large coffers of his own, had served king and country with honor. He had wed her with nothing but the best of intentions. Which was more than she could likely say for the spouses of the women before her.

"We have heard so much about you, Mr. Cobbett," Lady Bannfield said, her green eyes snapping and her golden hair blazing like a flame. Her striking beauty had won her an earl for a husband. "Your acquaintance must now be exceedingly sought after, given your marriage into the earl's family. Quite a boon for anyone, I should say."

Given that the opposite had been on display for everyone in the

ballroom that evening, Pippa felt the barb in those words keenly. Myles, however, kept a pleasantly reserved expression upon his face.

"As you say, my lady."

Mrs. Havenbrough tittered behind her fan, though what she found amusing, Pippa could not have said. She spoke with a cloying sweetness that did nothing to mask her disdain. "I confess, I imagined a different sort of man for our Lady Philippa. You do not mind me saying, sir, but I thought she might marry a degree or two nearer gentility than a former officer. You have married up in the world."

A slap in the face might have been a better compliment. But while Pippa felt her cheeks grow warm, Myles actually smiled. A tight, strained smile. Still, his fortitude impressed her as he said, "I must agree. Her loveliness and kind disposition are beyond compare. I cannot say I have ever met a woman who is composed of both wit and angelic beauty." He looked pointedly down into Pippa's gaze, causing her heart to lift hopefully. Not that she needed him to defend their union, rather that she enjoyed he would choose to do so with such ease.

"Dear me, you sound as though you quite adore her." Lady Ian Crawford's eyes narrowed, as though she searched for a weakness in a fellow combatant. "Given the most distressing reports we heard on the matter of our dear Lady Philippa's situation prior to your wedding—when *was* your wedding, dear?—it is something of a relief to find her tucked so securely in your protection, Mr. Cobbett."

Only Pippa saw the way his jaw clenched, the way he fisted his hand slightly behind his back. Myles hadn't seemed to mind when the ladies remarked upon his reputation. Had they pushed too far by bringing up the rumors about hers? She needed to get him away from the spiteful hens.

"Any and all who know my wife, madame, could never doubt that one of the most remarkable things about her is the propriety and integrity she displays in her behavior. For someone to think any less of my lady...." He sighed after letting the sentence trail away, then his expression turning as calculating as Pippa had ever seen it. "Well. Let us only say that such people are so lacking in compassion and intelligence that we must pity them rather than expect better."

It took more control than Pippa possessed to hide her smile at that. Myles had effectively called into question the characters and understanding of the women standing before them. That they all reacted with some shock to his words meant they felt the sting of his words. Pippa, however, felt quite proud of her husband's quick wit. Though the poor man did appear more tense and pained than before. He had grown pale, too.

"Such a pleasure to see you all. If you will excuse us, I must introduce Myles elsewhere." She curtsied and led her husband away. Thankfully, Myles fell into step beside her quite naturally. She brought him to stand near an open window. Myles put a shaky hand through his hair.

FROM THE CORNER OF HER EYE, PHILIPPA NOTICED THE color come back into her husband's face. She stood on his blind side on purpose, keeping her own gaze trained on any who might approach them. But this meant she couldn't see much of his expression, could not tell if his good eye was open or closed as he took in slow, deep breaths of the night air.

"I did not anticipate this evening presenting such a trial to us both," she murmured from behind her fan, waving it languidly as though she hadn't any reason toward agitation.

"You are too patient with me, I think." Myles tipped his chin upward and turned just enough for her to see his good eye studying her. "I apologize, my lady."

"Whatever for? You aren't the one acting without common decency." Philippa glanced again at her former friends, only to find they had dispersed. She spotted two of them at once, speaking into the ears of other women of rank. They played with her reputation as cats with a butterfly—without care for how their claws shred her wings so long as it amused them.

Myles leaned toward her, and the fabric of his coat brushed the bare skin of her arm between her sleeve and glove. "My presence isn't helping as you hoped. Perhaps I should leave. I will send the carriage back for you, of course."

Though she opened her mouth to deny such a thing was necessary, she swallowed the remark in the face of his fatigue. The light in his eye had dimmed, the corners of his mouth turned down, and his shoulders had lost some of their proud bearing. Surely the comments of a few spiteful women had not done so much to her soldierly husband. Perspiration dotted his brow below his hairline.

"Are you unwell?" she asked, resisting the urge to strip off her glove and touch his forehead.

He hesitated, then turned away, giving her his scarred profile as he answered. "I am sometimes discomfited in crowds. The noise. The smells." He shook his head. "I will be well enough. The fresh air is already helping."

"I do not know that London air can ever be called such a thing," she said, trying to make light of the moment. He did not appear to have heard her, so still he remained. Philippa chewed her bottom lip, then swept the ballroom again with her gaze. "I have yet to see Adam and Elaine arrive. I am concerned something has gone wrong at the house. Perhaps we should both return and look in upon them."

He didn't accept the excuse as readily as she hoped. "You needn't end your evening for my sake."

"For your sake?" Philippa snapped her fan closed and tapped him on the arm to punctuate each word. "Mr. Cobbett, we are for home." She looked into the crowd again and met the satisfied smirk of her eldest brother from across the room. Let him gloat. She had no intention of remaining at the ball if it meant acting as a target for ridicule. "I find I have lost all interest in this company."

"If you insist, my lady." He offered her his arm.

She took it. "I do." Then she put her nose in the air. "You are familiar with the concept of a strategic retreat?"

At last, he smiled, though it was with little humor, and when he spoke, he sounded weary. "Indeed. We will regroup and form a new plan of attack."

Her new husband didn't thrive in crowds. Yet he had agreed to escort her to a ball. Had withstood insults given directly to his face. Out of duty.

Perhaps Philippa had miscalculated when she could show her face again in public. But that hardly mattered. It would just take a little more time than she expected for gossip to die down. She still had what she wanted. A marriage of her own making, her fortune coming into her hands very soon, and greater independence than she had enjoyed thus far in her life.

After they returned to the Gillensford townhouse, the butler informed them that the youngest child had a fever that had kept her parents home.

Philippa stood in all her finery with her heart going cold. "Has anyone sent for the doctor?" Myles stood behind her, and when she spoke, his hand went to the small of her back as though to support her.

Thankfully, her fear hardly had the chance to form. "He has come and gone, my lady." Hopkins bowed politely. "He believes the little one is teething. The child is resting now, with both parents in the nursery." The butler's eyes twinkled, and were he not so well trained, Philippa knew he would smile with his amusement. The new parents doted on their infant, but there was always an undertone of bewilderment when Isabelle cried without obvious reason.

"Thank you, Hopkins." Myles removed his hand from where he had touched her, and Philippa looked up at him with a sheepish smile. "I suppose I worry nearly as much as they do about the children."

"A common enough thing, when you care about someone." The corners of his eye crinkled a little. "Do you intend to go up and check on things?"

"And risk waking up an ornery babe? Not to mention a grumpy Adam." Philippa gestured to the nearest door, leading to the sitting room. "I thought I might take some tea and read a book. It is still quite early for those of us keeping London hours."

"I suppose so." His gaze flicked from the door to the stairway.

"You needn't linger with me," Philippa said quickly, though a twinge of disappointment accompanied the words. "I know you are tired."

But her husband gestured to the doorway. "Tea and a book are my favorite things to combat a headache."

"Truly? I cannot read when I am even the slightest bit ill. It always makes things worse." She led the way to the doors, opening them herself. During the day, a footman stood in each corridor, ready to help family members with even the smallest of tasks. But with evening upon them, and the family mostly abed, the servants had sought their own rest or other duties.

"Sometimes it is the same for me, but I am willing to risk it this evening." Myles followed her inside the room and sat down in a chair near the fire. He took off his right glove, then the left, and put them on a table next to him.

Philippa went to a small set of shelves in the corner. More books were in other parts of the house, but there was always a selection at hand in this room for anyone looking to pass the time. She took up a novel she hadn't read in years. She then looked over her shoulder at her husband's bowed head.

"I could read to you, so you can rest your eyes—" She pressed her lips together tightly over the last word, but not soon enough to cut off the plural *S*.

Myles didn't so much as twitch. "That is a kind offer. If it wouldn't trouble you, I think I might enjoy being read to. I cannot remember the last time anyone read something to me."

She relaxed. It seemed she hadn't offended him with her small slip. "And here I read aloud nearly every day." She came around the couch at the same moment the door opened, a maid coming into the room. Philippa gave instructions for tea, then settled in the chair on the other side of the hearth from Myles.

"Who do you read to?" Myles asked, and she realized he'd closed his good eye and leaned against the back of the couch.

"I used to read to my mother. She had headaches all the time. Or, at least, she *says* she does." Philippa chuckled and opened the book. "Since Elaine married into the family, we often read together. One of us sews or paints, the other reads. Sometimes I read with Nancy, too. I cannot think of a better way to enjoy a book than with another person."

"I look forward to giving the exercise a try, then." Myles folded his

arms across his chest, and she saw him tuck his left hand away. From habit? Or to hide it?

As she read aloud from *The Eve of St. Marco*, she glanced up at him more than once. He breathed evenly, his eye remained closed, and she couldn't be sure he was awake. When the tea came, her husband opened his eye without any sign of disorientation or sleepiness. He poured out, so she could continue reading.

For half an hour, she read to him. She sipped at her tea when her voice grew weary, then came to the close of a chapter. It felt like the right place to stop. Especially as she couldn't tell if her husband truly enjoyed the reading or if he only humored her. As soon as she closed the book's cover, his eye came open and he appeared as alert as ever. Then they talked quietly of the book, with her mindful of his headache, before he suggested they both turn in for the evening.

They went upstairs together, and Philippa noted that most of the lights were out. The corridors were dark and quiet. When they stopped before her door, she looked up at her husband with curiosity. He held a candle between them.

"Do you need the light?"

She shook her head. "My maid keeps a lamp for me when I am out. Does your valet not do that for you?"

Her husband appeared thoughtful. "I haven't employed a valet yet. I had not even entertained the idea of obtaining one. There is a footman who has been helping, when I require it."

Philippa's mouth popped open in her surprise. "Myles, you must have a valet."

His eye wrinkled at the corner again. "As you say, my lady." He bowed, then made to walk away. And Philippa raised her hand to stop him, then hastily tucked it behind her back, hoping he hadn't noticed. What reason did she have to ask him to linger there, in the darkness?

She slipped into her room, where a small fire glowed in the hearth and a lamp waited for her beside her bed. The cozy, inviting room had been hers for weeks now. Yet as she finally slipped beneath her blankets, Philippa didn't feel as content as she had before. Perhaps because she reflected on the ball. The failure there settled in her heart. As did the

disappointment of finding no one willing to speak to her, unless they wished to hint that her marriage was a scandal. Though quiet, her subsequent evening with Myles had been a gentle balm for that hurt.

Maybe she needed to wait another week before going to important societal functions.

People would surely forget about her hasty marriage eventually.

Twelve

Myles dreamed of the ball with Philippa. A vivid, gentle dream in which he danced with her. Men never danced with their wives. But perhaps there, in that time and space, they were unmarried. A hundred bodies surrounded them in the ballroom. As he went through the familiar steps, the room grew louder. People jostled him. Shoulders first brushed and then shoved heavily against his. His wife looked at him with concern puckering her brow. She opened her mouth to speak, to ask him a question.

Then Philippa's hand slipped away, and when Myles turned to find her—instead, he found a battlefield strewn with soldiers. His ears thundered with cannon fire. Screams. Myles had to wake up. Knew he must. And then he flew sideways as he had before—

He sat up in bed with a roar, clutching at the coverlet, the fabric bunched up in his hands. All he could smell was the memory of smoke. His body slick with sweat, he stumbled out of the bed and knelt beside it. He found the empty chamber pot beneath it and drug it out, retching. His blood thrummed in his ears, drowning out anything outside of himself.

It felt like ages before he could sit back, tipping his head against the

bed to stare upward at the dark ceiling. Gradually, his pulse slowed. He felt the cold of the floor where his heels rested against it.

The house remained dark and quiet.

No one had heard him.

His shame remained his own. He hadn't had a night terror such as that in a long time. And he knew, should he sleep again that night, his mind would present it to him again. That was always the way with the worst of his dreams. When he went to bed, Myles prayed for dreamless nights. Those were the only good nights.

He pushed himself up from the floor, and the room spun. He went to the basin of water, cold now from his evening ablutions, and splashed his face with water. Fumbling about in the dark, he managed to light candles and stir the fire to life before collapsing in a chair.

The mirror above his dresser had tilted with his frenzied movement, and from where he sat he could clearly see the spectacle he'd become. He wore only a long white shirt, loose from his throat to halfway down his chest. His eyepatch waited for him on the mantel, leaving the scarred seal of his other eye to reflect back at him through the shadows.

Not all soldiers who lived through battle thought themselves fortunate. He had heard more than one man refer to himself as "cursed" long after the sounds of war had faded. And it was true. Here he sat, surrounded by more finery than he had any right to enjoy, still plagued by the dark memories of the killing fields.

With a shudder, Myles looked away from his scarred reflection to the fire. "I must get hold of myself." Speaking the words aloud gave them the feel of a vow or a prayer. "I cannot shame my wife or her family. Or the men depending on that hospital."

When sunrise came, it found him already dressed. He needed his routine back. Marriage or not. He'd found the best way to cope was to go through the same motions, every day. Wake. Dress. Read. Walk. Eat breakfast. Go to a club. Spar. Take tea.

He rehearsed to himself all the things he had done before Philippa came into his life. He couldn't do it all. Not the same way. But maybe he could build a new order.

He went out the front door and into the world, determined to order his thoughts and regain control of his mind. The first important thing on his list was to find a place with a simple breakfast. Along the way to make that discovery, Myles acquired a newspaper. Each step upon the pavement of London streets returned a measure of strength to him. In the finer neighborhoods in which he walked, there were not yet many people out to enjoy the morning light. The lack of walls, of crowds, let him take his first deep breath in what felt like ages.

Once he sorted out his breakfast, Myles went to Boodle's. His father had held membership there for a short time, when he took a small political role in London during his youth. That fact, and Myles's military career, had gained him notice. His willingness to engage other gentlemen in informal fisticuff lessons had cemented his membership.

No one treated him any differently when he walked into one of the many club rooms filled with books, chairs, and tables. He selected a quiet spot in the corner and sat, content to read his paper in peace.

A shadow fell upon the newssheets as someone stepped between Myles and the window. He looked up, lifting his eyebrows and preparing to return a greeting. But the man who stood over him was a stranger to Myles.

"Mr. Cobbett."

Myles did not flicker an eyelash at the address. "And you are?"

The man's expression turned to an arrogant smirk. "Havenbrough. My wife is an acquaintance of Lady Philippa's." He crossed his arms and settled back on his heels as though intending to remain in the stance for some time. "I told her you were a member at my club, though I cannot think how, given what little recommended you. Prior to your marriage to a peeress, of course."

It took a moment for Myles to remember the man's wife. She had been one of the three spiteful women at the ball, eager to simper and offer words of false sweetness to Philippa. Given the way Havenbrough stood before him, Myles anticipated more of the same. "It does seem as though the club will let anyone who can pay the fee join." Myles feigned a disappointed sigh.

Mr. Havenbrough's jaw visibly tightened. "I understand you're something of a pugilist, Mr. Cobbett."

Myles raised his eyebrows at the change in tactics. Surely the man wasn't about to issue a challenge of some sort. Not that Myles was an expert at boxing, but he held his own and had even gone a few rounds with scrappers of professional capability. "I would not classify myself as such, Mr. Havenbrough. I enjoy the sport for the camaraderie and exercise it provides."

The frustration that had begun to layer itself within him made the temptation to engage in fisticuffs stir. Yet just looking at Havenbrough, Myles sensed the man would post little to no challenge. The part of him that rose like a wolf scenting the wind hunkered down again, more discontent than before.

"It seems the rumors I've heard are not far from the truth." Havenbrough smirked again. "Though how someone of Lord Montecliff's respectability could permit his younger sister to marry a common scrapper, I can't understand. Unless there wasn't much of a choice." The man had a tone that suggested an impolite amount of relish for the subject. "Perhaps no one else could handle the young woman. I understand she can be—"

"Careful how you finish that sentence." Myles didn't speak so much as growl the warning. "Pugilist or not, I take exception to a man who knows nothing of my wife speaking of her with less than absolute respect."

Rather than appear chastened, Havenbrough's teeth flashed in a less than friendly grin. "Sensitive, are you? I must have struck a chord you did not care for."

"Or perhaps he merely has better manners than you," a new voice said, and Moreton appeared beside Myles's chair. "I cannot say I know many who make it a habit to speak of ladies in a gentleman's club. Perhaps you are not acquainted with that unspoken rule."

Havenbrough bowed the barest amount. "Forgive me for intruding, Mr. Cobbett. I will leave you to your business."

Myles and Moreton both watched the man withdraw to a group of

others sitting in a ring of chairs, all of them watching his approach with interest. Finally, Moreton sat down in the chair nearest Myles.

"I didn't expect to see you here so early in the morning." Moreton glanced at the news sheet Myles had wrinkled in his grip. "I thought you had a luxurious sitting room, or perhaps a well-laden breakfast table where you read your paper these days."

Myles shifted somewhat guiltily and forced himself to relax his grip on the paper. "How can I explain?" Myles tipped his head in the direction of Havenbrough's retreat. "I missed the joy of fending off rude strangers."

Moreton chuckled and leaned back in his chair. "Emily received your lady's invitation to dinner tomorrow evening."

Philippa had invited his friends to dinner? "I hope you both accepted. The Gillensfords employ an excellent cook."

"Which makes me again question why you are here when you could be in a comfortable townhouse enjoying a breakfast prepared by said cook." Moreton wore his solicitor's expression—one which meant he had found a scent of deception and meant to follow it to its source. "We no longer run in the same circles, Myles, but I cannot help wondering if Havenbrough's rudeness is mild compared to what else is being said."

The conversation at the ball flashed through his mind, and Myles turned his attention to a nearby window. "Nothing of a sensational nature has overcome the news of Lady Philippa marrying a nobody. Though one would think that would be less interesting than the gossip previous."

When Moreton only stared at him in silence, a disapproving squint to his eyes, Myles dropped the paper on a table and bent toward his friend. "What do you want me to say? I have spent the last several days hardly stirring from that house. And while it is a house with great luxuries, there is also little for me to do. Except be measured by tailors, dress for parties, and appear perfectly content whenever I am in the same room as someone else."

Moreton laced his fingers together and adopted a professional tone.

"All in all, not an unpleasant existence. Especially as you have a lovely wife to keep you company from time to time."

"My wife has other occupations. She is enjoying her freedom for the first time since she made her debut in Society." And Myles didn't begrudge her that freedom in the slightest. After meetings with Mr. Tuttle-Kirk, she had gone shopping, attended committee meetings with her sister-in-law, and today would have her first at-home day as a married woman, sharing the morning room with Elaine to greet her guests.

She didn't need her tired and frustrated husband anywhere near her to dampen her enthusiasm or intimidate her visitors. Assuming she had any visitors.

"Ah, there. A flinch. What were you thinking, just then?" Moreton moved to the edge of his seat.

"How do you do that?" Myles glared at his friend. "I said nothing."

"Let a man sit in silence long enough, and if his speech won't tell you something is wrong, his mannerisms will. You flinched."

Though his exasperation was well-tempered with relief, Myles explained—in quiet tones—what had happened the night of the ball. Moreton nodded now and again, but otherwise said nothing until Myles finished the telling. Then, his friend spoke.

"What is the strategy going forward, since marriage alone hasn't made your lady more acceptable to her peers?"

"A strategic retreat," Myles admitted. "Attending functions without as much social distinction. For which I'm grateful. That ball was more crowded than a battlefield and stunk nearly as much."

"Ah-ha," Moreton murmured, a sad lift to his lips appearing. "This is coming more to the point of what is wrong with you."

Myles picked up his paper, ready to hold it up as a barrier should his friend prod too much further. "I am merely frustrated that I am uncertain how to help the situation. That is all."

"I can see the tension in your shoulders, Cobbett." Moreton lowered his voice still more as he spoke. "And that weariness in your eyes. Are you sleeping well?"

"Well enough." Myles opened the paper. "What are you doing at the club, anyway? I almost never see you here."

"I had a meeting with a client." Moreton let the silence hang between them again, but this time Myles kept his lips pressed shut. Finally, his friend sighed and came to his feet. "I need to return to my office. I suppose I will see you at dinner tomorrow evening."

"I look forward to that. Good to see you, Moreton."

The solicitor nodded once. "And you, Cobbett. Good day." His friend took his leave. Myles waiting another quarter of an hour before doing the same. The club had not been a place of refuge as he had hoped.

~

ELAINE'S FRIENDS LEFT A QUARTER OF AN HOUR BEFORE TWO o'clock. Across London, women of the finest families and households closed the doors to their elegant houses, whether they had returned home from visits or showed out a final caller. Now, it was time to prepare for an outing to Hyde Park, or tea and a nap to fortify themselves for evening engagements.

But Philippa remained sitting in the same chair she had occupied all afternoon, staring across the room at a landscape depiction of gloriously green hills dotted with perfectly white sheep. Hardly a realistic rendering, but the artwork had a certain cheerfulness to it. Yet Philippa's stare had little to do with the painting and more to do with her discontentedness.

She heard Elaine's last caller, a banker's wife and donor to the hospital, at the head of the stairway.

"Is your sister-in-law well?" the banker's wife asked, sotto vocé.

Elaine answered with her usual cheer, though Philippa could well guess "I believe so. You know how it is so soon after marriage. There are a lot of changes to a young lady's life."

A hesitant quiet followed, and then, "You have heard what people are saying?"

"Yes, but it troubles me not at all. My sister-in-law's only misfor-

tune is counting the wrong people her friends, Mrs. Claridge. No one who knows Lady Philippa could credit rumors that paint her as anything other than an intelligent and compassionate woman."

Though Philippa's heart warmed while listening to Elaine's defense, her stomach sunk with dread. This explained the lack of visitors coming specifically to see her. Perhaps Lady Fredericka and the earl had decided to punish Philippa's independence by encouraging whatever the gossips had to say about her hasty marriage. And about her husband's humble origins.

For the second day in a row, Myles had left the townhouse early in the morning. Without anyone aware of his plans. The day before, he had returned in time for dinner. She supposed it would be the same today. Considering she had invited his friends to dine with the family, she did not think he would be late.

And she didn't begrudge him his freedom. Not when she had so newly attained her own. Though she did wonder where he went.

When Elaine returned to the room with a tired smile, Philippa rose from her chair. "Thank you for allowing me to entertain with you today, even though none of your visitors came expecting to see me." In truth, several had seemed surprised to find Philippa in the sitting room.

"I hope you enjoyed yourself. You were quieter than usual." Elaine smoothed a cushion on one chair, then found a shawl she had discarded earlier in the day and wrapped it around her shoulders again.

"And had less visitors than I expected." There wasn't any point to avoiding the topic. "No one came to see me, Elaine. Not my married friends, not my unmarried friends with their maids or mothers."

"Not everyone knew it was your at home day, especially given the newness of your marriage." Elaine never told falsehoods, but her hopeful attitude faltered as she spoke. "Perhaps it is because you still share my address. That may have caused some confusion."

"Mother and Richard are doing their best to show public disapproval of my choices." Philippa absently wandered to the tea service and traced the rim of her teacup. "I expect I will receive a note from

one or the other soon enough, gloating over my lack of friends now that I have removed myself from their protection."

"There are good people in Society, Pippa. They will show themselves soon."

"What if they do not? How many people have already expressed to *you* their wariness to support the hospital, because you have a woman with a smudged reputation living under your roof?"

For the first time, Elaine hesitated to answer. Pippa's shoulders fell. "Elaine—how many?"

"No one has withdrawn their support yet," Elaine insisted, but the way that *yet* was spoken made Pippa's guilt grow. Something of that emotion must've shown on her face, as Elaine hastened forward to put her hands upon Pippa's shoulders. "Oh, do not look that way. We both know things will work out. Your mother didn't like my marriage to Adam at all, and we still have friends aplenty and more invitations than I can possibly accept."

"Because you had no scandal tied to your name, and you entered Society as a mature woman with children and a fortune behind you." Philippa shook her head and gently backed out of Elaine's hold. "The circumstances are quite different. Everyone bandied my name about with Lord Walter's, thinking we had snuck off into the shadows to paw at one another." She shuddered and went to the window, glaring out at the world. "And then I leave my titled brother's protection, marry someone my mother loudly disapproves of, and here we are."

Elaine approached, her chin tilted upward. "People will eventually lose interest, Pippa."

"What would you do, in my situation?" Pippa folded her hands before her, arching an eyebrow at the lovely former seamstress. "If you gave me your most honest counsel, what would you recommend?"

"Are you sure you want to hear it?" Elaine smiled despite her question. "Because my advice is likely not at all what you expect."

"Then I positively insist you say what you have to say." Pippa couldn't resist smiling back. "I am ready to try just about anything."

With a slow nod, Elaine looked away from Philippa and down into the street. "I would leave London entirely." When Philippa gasped,

Elaine spoke with firmness. "I would, Pippa. While you are here, everyone may purposefully ignore you. They will all speculate about you. If you left for the country, being out of sight would also put you out of their thoughts. The gossip would die a faster death. Beyond that happy event, though—you would have an opportunity to know better the man you have married."

Philippa drew back a step. "I can come to know Myles right here in London. In this house."

"Where it is safe?" Elaine added with a suggestive tilt to her head. "Philippa. I don't know if you have realized it or not—but your husband is as out of his element as I was when I inherited Tertium Park."

"We have an agreement," Pippa murmured, looking away from her sister-in-law. "An understanding. He has his freedom, and I have mine."

"That isn't a marriage, darling." Elaine lowered her voice to a near whisper. "It's barely a partnership. Beyond that reasoning, the two of you must present a more united front to Society if you wish to be accepted into its fold again. Despite what I achieved in our small country circle, I would have been a complete failure in London without Adam."

Philippa could admit the truth of that. Adam's connections and charm had smoothed Elaine's path. Their marriage hadn't carried even a whiff of scandal with it. Even those who didn't know Adam and Elaine loved one another deeply merely assumed he had married her to keep her substantial inheritance in the family—not something anyone in Society would look down upon.

"Try as you might to become better acquainted with your husband in Town, you could better dedicate your efforts to that cause in the country. Where there are fewer distractions."

"I meant to finish the Season in Town," Pippa said. "I am not ready to abandon those plans. Besides, Myles agreed to a marriage of convenience. I'm not even certain he would want to leave London." Though he hadn't enjoyed that ballroom. By the time they left, he had almost appeared ill.

But that was only one ball. And it had subjected him to the nasty remarks of others. He had chosen to live in London even before meeting her. Why would he wish to leave?

"You asked for my counsel." Elaine didn't seem at all annoyed with Pippa's response. "And that is what I will say. Leave London to relieve the pressure you and he are under. Come to know one another. Return next Season as a unified couple, and take the *ton* by storm."

Though Philippa wanted to put her sister-in-law's advice from her mind, she found herself turning over the merits of the idea for the rest of the afternoon. By the time the dinner hour arrived, and she waited in the drawing room adjacent to the dining room, she had grown rather nervous with thinking Elaine could be right.

Myles appeared, dressed for dinner and as solemn-faced as usual, before anyone else had joined Philippa.

"Any sign of our guests yet?" he asked. His gaze fell upon her only briefly, then quickly tripped across the room to the clock upon the mantel.

"I am certain they will arrive at any moment." Philippa rose from her chair. "Did you enjoy your day?" She hadn't seen him until that very moment. A wife did not ask her husband how he spent his time, she well knew. It would be impolite. It wasn't her place. Especially given their arrangement. She doubted he was off in a gambling den or any other place riddled with inequity. But still. The curiosity remained.

"I did. Thank you. And you? Did you have many visitors?" He crossed the room slowly, taking up a position on the opposite end of the rug from her. As though he did not wish to come too close.

That couldn't be the case. They had been friendly enough before this moment. During their conversations prior to marriage, and after, they had spoken with an understanding of one another. Hadn't they? Did it matter?

"Not as many as I expected." She could admit that much and save face. There was no point in making him worry. Not that he would. *Bother*. Elaine's advice had turned Pippa upside down, making her double-think everything. "Elaine thinks it will take more time."

"Ah." Myles lowered himself into a chair, keeping the left side of his face turned slightly away from her. "Do you agree with her?"

Pippa started. "I—I suppose I must. To an extent." Yes, it would take time. But surely she needn't leave London. Not when her time was finally her own. Yet it didn't fall to her to make the decision alone, surely. If she asked Myles, and he preferred London, it would certainly settle her mind. And yet—what if he wished to leave? Did that follow that she must abide by his desire, rather than her own? Or compromise?

She had promised to live under the same roof with him for a year as they came to know one another, and as they worked together to build the kind of life they each wanted.

Pippa ought to ask him. She parted her lips to do so when a knock on the door forestalled her. Myles raised his visible eyebrow at her and waited for her to answer the knock. "Enter," she called, putting aside the question for another time.

In came the butler, introducing their guests for the evening. Mr. and Mrs. Joshua Moreton, the only friends she had actually heard her husband mention. Which meant their good opinion mattered to him, and Philippa meant to have it.

Elaine and Adam joined them shortly after, and while the men spoke on one side of the room, the women came to know one another on the other. Mrs. Moreton and Elaine had similar temperaments, though the former seemed far quicker to laugh than the quieter Elaine. By the time dinner was announced, the women were deep in discussion about the coming of summer, and how glad they would be to leave long sleeves behind in the warmer weather.

The dinner hour passed happily, and the after-dinner conversation proved entertaining, too. All the while, Pippa kept an eye on her husband, noting how different he seemed in company with his friends. He was relaxed. He spoke with a dry wit that surprised her. And he smiled more than she had seen him smile the whole of their knowing each other.

And she began to wonder if maybe Elaine had a point. Maybe it would behoove her to come to know Myles better.

Thirteen

"What are we looking for at this one?" Myles asked his wife, looking up at the tall brick building before them.

"Furniture for our future home. When we find it." She grinned at him and tugged upon his arm.

Myles escorted Philippa through the warehouse district, a place he had never visited before. A week had passed since their dinner with the Moretons, and Myles had spent every day except Sunday wandering about London in the mornings.

He returned to the house in the afternoon to meet with Gillensford to discuss the hospital and soldiers' affairs. They would walk through a potential building sight the next day. Gillensford had hoped to secure an old building and repurpose it, but Myles had nearly convinced him that something built specifically for their purpose would prove a better investment.

During dinner the evening before, Philippa had asked if he would accompany her on what she called a "shopping expedition." Though her phrasing had amused him, he hadn't realized how literal she meant the phrase. They had started directly after breakfast, and he found himself wishing they had brought along elephants to ride and porters to carry a supply of food and water. It was nearly time to return to the

house for dinner, and his feet hurt as they had during the longest of his military marching campaigns.

His wife had tried to engage him in conversation in the evenings, showing interest in his day and his work with her brother. He tried to avoid saying overmuch about the number of times he met people who knew her. Men and women who raised their eyebrows, made what they thought were cutting or witty remarks, then went on their way. He had even glimpsed her eldest brother the previous afternoon, and the man had pretended not to see him. More than a few people on the street saw that moment—a social slight, though not the cut direct.

Things weren't getting any easier for either of them. Philippa's remarks about her days always lacked any mention of visitors or friends, except for a few visits exchanged between her and Emmeline Moreton. Emmeline had won Philippa's friendship quite easily, as Myles had hoped.

They entered the warehouse, where bolts of thick upholstery fabric hung on walls and furniture was scattered throughout large rooms. Rows of chairs stood together, each one intricately carved, and tables were in another room entirely. Philippa led him from one collection of couches to another, occasionally pausing to discuss the merits of a specific design. Myles tried to show an interest, though one chair looked the same as another to him.

Furnishings mattered a great deal more to his wife than to him.

A clerk followed them about with a notebook, jotting down observations Philippa made. Though they were not making a purchase today, the clerk had offered to send home with her a list of her favorite items and swatches of fabric. Setting up a home together would be a costly affair, with far more decisions than he had considered.

When they finally left the warehouse, Philippa twined her arm through his and smiled up at him. "I have never chosen furnishings before. Everything we have at our country estate is terribly old. And Elaine is only leasing the townhouse, which came with all its furniture. Starting with nothing is rather thrilling."

"And expensive," Myles added with a chuckle. "Have you given much thought to searching out a house in London?"

"Not yet. I cannot decide what size would be best for just the two of us."

Just the two of them. For now. Though he hoped, by year's end, she would consider adding children to their arrangement. Among other things. Marriage to a beautiful woman who had no intention of falling pregnant meant keeping his distance both physically and emotionally. Which proved harder the more time Myles spent near Philippa.

Her beauty was alluring, especially when she smiled or spoke of things which excited her. And she was clever. She read the newspaper and could converse on a number of topics. She enjoyed laughing. She adored her nieces and spoke often of the nephew away at school. He found everything about his wife utterly charming.

Which meant staying away from her as much as possible. Spending the long day walking through warehouses and shops with her had been difficult. For one thing, it meant fighting to keep his interest and growing awareness of her hidden. For another, the only distraction from his wife was the constant awareness of the crowds shifting and pressing in around them.

His head had started to ache an hour before they finished. And his shoulders carried the tension of the last week, try as he might to ignore it.

Back outside, horses came and went in the street at such speeds that Myles did not trust to cross them. Not with Philippa on his arm and a blind eye. "Let us walk a little more in this direction. Perhaps we will find a carriage for hire without crossing the road."

"I knew we ought to have kept our driver," she said. "Though I suppose it wouldn't be fair to our horses to make them stand about all day, waiting for us."

"Leave it to me." Myles patted her hand reassuringly. They had gone a dozen steps more when a loud crash—the sound of metal striking something hard—exploded nearby. With the crash came a horse's scream, and angry shouting as a driver tried to calm his beast. And Myles—Myles pulled his wife against the building nearest them. His heart raced within his breast, his head swiveling quickly as he tried

to find the source of the sound—the source of danger. Blackness crowded in upon him. Another loud crash made him duck his head, forcing Philippa down with him for protection.

Cannon fire and the screams of men both roared within his ears so loudly that he shook, and then he felt his wife's hand slip away from him. Someone shook him. Slowly the surrounding sounds faded away, leaving the worried words of his wife to float into his awareness.

"Myles? Is something wrong? Myles, are you unwell?"

He opened his eye, uncertain when he had closed it. Unaware of how much time he passed. He slouched against a building. Behind Philippa's shoulder, traffic moved as normal on the street. Though he thought a few faces on the walk peered at him before their owners hurried by. Pretending not to see him, a grown man, behaving as a lunatic.

At last, he lowered his gaze to Philippa's lovely face, pale now with worry, brow wrinkled in concern. Her beautiful eyes were large and fearful. Of him? Or for him?

He slowly adjusted his posture, still leaning a touch on the brick wall for support. "Did anyone see?" he asked quietly, his hands shakily adjusting the hem of his waistcoat, and then his jacket.

Philippa did not look away from him. "What happened?" she asked in a whisper he barely heard. "One moment we were walking, and suddenly you pulled me to this wall. And you looked as though you had seen some sort of horror."

"That noise..." His words trailed away as his eye caught what had set off his war-wounded reactions. Several feet in front of him was a shop carrying pans and pots of all sizes, and a young man was stacking several in a cart. Perhaps he had dropped a few. Or slammed one against another. A completely innocent event. An innocuous sound.

Myles shook his head, trying to clear it further, while his face grew hot, and his stomach churned. His wife continued to stare at him, waiting for some kind of explanation.

"I think we had better return home," he said at last, pushing himself fully upright. He offered her his arm without looking at her, and he felt her hesitation as she took hold of him again. He kept his eye

forward until he found a carriage for hire. Then he assisted his wife inside and took the seat next to her, staring out the window. The way they sat, she was upon his scarred side. He hadn't meant to do that, but sitting across from her would've invited more staring and scrutiny.

She did not let the silence last long. "What happened, Myles? Did you have some sort of dizzy spell? Or a faint?"

He shook his head. Refused to look at her. "Nothing of the kind. It will not happen again." The sick feeling in his gut increased with those words. In truth, he couldn't promise her such a thing. When Myles had first returned home, many noises had startled him. Loud shouts. A runaway horse. They had left him trembling and sick, lost in memories of war rather than aware of his present circumstances. But it had been months since he had experienced such a spell. He had hoped they were a thing of the past.

Like his dreams, these waking nightmares could come and go without warning.

Her slim fingers grazed his forehead, and Myles reacted without thinking. He snatched her hand away, whirling to face her with a fierce glare. He hadn't seen her remove her glove or reach for him. Because of his half-blindness.

Her eyes went wide, but she held perfectly still. Watching him.

Shame raced through him with heat and speed. He gentled his hold upon her bare hand, then released it altogether. "I apologize. I am unused to being touched."

Rather than appear offended or hurt, Philippa tipped her chin back. "I am checking you for a fever." She put her hand up again, daring him to pull away as she glared. He held still, surprised that she would wish to try a second time. Her palm across his forehead was smooth and soft, a gentle touch that he yearned to lean into but dared not show such a need.

He wasn't used to being touched, as he said. But he relished the simple contact. Especially as it was hers. Her hand on his arm had become common. But her skin against his? It was a beautiful rarity. Only ever accidental. And here she purposefully stroked the tips of her fingers against his forehead.

"Cool to the touch," she said, confusion apparent in her deep blue eyes. She withdrew her hand but did not immediately replace the glove. "Myles, please tell me. Have you been ill? Did all our walking today over-tire you?"

Myles lowered his gaze to her hands in her lap, watching as she twisted her unworn glove. Admitting to the brokenness of his mind had never been easy. He had only explained it a few times before. To a doctor, who had advised rest and fortifying himself with liberal doses of laudanum. His mother and father, who had looked upon him with pain and helplessness. To Joshua Moreton, who then spent hours every day looking in on Myles.

How would his wife react?

"Perhaps we could speak of it later." When he had time to decide how to tell her, how to explain that his weakness didn't make him any less of a man.

"After dinner," she said at once, that determined glint in her eye returning. "I will not be put off for long, Myles. If you are ill, I must know." She gentled her stern words by laying her hand upon his, and he wished he had found reason to remove his gloves, too. What would his wife think if she knew his thoughts?

He nodded once in agreement, turning his gloved hand over to lace with her fingers. Offering a gentle squeeze, a nonverbal thanks, for her words. "After dinner."

He did not know how he wanted their conversation to proceed. But he dreaded seeing pity in her eyes. Or disgust. They both fell silent for the remainder of the carriage ride, and Philippa had the kindness not to remove her hand from his.

~

DINNER THAT EVENING INCLUDED GUESTS, COME TO discuss the children's school that Adam and Elaine had founded. Three couples joined them at the table, all married, and all from the highest points in the merchant class. Those not born to privilege, but to the knowledge of hard work, were far quicker to give to the little

school to ensure it remained open and financially stable for years to come.

Pippa assisted Elaine in hostessing duties, but that didn't serve as much of a distraction from watching her husband. He hadn't shown any further signs of illness since their return to the townhouse. He also said as little as possible during the meal and afterward in the parlor.

When the guests left, the hour closer to midnight than Pippa liked, both couples climbed the stairs to the second floor of the house. Adam and Elaine drifted down one corridor, toward the stairs, in order to go up to the nursery as they did every night. To take one last look at their little ones before retiring for the evening.

That meant they did not see as Pippa stopped at her bedroom door and kept her arm securely tucked through her husband's. "You haven't found a valet yet, have you?"

He stared across the way to his bedroom and shook his head. "Not yet."

Which meant his room would be dark, without a lamp or fire lit. Pippa sighed and pushed open her bedroom door, tugging him inside behind her. Quite suddenly, her husband dug his heels in.

"Wait—" He disentangled his arm from hers. "We can speak tomorrow—"

"I am not giving you the chance to slip out the door before I am even awake." She stepped into her room and turned around, gesturing for him to enter. "Come in, Myles."

He remained in the corridor, half in shadow, staring at her with one wide eye. "Are you certain?"

Though her cheeks warmed, Pippa couldn't resist a short laugh. "I have no ill intentions toward you or your virtue, husband. I promise. I only wish to have a short conversation with you."

For a moment, he glowered at her, though a flicker of humor had appeared in his eye. "I have no fear for my virtue, my lady. I am a married man, after all." But his steps were hesitant. When she closed the door after him, he stepped hastily away from her, keeping to the wall rather than walking to the fire and the two chairs pulled up before it.

She had never heard of a man growing timid in a woman's bedroom. Especially a married man. But perhaps she misunderstood the situation. Maybe he only wished for her to feel unthreatened. If so, his hesitancy struck her as most charming.

Pippa stripped off her gloves and dropped them on her dressing table, then she took her favorite chair before the fire. Once there, she plucked the waving white feather from her hair and dropped it onto the small table at her elbow. "Myles, please sit. Make yourself comfortable."

He cast her a suspicious look before approaching, slowly. He sat in the chair as gingerly as if he expected to spring up again at a moment's notice.

Did she make him nervous? Or did their topic of conversation unnerve him?

Pippa folded her hands together in her lap and studied her husband. How many times had she traced his profile with her eyes? Or wondered at what it must be like to wear an eyepatch, going through one's life with half the sight one was used to? He had such a handsome face, even with the scars marring half of it. Tonight, he wore his usual stern expression. Though she saw the pull of muscles along his jaw that spoke of greater tension.

"Will you tell me what happened today?" she asked when they had sat in the quiet for so long, she knew he would not speak first.

Myles shifted, his gaze briefly meeting hers before darting to the fire again. "There isn't a word for it," he said, his voice so low that it mingled with the sound of the crackling fire. "Call it a waking nightmare, or the memories of war, if you like." He shifted in his chair, removing his dinner gloves with an attention she knew they did not merit. "Today, I heard a sound. Something simple, that you likely did not even hear. But to my mind, it was deafening. It overwhelmed my senses and my mind. Instead of standing on the street beside a beautiful lady"—he smiled tightly up at her, as though he hadn't even meant to offer the compliment—"I felt as though I stood in a field in France or Italy. Facing the enemy all over again."

Turning that explanation over in her mind, Pippa cast her mind

back to that confusing moment. Her husband had snatched her away from the walk and thrown them both against a solid wall. There he had stood, eyes blazing and face pale, unmoving except for a tremor that went through his body.

"I wanted only to escape," he said, voice hoarse. "But how does one escape the ghost of a memory?"

"Is this the first time such a thing has happened?" she asked, studying him with new respect. Admitting to a weakness in body was one thing—but a man, admitting to an imperfection of mind? Unheard of, in her opinion. All British men were expected, even raised in such a way, to withstand the unpleasantness of the world around them with detachment.

"No." Myles finally met her gaze, darkness mingling with pain in his expression. "Though it has been a long while since I have undergone such a...such a spell."

"Have you spoken to a doctor?" Even as she asked, she had little hope regarding the answer. The human mind wasn't something any physician could claim to understand.

Myles leaned forward, clasping his hands between his knees. She looked down at them, noting the remnants of fingers on his left hand. Physically, he had lost much. But again, she wondered at all the scars she couldn't see. Scars on his heart.

"The only doctor I spoke to urged me to get more rest. He theorized that a well-rested mind was less apt to make mistakes—thinking I am at war when I am only walking down the street. He also suggested opiates." Myles shuddered. "But I will not risk myself or my future on something that forms a lifelong habit of use."

"Did the rest help?" she asked, privately agreeing with his stance on taking something that would dull feelings rather than solve the problem.

"For a time. Through my own observations, I find that having a routine helps. Doing things to exercise my mind and body means a better rest at night. Sometimes, that keeps my mind from wandering into the past." He shrugged and looked down again, flexing his hands. "I am sorry you had to witness a moment of weakness today."

"You and I are married." Pippa resisted the urge to reach out to him, to breach the distance between them with a touch to his hand. He hadn't seemed to like her initiating such contact in the carriage. "We must look after one another. Now, and always. I want to help you, Myles. In whatever way I can."

He looked up at her through a lock of hair that had fallen across his forehead. One corner of his mouth tipped upward. "I should have told you about it before I agreed to marry you."

Pippa shrugged and offered him a smile, attempting to reassure him. "I cannot see how it would have made a difference. You are an honorable man. You suited my every requirement in a husband."

"There is more," he said slowly, as though it pained him to admit to any other weaknesses. "The headache at the ball...that is not uncommon in such circumstances. One reason I attend the church in Chelsea is because of its size. There are never crowds of people inside. They wouldn't fit."

"Crowded events make you ill," she said, "and when you are not rested, your memories of war assault you." That would make life in the middle of London Society difficult for her husband. But then, many a woman went about town without her spouse. London's elite accepted that the social whirl of dinners and dances was more for the benefit of ladies, anyway. Men merely put up with the parties and planning to appease wives.

When her husband clenched his hands into fists, she focused again on him. "Is there something else?" she asked, studying his features. "The more you tell me, the more I will understand how to help."

A laugh preceded his scoff. "There is nothing you can do to help me, except exercise patience. There *is* more. I have nightmares. Vivid, disturbing dreams. I wake feeling lost, the scent of smoke choking me. Sometimes, I cry out. In my rented rooms, I disturbed the neighbors more than once." He shuddered and dropped his face into his hands. Shame poured from him, until tears pricked at Pippa's eyes.

"I think we ought to talk to another doctor," she said softly. "A military doctor, perhaps, who may have seen such a thing before."

"I know many men who experience such things. We do not speak

of it often. It is only something understood between old soldiers." Myles shuddered. "There is nothing a doctor will do."

"How do you know?"

"One of your brother's contacts in preparing the military hospital is the Royal Navy physician. Sir Gilbert Blane. Have you heard of him?"

It took her a moment to place the name. Then she nodded with some excitement. "He is one of the Royal Family's physicians. I have heard of him."

Myles leaned back in his chair and turned again to the fire. "He regularly tours the hospitals of the Royal Navy. One of the letters he sent your brother, about the hospital, suggested that a lunatic asylum would better serve the military. Most asylums in England hold dozens of former naval men apiece, you know."

"I didn't know," she whispered. "A lunatic asylum? How is that helpful to one such as you? You are not mad. Only conversely affected by your memories."

A gentle smile touched his lips before turning bitter. "For some, it is one and the same. Sir Gilbert has proposed that the best way to manage men with such difficulty isn't to offer any treatment that would allow them back into the world, but he encourages that they become long-term residents of asylums and hospitals. And he has said that a strict schedule, something that encourages a man to maintain order in his life and around him, is the most beneficial thing. He suggested the hospital—or asylum—have extensive gardens for which the inmates will be responsible."

"Gardens." Pippa studied her husband. "I take it you are not much of a gardener."

Myles released a mirthless laugh, shoving his left hand through his hair, leaving it standing on end. "No. I am not a gardener."

"Why do you leave the house every day?" she asked softly. "Is it worse for you, to be here?"

His expression changed again, his chin lowered while he looked up at her. "After we wed, I grew restless. I had more...vivid, shall we say, nightmares. I thought the answer would be to return to my old

routine. Walking the city. Eating breakfast in a quiet cafe. Attending a club to read or engage in a boxing match."

"But those things did not help," she mused, tapping the arm of her chair. "Or perhaps they have, and things would be worse if you had not returned to your former schedule." She stood and paced away from the fire, then back.

She had chosen Myles to wed based on his humble background, and his honorable behavior. Learning about his circumstances, how he lived with so little, had made her feel as though marrying would be a boon to him, too. Something which would improve his life. Yet she had put him into situations that disturbed his peace of mind.

The life of a London gentleman was likely just as uncomfortable for Myles as the life of a gardener would be. And yet he had agreed to it, because she had asked. Because he wanted to help her and do a kindness for his family and others. Myles had sacrificed to marry her.

Guilt smote her heart, and Pippa leaned her forehead against the mantel. Peering into the flames. "I wish I had known before," she murmured softly. She might have done more for him. Instead, all she had worried over was the lack of invitations she'd received for balls and evenings of entertainment. Pining after crowds of people and diversion while her husband suffered nightmares.

And none of the people who made up those crowds even wanted her around. Not at present, while suspicion and scandal still clung to her reputation. With her own brother and mother determined to punish her for her independence.

Myles stood, and she turned to face him, ready to offer up more reassurances. But his expression stopped her words. He appeared utterly defeated, his shoulders slumped, and the corners of his mouth turned down.

"I should have told you before we spoke of contracts and marriage. You didn't know what you were getting in a husband at all, did you?"

"That isn't quite what I meant." She tried to smile, but he was already shaking his head.

"I had best retire for the night and leave you to your rest. We both know, I sorely need to take my own. I have no wish to embarrass you in

public again." He turned away before she could reach out to him, and he was already at the door when she finally forced out her words.

"Myles, you didn't—"

"Goodnight, my lady." He opened the door and left, closing it behind him with quiet finality.

Pippa started across the room, thinking that she must speak to him to clarify things. But she stopped when she reached the door and leaned against it heavily. What could she say to him?

Fourteen

I wish I had known before.

Myles couldn't rid himself of Philippa's words. Had he deceived her when he signed the marital agreement? It had never occurred to him the need to disclose his nightmares to her. Yet now, marriage joined them to one another, and all the consequences of her actions were his, and that all consequences of his choices were also hers.

"I think we had better consider a location outside of London, if we intend to build something new." Adam Gillensford shuffled through several papers on his desk. Each one described a London property or land for sale. He jotted down figures and square footages of each location. "It wouldn't be terrible to have more land, for gardens and such. Especially if we could provide our hospital kitchen with its own produce."

The study wasn't large, but there were two desks within. Myles had found the furniture arrangement strange until he happened upon Elaine and Adam working in the room at the same time. She wrote business correspondence and had a hand in each of their ventures. Their partnership in marriage was a fascinating study. He'd never heard of anything quite like it.

Myles picked up a list of properties outside of London that the solicitor had provided to Gillensford. "Land would provide a greater ability to build something according to our unique specifications, too. But then you run a small risk, given that you'll have less oversight if the location is far from your London and country addresses."

"Agreed. And I know of nothing in our county that would suit. Though I suppose I would need to contact someone more familiar with property in that area." Gillensford started stacking papers, a sign that he was finished for the afternoon. "Enough with business. We have talked of nothing else these last two hours."

Before Myles could stand to leave, or offer up a new topic of conversation, Gillensford said, "How is my sister?"

A difficult question to answer at present. "We all live in the same household," Myles said, somewhat confused. "You know as well as I do, I should think. I have not seen her since last evening." He had carefully avoided the rooms in the house where the women spent most of their time. He had broken his fast in his room and taken tea in the study.

Gillensford leaned back in his chair, as though settling in for a long conversation. "That isn't the best answer, Cobbett. Not when you are married to the woman. I know your arrangement with Pippa isn't traditional, but I thought you the sort of man who would not allow things to stand that way for long."

Myles frowned, uncertain how to address what his new brother-in-law seemed to imply. "I have no intention of taking advantage of our situation—"

"Not what I meant," Gillensford said, the words clipped. "You are an honorable gentleman. I merely thought, given that you are both young and intelligent people, that you'd have decided by now to get to know one another better. Form a relationship based on more than a financial need."

"A friendship?" Myles asked, already sinking deeper into his chair. He knew the answer before Gillensford gave it.

"That would be a start." The other man scrubbed thoughtfully at his chin. "I must admit, I am not eager for this conversation between us, Cobbett. But my wife has expressed concern over Pippa's state, and

when my wife is concerned, I must be as well. Even if it means a difficult conversation about my sister."

"I hope I haven't given Elaine any reason to worry." Myles shifted again, tucking his scarred hand beneath his right arm. The room grew uncomfortably warm, with the afternoon sun slanting in through the window.

Gillensford chuckled. "You and Pippa have both given my wife cause to worry. You two are rarely in the same room together for more than the time it takes to eat a meal. You hardly know each other. You are acting more like a house guest than a husband, and she is finding that Society isn't ready to forgive her yet for thwarting everyone's expectations. Yes. Elaine is worried. Living with us, in a London townhome, isn't the best way to begin your marriage, either. Even if it is a contracted agreement rather than a romantic attachment." He gestured sharply at Myles as he spoke. "It's far too easy for the two of you to avoid one another."

Though tempted to tell Gillensford that Myles and Philippa's marital arrangements were none of his business, living in the man's house made it difficult to brush aside the topic. Instead, Myles tightened the fold of his arms and shrugged somewhat defensively. "What would you have us do? Philippa is searching for a house to lease in London."

"Another large house where you two can avoid each other," Gillensford guessed. "That will not solve the problem." He stood and put both hands on his side of the desk, leaning forward. "I think you should both leave London for a time. Let the gossip die down. Go somewhere that the two of you can spend more time together."

"That isn't what Philippa wants." Myles knew that point well enough. She wanted freedom. The ability to float along in London Society without her mother's sharp eyes and sharper tongue to keep her in check. Yet that wasn't what marriage had provided to her. Not yet.

"Hang what Philippa wants. When she was twelve, she wanted a Roman chariot, but then was perfectly content with her own pony." Gillensford thumped the desk with a fist, though his words contained

no actual heat so much as frustration. "Take her away, Cobbett. Show her there is more to marriage than attending social events on your arm."

While Gillensford meant well, Myles had to shake his head at the suggestion. "I'm not sure that's my place." Philippa had made certain he understood she had no wish for a husband to command her. "Though I will take what you have said under consideration, of course."

Though Gillensford appeared ready to protest and belabor the subject, a knock at the door interrupted him. The butler had appeared to inform Gillensford of a visitor. Before leaving the room, Gillensford gave Myles one last look of exasperation. "This topic isn't closed between us, brother-in-law."

Myles chuckled and left the study as Gillensford did, but while the other man went downstairs to greet his visitor, Myles went up to his quarters. He'd had a letter from his mother, expressing her delight—and shock—in regard to his marriage. She had also pointedly asked when he and his bride intended to visit his childhood home. Ambleside. He hadn't visited in two years. It was easier to stay away than to return. Financially and emotionally. He hated to be coddled and fussed over by his family, even as he loved their affection and how liberally they bestowed it upon him.

Philippa was leaving her room as he entered the hall, and she hesitated with her hand still on the door handle. "Myles," she said, her voice uncharacteristically soft. Uncertain. "How...how have you been? Today, I mean."

The inquiry stung. "I have had no further incidents such as yesterday's, if that is what you mean." Did she now think him subject to frequent fits of memory? He had woken from an unpleasant dream in the middle of the night. But he had disturbed no one. Even if sleep hadn't returned to him.

She appeared confused, then hurt. "That isn't what I meant at all. It is only that I haven't seen you yet today, and our conversation last night did not end well."

He continued to his door, refusing to feel guilty. "I am well enough. I thank you for your concern."

"Myles," she said again, forcing him to pause when he had taken a step into his room. "Will you not ask after me?"

He swallowed his pride and turned to face his wife, who truly didn't deserve his ire. Guilt made his tone less amiable. Guilt that he had trapped her in a marriage with him, a broken man. "I apologize, my lady. How do you fare on this fine day?"

Her chin came up at the same moment a wan smile appeared on her lovely face. "I am tolerably well, considering that I received a note from a friend—or at least, someone I thought a friend—asking me *not* to attend an evening of music at her home this evening. I agreed to play for her weeks ago, you see. Before we wed."

His spirit sunk further. He dropped his hand from the door and gave her his full attention. "That is terribly rude of her, to deprive her guests of your talent." He tried to make the words sound light. Tried to offer her a commiserating smile. "None of this has gone the way you expected, has it?"

Slowly, Philippa shook her head. "Not at all how I expected. But it is not your fault at all, Myles. It is my mother and brother, I think. And the likes of Lady Darwimple and Lord Walter."

"If only we could ship the lot of them off to some other corner of the kingdom," he said, leaning against his doorway. Gillensford's suggestion teased at his thoughts. Dare he ask if she wanted to flee London?

"That would be utterly convenient." She leaned against the opposite wall, mirroring his stance. "But since we cannot move them about like pieces on a chessboard, I have thought it would be wise to change my strategy. Have you any suggestions?"

There it was. The perfect way to extend the idea. And he already had an excellent excuse waiting, in the form of his mother's letter, upon his writing desk. "How would you feel about another strategic retreat? This time, to the country, where the enemy has fewer resources."

Philippa said nothing for the space of three heartbeats. She stared at

him. Yet the quiet didn't feel awkward in the corridor. Instead, the atmosphere felt rather comfortable.

Slowly, a smile turned her lips upward. "Have you been speaking with Elaine? She suggested that very thing to me."

Myles chuckled. He shouldn't be surprised. If Gillensford had spoken to him, Elaine had likely spoken to her sister-in-law. Hopefully, not with quite the same suggestions. "I have not said a word about visiting the country to Elaine. Though I have recently had a letter from my mother, encouraging a visit."

It wouldn't leave them much time alone in each other's company, as Gillensford had implied was necessary. But it would be a change of pace. He would be in a safe place, too. Myles had never had a waking attack of his memories while at his family's home. And maybe, if Philippa met his family, she would think more kindly of *him*.

If he could spend time there, even so short as a week, that might fortify him well enough to continue through the rest of the Season.

His wife tipped her head back, staring upward at the ceiling as she hummed a thoughtful note.

"Your family home is in Bedfordshire, is it not?" Philippa actually appeared to consider his suggestion. "Kempston." They had spoken little about his family, though she had received all that information from his solicitor.

"Green End, to be precise," he said, observing her with growing curiosity. "Fifty miles from London." That piece of information might change her interested expression to one of alarm.

Except it didn't.

"That sounds lovely." Philippa leaned away from the wall, her posture perfect once more. "When would you like to depart for Green End? What is the name of your father's estate?"

"You truly wish to visit my family?" He straightened away from the wall, too. "Ambleside. My father's estate is Ambleside."

Philippa nodded, her eyes bright with enthusiasm. "If you believe a strategic retreat is in order, I will bow to your superior battle experience. And what better place to go than to your family? I should like to meet them."

"My father is only a very minor baron," he reminded her. Then he thought to offer a warning. "Their home isn't as grand as what you are used to, I would wager."

Waving her hand dismissively, Philippa assured him, "I haven't any expectations on that account. Though I imagine your mother is a lovely person, given what I know about her youngest son."

"Though I am not an impartial party, I have always thought her one of the best women on earth." His hand went to the door handle again, though with reluctance this time. "I will write my family at once. We could leave whenever you wish. If you truly want to make that journey."

"I do. Stop trying to dissuade me." Her smile sparkled, and she took one step toward him. "We should give the letter time to arrive before we do, I suppose. Do you think three days from now is enough?"

Three days? How could she seem so eager to leave London, when he'd been certain she would never entertain the idea of exiting the social wilds for the country? Yet here he stood, not having had to do much to convince her at all—

He'd been quiet too long. She spoke with less certainty, and a lower voice. "Unless you do not think that is enough time for your family to prepare?"

And suddenly, he was the one reassuring her. Speaking gently. Hoping that the smile he offered, as strange as it must look on his scarred face, was calming. "Considering how much my mother wishes to meet you, I think it is more than enough time."

Philippa appeared relieved. Then she bestowed another charming smile upon him. "I had better leave you to your letter writing, then." She took a step away, still facing him. "Thank you, Myles. For inviting me."

Then she turned and walked away, each step graceful and light. For a moment, Myles felt nothing but admiration for the woman he had married. As well as the creeping realization that he was not at all good enough for her. The third son of a baron. A broken man. And she, the daughter of an earl, the very picture of beauty.

He entered his room and pushed his hand through his hair, leaning heavily against the door. What would she make of his family? What would they think of her?

Adam Gillensford wasn't the sort of man to gloat, but when he and his wife learned of Myles and Philippa's plans, they would likely feel as though they had accomplished some kind of victory. But Myles knew well enough that a visit to Ambleside, while pleasant, wasn't likely to change Philippa's mind about Society or their marriage.

As he sat to write his mother, Myles reassured himself aloud, "All I need is enough time to shore up my defenses." That was all he allowed himself to hope for.

Fifteen

The exceptionally mild weather meant a peaceful journey from London to Kempston. Philippa had entrusted her brother with hiring a private coach to take them all that way, changing out horses as needed to decrease the time spent on the road. Myles knew the route they took well enough that they only stopped at the highest of quality inns along the three-day journey.

Pippa's maid traveled with them, ostensibly reading a book. Myles had yet to find a proper valet, so the maid was the only servant with them. The hours of time in the carriage were not so awkward as Pippa had thought they might be. Rather than sit in silence, Myles took the time to tell her about his family's history.

His father was only the second baron of his title, and the barony hadn't come with much land or income. It had been bestowed on Myles's grandfather as a small favor rather than a grand gesture of gratitude.

As the fields and woodlands of the countryside drifted by her window, Pippa soaked in all she could about her in-laws.

That small favor had made the first Baron Greenwood, George Greenwood, a lord. Which opened doors for the family and allowed them entry into a world that they didn't quite belong to. Myles's

parents, Matthew and Elizabeth Cobbett, Lord and Lady Greenwood, hadn't cared overmuch about titles or London. They were happy to stay in their middling-sized village with their six children, content with the world and all that was in it.

"Tell me about your brothers and sisters," Philippa said. With three older brothers and an older sister of her own, she had an idea of how a family of such a size would run. Except Myles seemed inordinately fond of his siblings, while she only felt such closeness toward the brother nearest her in age.

"There is George, named after the first baron, and Winston. We called him Winnie, most of our growing up, which he despised. Then my sister Mary. I came fourth. A few years after, my sister Margaret came along. Then finally, Elenor."

He sketched the layout of the house for her, writing the name of each room within its box. The house was, as he said, small for a member of the nobility. Minor though they were. Growing up, Myles had shared a room with his second-oldest brother, while the eldest had a smaller room of his own. The sisters had shared rooms similarly. Which meant the family had six bedrooms, but never room for visitors without displacing a member of the family.

"With only my youngest sisters and parents at home, I am certain now they have more rooms than they know how to use," Myles said with a grin.

They arrived in Kempston in the early afternoon, and the carriage rolled to a stop in front of a tall brick-and-timber house—an early eighteenth-century design—shortly after. The sun shone brightly, and the garden in front of the house was well crafted to appear wild and meadow-like, with a white-pebbled walkway from the drive up to the front door.

No sooner had Myles handed Pippa down from the carriage than the door of the house had opened, and several people came spilling out. Many more people than his parents and two sisters.

A stream of children came first, all of them jumping and shouting for "Uncle Myles" to greet them. After the children were three ladies and two gentlemen not old enough to be the baron and baroness.

When the lord and lady of the house finally came outside, both of Pippa's hands had been claimed by little girls in matching yellow gowns.

The children swept Pippa and Myles forward to the door, where a man with gray hair and Myles's distinct features stood waiting for them. The woman on his arm was considerably shorter than Philippa, with silver-blonde hair mostly tucked up into a white cap.

"Welcome home, Son," the baron said. "You must introduce us properly to your bride, before she thinks we are all as wild as these children."

The children giggled and released Pippa so she could curtsy as Myles made all the necessary introductions.

"I didn't know you already had guests," Myles said after introducing Pippa to the other adults. His second-eldest brother, Winston the vicar, was visiting with his wife. The eldest sister, Mary, had come with her husband and children, too.

Myles appeared distinctly uncomfortable. Surprising, given how much he had enjoyed telling Pippa about his relatives.

"Visiting family is not at all the same as *guests*," Lady Greenwood informed her son with a lofty tone. "Do come inside, Lady Philippa. Let us make you comfortable. I imagine, after that journey, you would prefer a moment of peace before we overwhelm you with our questions and conversations."

Pippa followed happily. "I hope my bringing a maid will not put you out."

"Not in the slightest, so long as your maid doesn't mind sharing an attic room with one of ours." Lady Greenwood tucked Pippa's arm in hers as they climbed the stairs from the ground floor to the first floor. "Most of the family sleeps here, of course. The children are upstairs in the nursery, then the attic is for the servants. All except the kitchen staff, who live in the village with their families."

The baroness started pointing at closed doors as they walked along the corridor. "That is Margaret's room, and there is Elenor's. You haven't met Elenor yet, of course, but she will be home by dinner this evening. And on the opposite side, Winston and his darling Laurel are

in that room, with Mary and her Mr. Fountain. Whose name is George, of course, but we all call him Mr. Fountain so as not to confuse him with *our* George."

Pippa realized they were running out of bedrooms at almost the same moment Lady Greenwood pointed to one of the last two doors. "The baron and I share this room, just across the hall from where you and Myles will be staying."

She turned her back to Pippa to push the door open. Likely a fortunate thing, as Pippa's mouth popped open in protest. She closed it again and looked over her shoulder, hoping to make eye contact with Myles. So he could *do* something. Myles wasn't there. Apparently, she alone had been ushered up the stairs, assuming others trailed behind. But what a silly assumption.

"Come in, dear," Lady Greenwood called from inside. "We will send your maid up at once, so you can make yourself comfortable."

With hesitant steps, Pippa entered the corner bedroom. Light streamed in from windows on two walls, and a breeze lifted the white curtains in a welcoming way. The room was painted a pale green, the rugs embroidered in blue and ivory. A small hearth on one wall would provide a fire at night, with two cozy chairs on either side of it. Much like her room in Adam's townhouse. But smaller.

"The dressing room is through here." Lady Greenwood opened a narrow door that Pippa vaguely noticed, as her entire attention had fallen upon the canopied bed in the center of the room against the wall, between two open windows.

One bed. Smaller than the one she slept in, *alone*, in the townhouse.

"We did not think you would mind the arrangement, though it is cozy, as you are newlyweds." Lady Greenwood closed the dressing room door, her back still to Pippa. "Though I daresay, our household is not what one would normally expect of a baron's estate."

"It's lovely," Pippa burst out, hoping her new mother-in-law wouldn't notice the way her cheeks burned. "Myles already told me all about his childhood home. He loves it so, and wanted to be certain I would find it familiar. Even though this is my first visit."

Myles had assured her they would have their own rooms. Or at least, implied that they would. He'd seemed surprised at the additional houseguests. Had he already realized what their situation would be?

It wasn't as though she could explain to Lady Greenwood the nature of their marriage. Not if Myles had neglected to do so.

"I am glad you both came," Lady Greenwood said, voice soft, eyes aglow with joy. Completely unaware of Pippa's inward anxiety. "Myles hasn't visited in ages. It is good to have him here, and especially wonderful to welcome you into the family."

"Thank you, Lady Greenwood." Pippa prepared to curtsy as her mother-in-law took her leave, but the diminutive woman surprised her by enfolding Pippa in her arms instead. The maternal embrace brought a prickle of guilt to Pippa's heart.

"He is a wonderful man, Lady Philippa. We are so glad you could look past the outside and see him for who he truly is."

Pippa, released from the embrace, didn't know what to say to that. So she said the first thing that came into her mind. "Please, Lady Greenwood. Call me Pippa."

~

MYLES SPENT THE AFTERNOON LETTING THE CHILDREN crawl all over him. He held nieces in his lap, allowed a nephew to ride him from one room into another, and took his sister's youngest infant in his arms while she herded the rest of her children up to the nursery.

Winston sat with Myles while everyone else in the household disappeared. Their parents went upstairs to dress for the evening meal. Their brother-in-law stepped outside to smoke his pipe. The women would settle their children and then see to their own preparations.

Philippa remained in their room. His mother had informed him they had a delightful conversation before she left his bride to take a nap. "You picked a lovely lady, Myles," his mother had said, her eyes brimming with tears, before she had left the room.

Mary's youngest boy was only four months of age and sound asleep

in his uncle's arms. "How is it," Myles mused, looking down at the tiny eyelashes of the baby, "that we all start so small?"

"It is part of God's grand design." Winston crossed one leg over the other. He was a larger man than Myles, with a chest like a barrel, and an infectious grin. "We all begin helpless. We depend on others for comfort, protection, and knowledge. Much as God would have us become as little children, to humble ourselves and trust him to care for us, as children must trust their mortal parents."

Somehow, Winston could speak of such things without sounding like he stood at a pulpit. He made the sacred sound familiar rather than forced. Something that Myles had always admired about his older brother.

"I suppose having children of one's own is meant to keep that lesson at the forefront of our minds." Myles settled comfortably in his place. "How many children do you have? I have lost count. Two dozen, at least."

"Five," Winston corrected with a smirk. "And one additional child due before Autumn."

Myles's eyebrows lifted. "Congratulations to you and Laurel. More so to her, since she is doing all the work."

Chuckling, Winston offered a shrug in response. "I am well aware that I do not deserve her. I think that is another part of God's plan, at least for me. He sent me an angel of a wife so I am forever working to be worthy of her." The vicar folded his arms over his broad chest and nodded to the baby in Myles's arms. "You have always been fond of children. I imagine you are hoping it will not be long until you have your own."

It was the first time anyone had mentioned the expectation of children to him. And he had only briefly spoken to Philippa of his hopes for a family. Myles took care in avoiding his brother's eyes as he spoke a half truth. "I had forgotten what it is like to have children filling all the nooks and crannies of a house."

Though he told himself he avoided his family to avoid pity, the matter went deeper than that. Every time he returned to his childhood home, his memories of growing up in a family full of love and hope—

and a fair amount of fun—had proven bittersweet. Because he'd never create such a home of his own. Not on his low income. Not as broken as he'd become.

Now, hope tugged painfully at his heart.

He envisioned all too easily how it would be, to sit with his arm around Philippa while they watched children with her dark curls and blue eyes playing on the rug before the hearth, a baby in her arms.

But not yet. Maybe not ever. Philippa had waited all her life for the ability to come and go as she pleased. Having children would complicate that for her. And as much as he longed for his vision to become reality, Myles recognized that her happiness was much more important to him than...well...anything.

Winston's voice, though pitched low and quiet, pulled Myles away from his musings. "The number of thoughts I've seen play across your face in the last five minutes is rather impressive." His expression had changed, too. From content to curious. "Is there anything you wish to talk about?"

Myles shook his head, aware his smile would reassure no one given how weak it felt upon his face. "Not presently."

"Hm." Winston studied Myles for a moment and appeared on the verge of asking another pointed question when Mary came back into the room. She appeared rather out of sorts.

"What are you two still doing in here?" she asked, somewhat accusingly. "Get upstairs and dress for dinner. Family we might be, but we certainly aren't heathens without manners."

"That isn't what heathen means," Winston corrected with a grin.

Their sister glowered at him. "Do you know what *delinquent* means? Because your wife will make certain you do, if you aren't upstairs and dressed in the next quarter of an hour." She gently took her baby from Myles. "As for you, my littlest brother—"

Myles protested in a whisper as the baby shifted from his arms to hers. "I'm taller than you by a foot!"

"Hush. You know quite well what I mean." She tucked her sleeping child against her breast. "We are all trying to make a good impression on your Lady Philippa. The least you can do is pretend our mother

raised you with good manners." Affectionately exasperated, she cast them both a superior glance and left the room.

Winston stood the moment she was gone. "As I am well aware how my wife feels about having a delinquent husband, I had better be on my way. I advise you to do the same." He winked and left Myles alone in the room.

The mantel clock revealed that they had half an hour before dinner. Philippa had been in their room this whole time. Though he couldn't be certain if she was resting or avoiding his family. Or, perhaps, avoiding *him* now that their sleeping arrangements were decidedly not what either had expected.

Regardless of her reasons, Myles had no choice but to go up to their shared room. He had to dress for dinner. And he and his wife needed to talk.

By the time he stood before their bedroom door, Myles had a plan in mind. So, he knocked softly and waited for a response. The knock carried through the corridor more loudly than he wished, but Philippa's maid opened the door a mere second after.

"It's Mr. Cobbett, my lady," the girl said, hardly opening the door more than a crack. The little gatekeeper's stern frown made him smile, which made her frown even more.

Philippa's clear voice carried through the room to him. "Let him in, please. And you are dismissed for the evening."

The maid opened the door fully, curtsied to him, then stepped into the hall. She closed the door behind her with a quiet *snap*, leaving Myles and Philippa in the room alone. And there she stood, his elegant wife, dressed in a gown he had seen her wear once before, when her brother had entertained several minor lords at his dinner table. She had pearls in her ears and around her throat. A spray of white silk roses in her hair, too.

She looked every inch a lady, from her dark curls to the fine blue silk slippers upon her feet.

Myles gulped. It was that, or choke on his attraction to his wife. Her beauty drew him a step closer, but the flash of alarm in her eyes froze him once more. Though she held herself with the confidence of

one born in her position, she'd found herself in an unwanted situation.

"We are sharing this room," she said, bringing her hands up to her stomach to lace her fingers together. "So I take it that your family does not know about the unique arrangement we've made."

Myles released a quiet breath, then pushed his hair back from his forehead. "I haven't told them more than the most basic information. When we married. Your name. My change of address." He looked away from her. "I'll use the dressing room to prepare for dinner, if you prefer. Then we can go down together."

She nodded but didn't move from where she stood in the center of the room. Myles walked around the edge of the carpet, feeling her eyes on him the whole time.

"You still don't have a valet," she said, before he opened the door to the narrow room that held their clothing and luggage.

"I'll manage." He tried to reassure her with a smile. "We both will, I think." When she gave him a hesitant nod, he went fully inside and shut the door.

A narrow window let in the last rays of spring sunlight, and a lamp flickered in its place on the wall. There was just enough light for him to dress, though the room was stifling and uncomfortably warm.

His head started to pound, so he left while still holding a cravat in one hand. His shirt was open at the neck.

Philippa had settled into one of the chairs near the hearth. A book lay open in her lap. But the way her eyes snapped up to meet his made him doubt she'd actually focused on the book. He held up the cravat, sheepishly. "I need a mirror to tie this torture device around my neck."

Her eyes fell from his gaze to the open shirt, and his wife's cheeks turned a dark, rosy shade of pink. "Yes, of course." She lifted up her book and pointedly stuck her nose inside it.

Myles went to the mirror hanging above the bureau and started wrapping the cloth around his neck. He lay the whole thing on the back of his neck, then pulled it forward. Then back. Around again, then drape it this way and that. Finally, he held it all together with a plain silver stickpin.

"What are we going to do about our sleeping situation?" Philippa had apparently used the time it had taken him to dress to gather her courage enough to ask the question.

Myles looked down at his hands, realizing he'd forgotten to take his dinner gloves out of the dressing room. He flexed his left hand several times. "I have given it some thought. I would prefer to keep my family unaware of our agreement. It would..." How did he explain in a way she would understand? "It would distress them, I think. To know our match was made based on anything other than mutual affection."

"I understand." He darted his gaze up when she spoke, immediately noting the softness in her eyes. "I do, Myles. And I don't mind. I cannot think many mothers would be thrilled with a situation like ours. Especially one as caring as yours."

"Thank you." He relaxed somewhat, then nodded to where she sat. "I will sleep in one of the chairs. No one will be the wiser."

Philippa raised her eyebrows. "One of these chairs?" She stood and pointed in her seat. "Myles. That would be terribly uncomfortable."

"I've slept in worse places," he admitted, trying to smile through the memory of the hard, damp ground where he'd lain his head during the war. "I will steal a pillow from the bed. A blanket from a linen closet. That amount of comfort will be perfectly acceptable."

His wife pursed her lips, glancing down at the chair and then up at the bed.

Days in a carriage and uncomfortable beds in old inns hadn't exactly been easy. He'd looked forward to a downy mattress and warm blankets and pillows stuffed with feathers. But Philippa's happiness and wellbeing came first.

"I suppose..."

The long case clock in the entry hall chimed the hour, its steady rhythm echoing through the whole house.

"We had better go down, so we aren't late to dinner. I wouldn't want your mother to think me rude." She started across the room, stopping at Myles's side. "I quite like her."

"I think she feels the same about you." Myles extended his arm to her, and she took it with a hopeful smile.

"Really?"

"And if anyone is blamed for our late arrival to dinner, it will be me. Just wait and see." He led her from the room, and they went down to dinner together without speaking another word on the subject of who would sleep where.

~

PHILIPPA WOKE FROM HER SLUMBER WITH A START. SHE'D had the most peaceful dream. There was a garden, full of bumblebees and butterflies. She'd been looking for someone. And then she'd heard Myles calling for her.

Awake, she heard him moaning. Speaking unintelligibly.

Blinking in the darkness of an unfamiliar room, Pippa listened carefully a moment. Then she realized Myles mustn't be awake. He was dreaming. And given the sound of things, they were not pleasant dreams.

He was having a nightmare.

She threw the covers off and put her bare feet on the cold floor, then stumbled blindly toward him in the dark.

They had exchanged enough covert looks after dinner for Pippa and Myles to understand one another. She had gone up to bed before him, ringing for her maid to help her undress. Then she'd slid into bed and left a lamp for him to take into the dressing room for himself. He'd stayed downstairs long enough with his brothers that she'd almost fallen asleep, lulled easily to rest in the comfortable bed. But she'd woken when he'd entered the room, her whole being aware of his movements up until the moment he'd settled in the chair to sleep.

She hadn't spoken to him. He'd assumed she slept. That seemed easier.

Pippa stubbed her toe at the foot of the bed and yelped, then covered her mouth. Except that was foolish. She needed to wake Myles, given the amount of distress in his voice.

The banked embers glowed just enough for her to reveal her husband's profile as she grew closer. His head was tilted back. His chest

moved up and down rapidly, matching the sound of his ragged breathing. Pippa hurried to his side.

How did she wake a grown man from a nightmare?

She touched his left hand where it rested, draped over the arm of the chair. And she whispered his name. "Myles? Myles, you are dreaming. Wake up, Myles."

He shifted. Then gasped as he leaned forward abruptly, and his hand came up to snatch at her arm. He gulped in air, and Pippa hurried to kneel before him. She put both hands upon his knees, peering through the semi-darkness at his face.

"I am here, Myles. You are safe. We are at Ambleside." She repeated the information to him again, then dared to reach up and lay the palm of her right hand against his scarred cheek.

"Pippa?" he spoke her nickname in a hoarse voice. His hand covered hers upon his cheek. Had her heart not already been pounding with worry, she might've noticed that it skipped when he called her that.

"Yes, Myles. I'm here." She brushed her thumb across his cheek, the feel of his rough skin and stubble reassuring her. "You had a nightmare."

He shuddered. When he spoke again, he sounded more himself. His voice warm and gentle. "I woke you."

"I am glad you did."

He abruptly stood, pulling her to her feet. "You will catch cold, kneeling on the floor in nothing but a nightdress."

She shivered, and he gathered her closer. "I am perfectly fine. You are the one having a terrible dream. Let me worry over you a moment, before you try to rescue me from a cold floor."

He gently squeezed her hand. "Thank you for worrying. But now, back to bed. I will be well enough. It was only a dream. And a mild one at that."

"Mild?" she repeated, aghast. He guided her back to her bed.

"I am well. You should rest."

But she didn't let him hand her up into the bed. Philippa kept hold of him instead. "You cannot be serious." Then she shivered again and

reached for his other hand, realizing how cold his skin felt to her touch. "Myles, *you* are the one who will catch cold. With the fire banked, this room is freezing."

"I have a blanket—"

"Your fingers are like ice."

"I am perfectly—"

"Get in the bed."

Perhaps her lack of patience caused Pippa to speak those words without thinking how they would sound. But once she said them aloud, compassion wouldn't let her take them back. Myles had woken from a nightmare. He was cold. The bed was warm and comfortable.

And large enough for two.

"Philippa, I cannot possibly impose on you in that way." His voice lacked any conviction, though. He sounded completely unsure of himself.

"You sleep on one side, I will take the other. We are married, after all. And you are still wearing trousers, I noticed."

In the darkness, he cleared his throat. Shifted from foot to foot. "It didn't seem advisable to be half naked in the chair. And...well. We might be married, but we certainly haven't agreed to—" His words became strangled.

"Myles." She closed her eyes tightly, searching for words in the corners of her mind. "It is very late. You are cold. We *are* married. And...and I trust you." Stunned silence answered her words. "You have always been protective and respectful of my wishes. A gentleman. And we both need our sleep, so you can enjoy your family tomorrow. Please. We will pretend that it doesn't matter. And sleep in the same bed."

Except it did matter. She had never shared a bed with another person in her life. Not even her own sister. And to sleep next to a man? Wearing nothing but her nightgown? Positively indecent. She'd never been so vulnerable.

As she shifted over to the cooler, previously empty side of the bed, and he settled into the warm spot she had left to come to his aid, Pippa knew sharing the bed mattered a great deal.

She closed her mind to pondering on the *why*, and instead she

rolled to keep her back to her husband. She closed her eyes and curled herself into a ball. As far from him as she could.

"Good night, Philippa."

She smiled to herself. "You know you can call me Pippa, Myles."

A beat of silence, and then, "You do not mind?"

She smiled to herself in the darkness and tried unsuccessfully to ignore the way her heart skipped. "Not at all."

"Then good night, Pippa." When he spoke her name, the one reserved for those she loved, it wrapped around her like a gentle embrace.

"Good night, Myles."

Despite their situation, and how unfamiliar sharing her blankets ought to feel, Pippa didn't remain awake long. She slipped into a lovely, deep sleep. Her dream self went back to the garden. And this time, she found precisely who she searched for.

Sixteen

As an early riser, Myles had the good fortune to wake before his lady wife. When he woke, his awareness of his surroundings came slowly. The early hour meant the room was still in shades of blue and gray. Philippa's soft, slow breathing pulled his gaze to her, but as he turned his head to admire her peaceful slumber, he realized she had moved closer to him in the night.

Philippa pressed one bare foot against his calf. He felt the contact, from the tip of her toes to the soft curve of her heel. She slept with her back to him, leaving him a glimpse of her profile to admire.

Of course, recollecting how he had wound up in bed next to his wife made him wince. She'd woken him from a nightmare. Then insisted he not sleep another moment in the uncomfortable chair and the cold room.

He had given in to her demands. But at what cost?

Gathering himself to sneak out from beneath the bedcovers, Myles took in a deep breath. And inhaled the soft scent of his wife. She smelled of cotton warmed in the sun and honeysuckle blooming on the vine. Everything about her was soft and beautiful.

So much the opposite of what he was. Half blind. Scarred. Hardened, and brittle enough to break.

That realization gave him the strength to leave the room. Without disturbing Philippa.

True, his cravat was crooked. And he wore clothing more suitable to rambling about the countryside than sitting in his mother's garden, where he soon found himself, but at least he had clothed himself decently enough to make his escape.

Why did he always feel the need to run away from his wife?

Myles marched down a dirt path, through a low gate covered in ivy, and into a stand of trees. There weren't many trees, of course. They acted more as a break in the view from the house than as any sort of wood. But they were sturdy. They provided ample shade, and two branches bore swings in their branches.

The quiet didn't last long.

A tromping of feet from the direction of the house surprised Myles. He hadn't thought anyone else would be awake, much less capable of following him. He peered through the trees to the dirt path and spotted Winston.

And a few of Winston's children trotting along beside him.

"There he is," shouted the eldest, Winston's eleven-year-old daughter. "We found Uncle Myles."

"I thought it would be harder," the nine-year-old son declared. "Uncle Myles, were you even trying to hide?"

"Papa said he was," the six-year-old boy said smartly.

Winston had always been far too perceptive. That trait that made it impossible to keep secrets from him likely aided him as a clergyman.

They were close enough now that Myles could see the grin on his brother's face. "Mind your manners, or it's back to the nursery with all of you."

"I want to swing first!" shouted his daughter. The three children raced to the two swings, their interest in Myles given up in favor of something more diverting. Winston shook his head at them, then settled next to Myles on the old iron bench.

Myles eyed his brother with amusement. "Though I suppose a vicar might keep early hours, I didn't think you'd pass up an opportunity to stay in bed at Ambleside."

"I could say the same thing about soldiers and their early hours," Winston muttered, tilting his head back and crossing his legs at the ankle. He closed his eyes. "Especially newlywed soldiers."

Myles faced away from his brother. "I left Philippa sleeping."

"Did you?"

"Yes."

"Hm." Winston cracked one eye open to look at Myles. "What did she make of the family last night? I was curious, given how early she retired for the evening. I hope we didn't make her uncomfortable. Mary does have the tendency to say whatever is on her mind—"

"She was only tired. She was asleep before I even entered the room." Myles had to smile at that. His wife had *pretended* to be asleep when he came in the night before. "I think she enjoyed meeting everyone. Philippa's family isn't like ours, though. They are... distant to one another. I think she only gets along with one of her brothers."

"The one opening up that hospital?" Winston asked, and when Myles raised his eyebrows, his older brother grinned. "Mother read your letter out loud to everyone when it came."

"Of course she did. Yes. The brother opening the hospital." Myles led the conversation in that direction for a time. It was easier to speak about the Gillensford hospital than his wife, or his marriage. And Winston showed genuine interest in the endeavor. He'd been an essential part of Myles's early recovery from war. And he'd counseled many returned soldiers as a vicar.

Before too long, Myles felt comfortable again. At his childhood home, listening to one of his nieces and two nephews playing, and speaking with his brother, he could forget about himself. It was easier to enjoy the present moment.

"Here they are," a new voice sang through the trees. "I knew we'd find them out of doors." Mary and Winston's wife, Laurel, had arrived. A small gaggle of children came with them. And behind the mothers and children, walking arm in arm, was Myles's father and Philippa.

Myles rose to his feet the moment he laid eyes upon her. She looked beautiful, wearing a simple ivory gown with her dark hair piled loosely

atop her head. Ringlets of curls framed her lovely face, and her rose-colored lips pulled back in a joyful smile.

Winston slowly came to his feet, too. He must've read the admiration Myles held for his wife quite clearly, given the amused warning that followed. "Steady there, Myles. Remember. There are children present." He chuckled, then stepped forward to intercept Laurel. "We haven't been missing long, surely."

"Long enough that the breakfast table is laid and waiting." Laurel stepped into her husband's embrace, and their two youngest children immediately ran to petition for their own turns on the swings.

Myles's father was speaking quietly to Philippa, teasing a laugh from her. And Myles wished very much he could perform such a trick. Maybe he could try.

Philippa's gaze landed upon him, and somehow her expression brightened still more.

His father spoke first. "Myles, your wife is a delight. Thank you for bringing her to us." He patted her hand where it rested on his arm. "I've just found out that the two of you have never danced together. I told Pippa we would be certain to remedy that while you visit."

"Did you?" Myles raised his eyebrows at his wife. "Though we have never been partners, we have stood up for the same dance. And we even joined hands a time or two."

"That isn't the same thing," his father insisted. "Perhaps we can hold an informal party for the two of you. A congratulatory evening, of sorts, with entertainment and dancing. What say you, Pippa? Are you game?"

"It is a very kind suggestion, Father Cobbett." Her smile softened as she turned it to Myles. "But I think the two of us are hoping for more quiet after the gaiety of London Society. The last ball we attended left both of us exhausted."

"Yes, but our Ambleside parties are not so large affairs as those in London. Only our nearest neighbors need come." His father appeared thoughtful a moment. "Perhaps five and twenty couples. Enough to make our rooms feel crowded while still leaving room to dance."

"Good heavens." Philippa laughed and shook her head, setting her

curls to bouncing. "That is far too many people for me to meet all at once. Especially in one evening. You know, I think I would much prefer something out of doors. London is terribly crowded, and I have missed the country air."

Like a bolt from heaven, the realization struck Myles that his wife was attempting to steer his father into an avenue of entertainment that would be less likely to make *Myles* uncomfortable. A lack of crowds. Fresh air. Less stiff formality.

His heart crossed the last threshold from admiration into love. In that very moment. Without Myles thinking on it. With him unable to do more than stare at her in awe and adoration.

Somehow, in a slow and quiet way, he had fallen in love with his wife.

His father had already responded to her, and they were both now looking at Myles. Waiting for him to say something. His father with eyebrows raised and a crooked smile. Philippa with a curious narrowing of her eyes.

Despite his sudden realization, he had to act as unaffected as possible. "I beg your pardon. What did you ask me?"

Philippa released his father's arm to come to Myles's side, her eyes searching his. "Your father asked if we might like a celebratory picnic held in our honor, this Sunday after church." Then her fingertips touched his wrist. His palm. And he threaded his fingers with hers. "Though I am concerned about the number of people I must then be expected to identify as friends." She had given him a way to escape yet again.

Myles squeezed her hand gently. "I think a picnic would be perfect. I will be there with you." He could handle a picnic. Especially with Pippa by his side. His lovely, kind-hearted wife, who had left London to see to his comfort rather than her own. Then pretended to have a difficult time with crowds when the reality was that she thrived in the midst of them.

Guilt stung his heart. She had left London for his sake. He knew it now. The gossips were an excuse. For some reason, Pippa had decided

to look after him. When he felt it ought always to be the other way around.

The baron clapped his hands together, startling Myles out of his admiration of his wife. "That's settled then. Let's all go to breakfast and plan things out properly with your mother." He winked at Pippa. "She has hoped for a reason to show you off to the neighborhood, my dear."

Pippa laughed, and another piece of Myles's heart belonged to her.

Without warning, their marriage of convenience had turned into something much more precious to him.

~

After breakfast, Pippa and Myles were practically pushed out the door by his parents. "Show your wife all the best places for a picnic," her new mother-in-law insisted. "Pippa must choose where we hold our afternoon gathering."

Pippa barely had time to slip on a bonnet and gloves, and Myles only popped on an old tricorn hat that had seen better days before leading her out into the countryside behind their house. A few of his nephews had tried to accompany them, but somehow Uncle Winston had bribed them away with the promise of a fishing expedition, leaving Pippa and Myles alone on their ramble through the trees and then a meadow.

"I hope you do not mind my family's eagerness too much," Myles said, his hands tucked behind his back. She walked alongside him, plucking up a wildflower here and there as they went. "They want you to like it here, so you will come back, towing me with you."

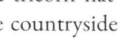

"They certainly needn't expend too much effort on my account," Pippa said, lifting a daisy to her nose. "I am charmed by all of them, Myles. By all of this." She gestured with the flower to their peaceful surroundings. Butterflies fluttered alongside them, going from flower to flower. The sound of the grass rustling in the breeze and the hum of bees were far better sounds than clattering wheels on cobblestone streets. "I spent

much of my childhood wandering about the estate where Adam and Elaine live when they are not in London. I spent all of last summer riding Bunny about, free as the wind." She smiled wistfully at the thought of her mare. A horse she feared she would lose to her brother's spite. Best not to dwell on something that hadn't occurred yet. "I quite enjoy the country."

Myles cocked his head to the side, his dark brown eye singly focused on her, his brow creased in puzzlement.

She tapped his sleeve with her flower. "You thought I preferred London to everything else, didn't you?"

He shrugged and turned his face away, allowing her to admire his profile. "I know your life in London is important to you. The freedom you wanted to enjoy is all there—not in a place like this." He waved at the meadow and trees.

Pippa raised her eyes to the clouds above her, picking out snatches of blue between the gray and white of an English summer sky. "That is the point of freedom, isn't it? That you can come and go as you please, whether it is to and from the theater or a fishpond."

"The company is likely better at the fishpond," Myles muttered, and Pippa allowed herself to giggle. An amused smile turned his lips upward. "My apologies. Comparing people to fish isn't kind."

"Yes. The fish might take offense."

Myles's laugh seemed to surprise him as much as it did her, and the richness of his voice made her shiver with pleasure. He didn't laugh enough. Though she certainly saw more of his smile of late than she had in London. How had he ever agreed to marry her, knowing she would drag him from one despised event to another?

He'd wanted to rescue her, of course. And provide for his younger sisters. Sisters who had, that very morning, plotted carefully which bachelors in the neighborhood they wished to invite to the picnic. Did they know yet that Myles intended to enlarge their dowries?

Pippa cradled her wildflowers closer. Had there ever been that same giddiness of feeling when she had considered suitors? She couldn't remember such excitement when she thought of one man over another. And she had quickly decided not to bother with courtship

and marriage at all. Not after she saw how miserable her siblings were in their matches. All except Adam and Elaine.

She peered up at Myles from beneath the brim of her bonnet. "Did you enjoy growing up at Ambleside?"

He slowed to a stop, then swept the surrounding countryside with his gaze. "I think my childhood as close to perfect as it could come." He led them up a small hill. "The years I spent running across hills and climbing trees with my brothers and sisters didn't prepare me for the life of a soldier—but my father's lessons of honor and duty made the more difficult days bearable. My mother's example of compassion kept me from focusing inward, where I likely would have spiraled into the same darkness and despair I sometimes see in the eyes of other men who spent their youth making war."

Was that the secret to his character? Good parents. A gentle childhood. Having seen where he grew up, she could appreciate all that was beautiful about it. Yet the Cobbett family, despite his father's title, wasn't wealthy. Not when compared to her own family's coffers. What was it that made their family so happy?

When Pippa didn't respond, Myles stopped walking and looked down at her. "My apologies, Pippa. We are supposed to find a place for a picnic. It should be a diverting task, and I've grown morose."

"I am not at all offended by your conversation, Myles. If anything, I am intrigued. Your character puzzles me at times."

His eyebrows rose. "In what way? I cannot think myself too mysterious. Though the eyepatch, I am told, lends me a certain air of peculiarity."

She giggled, like a flirtatious maiden rather than a sophisticated woman of Society. Then she cleared her throat. "Your eyepatch, sir, is absolutely charming. I would say it hints at a roguish quality. But anyone expecting to meet with a scoundrel will be terribly disappointed. You are an excellent product of your parents—honorable and good."

He stared at her in silence, his lips curving upward softly. "You are too kind in your assessment."

Before she could return compliment for compliment, he bent and

plucked a bright purple flower—a wild sweet pea bloom. But rather than add to the collection in her hand, he tucked the stem carefully behind her ear. His fingers brushed her skin. Realizing how close he stood, Pippa momentarily forgot how to breathe.

His lips no more than a hand's breadth from hers, Myles murmured, "When you put roses in your hair, I always wonder why a woman would wear any other ornament. You need none at all, given your beauty, but the flowers...." His voice trailed away, and he dropped his hand limply to his side. Then he cleared his throat. "Forgive me. This time, I've wandered into a topic I know nothing about." He stepped back before he gave her a little bow and stalked away, leaving Pippa to watch after him in confusion. Her heart dropped as she let out a disappointed sigh.

Though she wasn't entirely certain why she ought to be discontent, she felt it keenly.

She followed after her husband, cresting the hill, to find he had stopped on the other side. He watched two riders approach them. A man and a woman.

"Do you know them?" Pippa asked, looking from her husband to the couple.

"Not that I'm aware. But I think we are about to make introductions."

Pippa looked up again as the gentleman called from atop his horse. "Good day to you both. Might you be familiar with this neighborhood?"

Myles stood strong and handsome at her side, posture perfect and confident. "Indeed. My father is Lord Greenwood. I am Myles Cobbett. This is my wife, Lady Philippa Cobbett." He sounded proud to present her as his own, and Pippa glanced at him from the corner of her eye while her cheeks grew warm for no reason at all.

The man dismounted and bowed. "A pleasure to meet you both, Mr. Cobbett. Lady Philippa." He went around to the woman and helped her down, one hand lifted up to take hers as she slid down from her horse. "Allow me to introduce myself and my wife. I am Sir Isaac

Fox, and this is Lady Fox. We are from Aldersy, the west coast of Suffolk."

It was as he released his lady's hand, allowing her to perform a curtsy, that Pippa realized he had pinned up the left sleeve of his coat, as he had no arm to fill it. Her mouth popped open in some surprise, but she hastily covered her rudeness. "I hope we have not interrupted your ride, Lady Fox."

"Not at all," the woman said, her smile subdued. "We are glad to have found you both, actually, as I think we are rather lost. We meant to ride out to Huntington Park, but I have the feeling we are wandering in circles. Progressively larger circles, to be sure."

"My fault," the baronet said with a chagrined smile. "We could've stayed right where we were, but I learned that friends of ours are staying at Huntington Park, and we wished to surprise them with a visit."

"You are not too far off." Myles wore a gracious smile, an expression Pippa had not seen often. It wasn't his polite smile for a London gathering. This was more genuine. More comfortable. "Huntington is a mile east of here. If you go that way"—he pointed north— "you'll find a track through those trees. Follow it east, and you'll come through Huntington Park's plum orchard."

"Ah." Sir Isaac looked northward. "Thank you for the guidance. I think we will walk that direction, to avoid losing our hats to the trees."

"Are you in need of any other assistance?" Pippa asked, looking directly at Lady Fox. The woman wore a dark blue riding habit and a black beaver hat, with a bluebell tucked in the ribbon around its brim. Curls of her hair, a shocking shade of red that reminded Pippa of Elaine's copper tresses, peeked out from beneath the hat's brim.

"Not presently." She fiddled with the horse's leads in her hand, looking to her husband a moment before asking a question of her own. "Tell me, do the two of you live nearby?"

"No," Myles and Pippa answered together, then he smiled down at her. "We are newlywed, visiting my family."

"Ah, congratulations to you both." Sir Isaac tucked his horse's lead between what remained of his left arm and his side, then offered his

right arm to his wife. She took it, her horse's lead in her other hand. "We were married not so long ago ourselves."

Given that his wife looked to him with undisguised adoration, Pippa easily guessed that theirs was a love match. How wonderful. For them. And Elaine and Adam. She darted another covert glance at her husband, and for the first time, she wondered. Wondered if he had hoped for such a thing before the war stole his eye and left him scarred, without occupation.

"We are on our way to visit my brother-in-law and sister. They are guests of Mr. Lockheed. Lord and Lady Inglewood. Have you met them?"

"No, but we only arrived yesterday," Myles said. "That name is familiar. I think Lord Inglewood must've visited this neighborhood before. He is a member of the House of Lords, is he not? A more progressive member, if I am not mistaken."

Sir Isaac chuckled. "Indeed, you are not. He's likely in this part of the country to find like-minded men from the House of Commons." He shrugged and addressed his next comment to Pippa. "The man detests London, so he always escapes at the first chance to do his politicking in the free air of the country."

"How long will you be visiting the neighborhood?" Pippa asked, a sudden idea coming to her.

Lady Fox answered cheerily, "Another week. We are staying with Doctor and Mrs. Johnson, of the Clock House."

Pippa blinked. "The Clock House?"

Her husband grinned down at her when she gave him a questioning look. "We will be certain to visit so you can see why it bears that name." Then he shared a more friendly smile with Sir Isaac, tinged with curiosity. "Doctor Johnson and I are good friends. I suggested the Clock House to him when he married. I'm pleased he took up the lease."

"It is a charming location." Lady Fox tilted her head to the side. "Do tell me, how do you know Mr. Johnson? He is from Suffolk, near our home. I always wondered what brought him so far from there."

"We served in the army together. He was the doctor attached to my

regiment for a time," Myles answered, and gestured to the eye patch he wore. "He saved my life."

Sir Isaac and his wife exchanged a look of wonder. Then the baronet appeared quite excited. "Doctor Johnson was *my* doctor. Acting the part of surgeon, of course. He took my arm off to save *my* life." He gestured to the empty left sleeve of his coat. "In Toulouse, *after* the first surrender of the French Empire."

While the significance of that statement meant nothing to Pippa, she saw that Myles appeared impressed. And sounded it, too, when he said, "Wellington's last battle at Toulouse. I was at Quatre Bras. Attacked just before dawn by cannon fire."

"Ah. I suppose a cannonball didn't take your eye?" Sir Isaac stood relaxed, his expression almost jocular.

Myles's tone matched, as though the aspect of losing limbs and vital organs was an everyday occurrence. She'd never seen him appear at ease when discussing his injuries. "A tree took the cannonball, the tree's shrapnel took the eye."

Alarmed, Pippa looked to Lady Fox, who only smiled and shrugged.

"I have no wish to keep you from visiting your friends," Myles said, his expression amiable. "Though I would be interested in speaking with you, and Dr. Johnson, more. We are having a picnic in two days' time. May we include you—and your friends, Lord and Lady Inglewood—in the invitation?"

"If my lady has no objections." Sir Isaac looked to his wife for confirmation.

"I do enjoy picnics." Her smile curved upward, and something of significance passed between the two of them, something Pippa thought looked suspiciously like a joke.

"Then it is settled." Sir Isaac's horse nudged him at the same moment he spoke, leading the man to cast a glare over his shoulder at the beast. "And we will be on our way. I look forward to that picnic."

"Thank you for inviting us." Lady Fox curtsied, and after they took their leave, both couples parted as though they had met on a street in London rather than in the middle of a meadow.

Pippa looked over her shoulder one last time, seeing the couple vanish beneath the trees. “They seemed a fine couple.”

“Indeed.” Myles sounded in good humor. “I hope they found us the same.” Then he took her hand and tucked it into the crook of his arm. Pippa met his gaze, finding a warmth there that made her heart jump. She looked away. Then saw the perfect place for a picnic.

“There.” Pippa nodded, unable to point with one hand secured by her husband and the other holding a bouquet of flowers. “Those trees, and the little pond. We should have our picnic there.”

Myles grinned and gave a short nod of agreement. “As you wish, my lady.”

His smile, the beauty of the afternoon, and the heady scent of the meadow and wildflowers, all made her head spin. Something between them had altered, and it had happened as slowly as spring turning to summer. She felt it. Though she could not name it.

On their return walk to Ambleside, Pippa purposefully kept the conversation focused on the weather, the picnic, and what she had heard—in passing—about Lord and Lady Inglewood. Myles let her ramble. In fact, he even seemed to enjoy her sudden enthusiasm.

It wasn’t until much later that evening, when Pippa feigned sleep as Myles slipped into his side of their shared bed, that she wished she had been braver. Brave enough to ask if he had sensed the change between them. And if he knew what it might mean.

Seventeen

The day of the picnic started with overcast skies and a drizzle of rain, and Myles found himself in the unenviable position of reassuring all the ladies of the house. Including his wife. He had just left his mother in the sitting room, where she vented her worries upon the pianoforte in the next room, and entered the study where his wife attempted to wear a track into the carpet.

"It must stop soon," Pippa said, marching away from the window to where Myles sat in a chair. "Your poor mother. She worked so hard to invite everyone. I hate to think of her being disappointed."

Myles gave his wife a measured look, narrowing his eye at her. "She is only worried of displeasing you, Pippa."

"I told her she needn't worry." Pippa chewed on her bottom lip, looking through the doorway Myles had come through. "Should I tell her again?"

The music in the other room had grown into a crescendo as his mother tried to drown out the sound of the rain.

"It won't do any good." Myles rubbed at his temple. "The rain will clear. You can tell by how bright it remains outside."

"Will people still come?" She wrung her hands and went back to

the window, staring up at the sky. "Or will they worry over the damp grass?"

"Country folk are made of a sturdier mettle than that, Pippa." Myles came out of his chair to stand beside her, close enough that the sweet scent of her honeysuckle perfume teased him.

Sleeping next to her the last three nights, pretending he didn't lay awake wishing he knew how to tell her what he felt, had left him tired and mellow. He wanted very much to take her into his arms to soothe away her worries. But they had barely touched more than hands since their arrival at Ambleside. Unless Myles counted the way his wife tucked her feet up against him every night.

He smiled to himself at that thought, and Pippa turned in time to catch the expression upon his face. "Why are you smiling?" she asked, aghast. "Your mother is playing out her frustration in the next room, and you are *smiling?* Horrid man."

That only made his smile wider. "Pippa, my darling, the rain will stop. I have no doubt of it."

She continued glaring at him, the expression more endearing than threatening. It took a great deal of self-control to keep from leaning forward to press a kiss to her forehead. Instead, he contented himself with tucking a loose curl behind her ear.

Pippa's eyes widened, and she tipped her chin up the better to search his gaze. "You seem...pensive."

Myles shrugged. "I am at ease, that is all." All he would permit himself to say.

"More at ease than I've ever seen you." She raised her hand, hesitated, then brushed lightly at his shoulder with her fingertips.

That certainly isn't what she meant to do. Had she been about to touch his cheek?

She sighed and lowered her gaze to his cravat, which made her frown. "You need a valet, Myles." Now both her hands came toward him, and suddenly his wife was smoothing and tucking at his neck-cloth. Her fingertips brushing the skin beneath his chin, the weight of one palm pressing against his chest.

Myles gulped and took hold of both her wrists, stilling her hands. "You

needn't trouble yourself," he rasped, then cleared his throat. He released her gently. She didn't lower her hands back to her sides, though. Instead, she rested both of them on the lapels of his coat. She frowned up at him.

"Are you catching a cold?" Then she *did* touch him, purposefully, placing her bare palm against his forehead. Then one of his cheeks. The one with the scarring. She didn't even seem to notice the oddity of that touch. Instead, she scrutinized him as carefully as any doctor would a prospective patient.

He leaned toward her. "I've caught something," he murmured. Her eyebrows raised in alarm, and her hand still rested on his cheek. Her lips parted, and Myles's gaze dropped there. She swayed toward him as her eyes drifted closed. As though she knew—and welcomed the fact—that he wanted to kiss her.

An alarming trumpeting sound made them both leap away from each other. Winston came clattering into the room, a child upon his back and another hanging on to his arm. "And so the mighty elephant parades through the jungles of India," he said in a booming voice.

Myles wasn't sure if he wanted to thank or strangle his brother. He'd been close to kissing his wife—to making a fool of himself and laying his feelings before her while he was half-asleep. The results of such a thing would be disastrous this early in their relationship. Even if they had spent the last several days in one another's company.

"Papa, look! It's stopped raining," the child on Winston's neck shouted, pointing at the window behind Pippa and Myles.

Pippa spun around to look out the window, too. "It has stopped," she said, bouncing on her toes. "Oh, this is wonderful. I must tell your mother." The playing of the pianoforte in the room across the hall hadn't stopped, though Myles had somehow tuned out his mother's private concert.

"I told you," Myles said softly, admiring his wife's figure as she stood before the window. When she turned, eyes aglow with happiness, he sighed like a lovesick fool. "Better hurry and let her know, before she begins playing Beethoven. Austrian composers are a sure sign of melancholy in this household."

With a quick smile cast up at him, Pippa nodded and hurried from the room, darting around Winston and the children now calling for him to be a bear rather than an elephant.

"Bears hibernate," Winston explained, falling onto a couch. "And then they eat anyone foolish enough to wake them before winter's end." He growled impressively, making the children squeal and run from the room, proclaiming that a bear was going to eat them. Winston chuckled and looked up at Myles. The amusement turned to surprise. "You looked perturbed, brother. Is something wrong?"

Myles shook his head and turned away, crossing his arms as he stared out the window. Nothing was wrong. He'd nearly kissed his wife. She'd seemed perfectly happy with the idea, too. Until an Indian elephant interrupted them. Perhaps that was for the best. Because kissing, though he imagined it to be a rather heavenly pursuit, wouldn't be nearly enough with Pippa.

Winston clapped a hand on Myles's shoulder, surprising him enough that he ducked and turned, pulling Winston's wrist behind his back and holding it there. "How did you move from the couch without making a sound?" Myles asked, holding Winston still.

"I made plenty of noise." Winston grunted. "You are simply too besotted by your own wife to pay heed to anything else."

That was likely true. Too besotted and lacking in sleep. Myles released his brother. "A clergyman ought not sneak up on people."

"And a former soldier ought to be brave enough to tell a woman he loves her." Winston narrowed his eyes at Myles, daring his younger brother to deny the supposition. "She hasn't any idea how you feel, does she? As pleasant as you two are to each other in front of the rest of the family, there is enough delicacy in how you two act when you think no one is looking for me to guess—"

"Winston." Myles had to cut him off. He looked to the still-open doorway. "This isn't any of your affair." He rubbed at his temple. "Please. Leave it alone."

Winston folded his arms and affected a superior expression. "I am right, aren't I? Heavens, man. If your wife doesn't know that you love

her, how did you ever convince someone of her status and wealth to marry you in the first place?"

It wasn't his brother's business. No one needed to know the circumstances that tied Myles and Pippa together in matrimony. The few who knew were back in London. "It doesn't matter," Myles muttered, turning away.

"I think it must." Winston didn't need to put a hand on him to stop Myles from leaving the room. Not when he said, "Because *you* matter, Myles. To all of us."

Myles glared through the open doorway, then closed the door. With his back still to his brother, Myles said quietly, "I am well enough, Winnie. You needn't concern yourself with me."

"You aren't getting out of this by using that old nickname. I'm a vicar now. Such things don't bother me. What about the nightmares? Do you still have them?" Winston's voice grew nearer. "Or the episodes —the waking memories of war?"

A shudder passed through Myles. "Sometimes," he murmured. "But that has nothing to do with Pippa—Lady Philippa."

"It does. Because I have seen you broken before, Myles." Winston stood directly behind Myles. "If you love your wife, and she doesn't feel the same, I am fearful of what that will do to you. I have already seen you lose more of yourself to war and loss than anyone can bear." Winston fell blessedly silent, but it was only for a moment before he asked, "Why did you bring her here, Myles?"

With reluctance, Myles turned around. He leaned against the closed door and rubbed at his good eye. "We are here to meet the family. And to get away from London for a time. The situation there isn't ideal for one of my... *delicate* constitution." He wrinkled his nose and lifted his gaze to his brother.

Winston snorted. "You're no more delicate than a donkey." But the concern in his eyes was genuine. "What aren't you telling us about this marriage, Myles? And why can't your wife know how you feel?"

"Leave it alone, Winnie." Myles moved away from the door, back toward the window. The sun broke through the clouds for one glittering moment. "Know that my marriage to Lady Philippa is of signifi-

cant benefit to our family. I intend to add to our sisters' dowries. Our parents needn't worry about them securing suitable matches."

"The dowries? This isn't a mercenary match for you, is it?" The disapproval in Winston's voice smote Myles's conscience harder than his concern did.

"No." And that was all the answer Winston would get.

Winston stayed silent for so long that Myles wondered if his brother had left the room without him knowing. He turned around, only to find Winston still there. Staring at him.

"Loving your wife is a good thing, Myles. So long as she feels the same." Winston's shoulders drooped with his concern. "But you had better find out soon. Before you've given away so much of your heart that you cannot live without it."

Myles could not think of a response to that. Part of the reason he hadn't tried to tell Pippa, hadn't even planned on it, was their contract. He'd agreed to give her complete freedom. The other part, though, had more to do with Winston's concern. If she didn't feel the same, Myles didn't know how he could survive the heartbreak that would bring.

A knock on the door broke the silent tension in the room. Laurel called from the other side. "Winston? Are you in there? I need your help preparing the children for the picnic."

"Coming, my heart." Winston cast his brother one last worried glance. Then he opened the door and disappeared, leaving Myles's thoughts more convoluted than before. And his feelings for Pippa remained as complicated as ever. He loved her. He wanted to protect her. Honor her. Be the reason she smiled, and laughed, and greeted each day with a vivacity that astounded him.

He wanted to be her reason to wake each day with delight and retire each night with contentment. How was he to accomplish any of that when he could not even convince himself to tell her the truth of his feelings? He hadn't worried about it that morning when he'd woken next to her. And while they watched the rain, a quarter of an hour ago, he'd nearly kissed his wife without sparing the consequences more than a thought. Perhaps that would've ended in disaster, and he should thank Winston for interrupting.

Myles left the room, muttering to himself, "I need more sleep. That's all."

~

Though Lady Fredericka hadn't been an ideal mother, she had certainly prepared Pippa for one important aspect of being a grown lady—mingling. As the guest of honor at the picnic, Pippa knew her duties well. She stayed near her new mother-in-law so Lady Greenwood might introduce her with motherly pride. When Sir Isaac and Lady Fox arrived, introducing the Earl and Countess of Inglewood, Lady Greenwood was overcome with delight.

After the appropriate introductions and remarks were exchanged, and the foursome walked to one of the trees where a rug and cushions and been left for the comfort of guests, Lady Greenwood leaned in close to Philippa.

"I have never entertained anyone above a baron, my dear. You simply must help to ensure our guests' enjoyment."

Pippa found her husband near the pond, teaching a swarm of children how to skip rocks. As she approached, he lowered himself to be eye level with a little girl, no more than five or six years of age, and held a stone up for her to examine.

"You see how smooth and flat this one is? Rather like a dinner plate. But smaller. A dinner plate for a doll."

The child giggled and nodded her understanding.

"Here. Put it in your hand. Yes. Now turn just so." He put his hands on the little one's shoulders and turned her so she stood at an angle to the pond's edge. "Thumb on one side, as I showed you. Arm back." The little girl stretched her arm backward, then threw her rock. It skipped three times before sinking.

"I did it! I did it! Did you see, Henry?" She tugged at a boy's arm—a much taller boy, who grinned down at the girl, then up at Pippa's husband.

"Thank you for helping, Mr. Cobbett."

"I want to try," another child said.

"Everyone go find the perfect stone, then you can try." The children scattered, some in pairs, but most on their own, searching the ground for rocks. Myles looked up at that moment, his gaze meeting Pippa's. His smile widened into a grin, and he came slowly to his feet. "My lady. We were having a stone-skipping lesson."

"So I see." Pippa looked down at her feet and picked up the first stone she saw—round and flat, like a doll's dinner plate. She approached with the rock in hand, turning it over in her gloved palm. "Would you be so kind as to give me a lesson?"

"You?" Myles's grin momentarily faltered, then he spoke with lightness. "And here I imagined you to be proficient in all the skills that mattered."

Pippa shrugged, affecting a frown. "Alas, I cannot claim to be an expert with this. Won't you show me how you perform the task, Mr. Cobbett?" She batted her eyelashes at him, and her heart skipped merrily as she neared him. Flirting with her husband seemed a brilliant idea. She liked seeing him happy. And the flustered, crooked grin he wore was reward enough for her silliness.

"Might I inspect your rock, my lady?" He held his hand out, and she placed her stone carefully in his palm. He nodded to her gloves. "It will be easier if you remove them. And less dirty."

She looked down at the yellow fabric, then brushed away as much dirt as she could with the other hand. Then she removed her gloves. "My rock, sir? Is it the right sort of specimen?"

"A perfect stone for skipping, my lady." He bowed as he deposited the rock in her hand again. "Now. You must stand at an angle to the water."

"Like this?" Pippa stood at a right angle.

"No, not quite." He came up behind her, and then laid his hands gently upon her shoulders. "Turn just so." He carefully guided her to rotate until she stood correctly. Then his fingers encircled her wrist as he turned her hand the right way. "Here, bend your elbow. Yes. Like that." Very slowly, he pulled back her arm. "Now, when you throw, think of making the stone hit the water at an angle. When you release,

snap your wrist as you would open a fan—in one, quick movement—and let go."

He stood so close, the buttons of his coat brushed the back of her gown. He guided her through the motion once, slowly. When he spoke, his voice was a soft murmur in her ear. "Like this, but with speed and force behind it."

"You make it sound simple," she said, her voice more breathless than she expected.

He released her, taking a step back. "Go on, Pippa."

She swallowed, then repositioned herself to skip her stone. Then, trying to return to the earlier mischief she'd felt, she looked over her shoulder. "Like this?" She threw the stone, angled perfectly, and counted the skips as they went. Four. Five. Six. Seven. Eight.

"Nine, ten..." Myles's voice faded as her stone disappeared beneath the water. When she turned to look at him, widening her eyes innocently, he narrowed his good eye at her. "Pippa. I didn't think you a fibber."

She laughed, finally. "I never said I didn't know how to do it—I merely asked you to show me how *you* skipped stones."

He looked back to where her stone had sunk beneath the water. Then at her. Then he released a short, deep laugh. He held his hand out, and she laid her bare hand in his. Myles drew her closer. "You *did* say you grew up playing out of doors. Who taught you?"

"My great uncle, Peter Gillensford. The one who left his fortune to Elaine." Along the shore, children had started trying their luck with their stones. None had returned for another lesson. But they all laughed and giggled. Myles had done that. "Do you think I might borrow you from your pupils?"

"As they have all devoted themselves to practice, I doubt anyone will mind." Myles allowed her to lead him away from the pond, toward Sir Isaac's party. "Look who came."

"Ah, and Doctor Johnson has joined them." He nodded to a tall, thin gentlemen with a lovely woman on his arm. "I would especially like to introduce the two of you, if you have no objections."

"None at all. I very much want to thank him for saving my

husband's life." Pippa squeezed Myles's hand and glanced up to see him looking at her with a softness she had begun seeing since their arrival in the country.

The afternoon passed in a blur of sunshine and laughter. The men ambled away from the women after the food and lemonade had been mostly consumed. Myles had taken Lord Inglewood and Sir Isaac to try their hand at the lawn games his family had provided. Pippa sat content in the shade between Lady Inglewood and Lady Fox. The three of them had spoken enough to have found connections between them, though tenuous. But it was enough for them to converse together comfortably.

"I have heard of the hospital your brother wants to build," Lady Fox said during a lull in their conversation. She glanced from Lady Inglewood to Pippa. "Sir Isaac wanted to attend the ball in London last month, but we had already withdrawn to the country."

"Oh, the Gillensford hospital for soldiers?" Lady Inglewood sat straighter. "I had nearly forgotten—Isaac mentioned it in passing to me when they first returned home." Lady Inglewood was the younger sister of the baronet, a connection that had been made immediately apparent to Pippa given their kindly-meant teasing of one another.

"We have great hopes for the hospital." Pippa turned her gaze across the pond, to the other side, where the men were heard laughing. She had met her husband at that ball. Something she didn't intend to announce, though she grew increasingly grateful he had come that night. "Myles is devoted to the project. He has seen so much sorrow since the war. I know he hopes the hospital will provide a safe, comfortable place for soldiers to recover from their wounds. Those that are readily apparent, and otherwise."

Lady Fox and Lady Inglewood exchanged a significant glance. "I know precisely what you mean," Lady Fox murmured. She held a fan and wafted herself languidly as she spoke. "Given the way your husband feels, and the significant wounds he acquired, I am perhaps right when I suppose that he has nightmares?"

Pippa stiffened, a defense of Myles rising to her tongue, but then

she saw the sympathy and knowledge in the other woman's eyes. And in Lady Inglewood's. "Does Sir Isaac...?"

"Things are getting better," Lady Fox murmured, looking into the distance. "At least, I sometimes think they are. I should not be surprised if his dreams stay part of our lives forever. No one can live through such darkness without carrying the memory of it with them."

Lady Inglewood laid her hand on her sister-in-law's, then smiled at Pippa. "I do not think my brother would have come away from his home for this visit without Lady Fox's support. The love of a wife makes all the difference in a man's healing. But then, new as you are to your marriage, you have likely already discovered that truth."

Startled, Pippa lowered her gaze to the rug on which they sat. "Yes, of course. I do all I can to support my husband." But had she? Was escaping from London enough?

"The most difficult thing for me, in those early months of marriage, was convincing my husband that I loved him just as he was." Lady Fox spoke with conviction and a determined tilt of her chin. "Our Society lays such importance on appearance, and on our gentlemen publicly eschewing all emotion. Isaac thought himself broken and therefore unworthy of my love. He didn't think he could tell me things without causing me pain, or worse, making me pity him."

Could Myles think such things about himself? He had said things...had apologized for things that she had dismissed in the past. Though she had compassion for her husband, was it enough? If someone thought themselves broken beyond repair—as Sir Isaac had—what would reassure them? If Myles hid how he felt, she could not help him.

"England needs the hospital," Lady Inglewood said, conviction in her words. "I hope your husband will discuss the particulars with mine. If we can help in any way, I should like to. For Isaac's sake, and everyone like him."

Pippa agreed with them, then allowed the conversation to drift from that topic even while she made up her mind to speak to her

husband. As soon as she had opportunity to do so. He needed to know how she felt. At least—some of what she felt.

A roar of laughter from the other side of the pond drew her gaze, and Pippa saw her husband among the laughing men. And then he looked at her. Despite the distance between them, she felt the moment their eyes connected. Her cheeks warmed as he touched the brim of his hat.

She shivered, despite the warmth of the day, and diverted herself with her fan. When she glanced up again, Myles still watched her.

And she wondered at the connection that had grown between them.

Eighteen

The night after the picnic, Myles delayed his rest as long as he could. He wanted to be certain Pippa had ample time to dress for bed and slip beneath the covers before he entered the room. Then she could pretend to sleep, and they could both pretend it meant nothing that he climbed into bed beside her.

They hadn't discussed the arrangement since that first night, when he woke from the nightmare. It was something they both understood. And if it meant he slept comfortably, next to the woman he loved, Myles didn't mind it at all.

When he entered the room, as quiet as ever, Myles paused in the doorway. The bed remained empty. For a horrible moment, he thought Pippa had disappeared. Left him. Went to sleep in another room, somehow. The thought chilled him, right through to his heart.

"Myles."

Her voice brought his gaze to her, where she sat in one of the chairs before the fire. The flames were low, and the shadows many. His beautiful wife waited for him, with a night-rail over her gown and her hair plaited down one shoulder.

"Pippa." He closed the door carefully behind him. "I didn't think you would still be awake or...up." It seemed their silent understanding

wasn't to remain silent any longer. "Do you wish me to leave for another hour?"

She shook her head, and for one moment Myles's heart skipped with hope. Would she invite him to stay? Had something changed—did Pippa want *more* at last?

"I wanted to speak with you in private. I thought there might not be a better time for such a conversation than now."

Despite his disappointment, Myles tried for levity in his response. "People are unlikely to interrupt us in our bedroom." Though the implication of that statement made him wince, he cleared his throat and approached the chair opposite hers. "I am at your service, Pippa. What is it you wish to discuss?" And why was she already dressed for bed? Her bare feet peeked out from beneath the hem of her white linen gown. He cleared his throat and sat down.

"Something that Lady Fox said today, actually."

"Ah. I liked the Foxes. And Inglewood. They are excellent company." And he hadn't thought it possible for them to offer offense to his wife, but why else would Pippa wear such a solemn expression?

With her eyebrows drawn together, and an almost pained smile, she said, "I like them, too. Very much. Lady Fox had much to say on the matter of the hospital."

That didn't strike Myles as any cause for concern. "As did her husband. I promised to write out all the details and send them that information along with how they might contact your brother." He tapped the arm of the chair with the fingers of his left hand. "What else did the baronet's wife say?"

Pippa shifted in her chair, clasping and unclasping her hands. Then she played with the ribbon at the end of her plaited hair and lowered her gaze. "She said something interesting about Sir Isaac. About what it was like, in the early months of their marriage. I had the feeling she wanted to give me advice. It seems he is also plagued by nightmares from his time at war."

"I am aware of that." Though it surprised him that his wife would divulge such a thing to a near stranger. And then, "Did you tell her I suffer the same?"

She lowered her gaze. "We spoke in confidence, Myles. One wife to another, about husbands who were wounded in war." She chewed her bottom lip, a nervous habit he found endearing. Despite the breach of his privacy.

"I suppose finding herself with someone in a similar situation was unusual." He could allow for that, despite the somewhat sick feeling in his stomach. "You said she offered advice." He didn't mean the words to sound clipped, yet he heard them that way.

Pippa folded her arms across her midsection. "Yes. Which brings me to the important part of this conversation. You must know, Myles, how much I admire you. I find you kind, and I feel safe when I am with you. You are a capable man."

He stared at her, confused. "A capable man?" he repeated. "What does that mean, exactly?" And why did hearing her say that make him feel distinctly incapable?

"Botheration," she muttered, looking heavenward as though beseeching the ceiling to open and the right words to drop in her lap. "What I am trying to say is that I do not feel—that is, I do not want you to feel any less of a man because of your injuries. Physical or otherwise."

She had not truly spoken such a ridiculous sentence. Had she? Myles stared at his wife, incredulous. Every insecurity he felt about his missing eye, his scars, his nightmares, tumbled forward to snatch at her words and turn them over and over. Dissatisfied with them. Recognizing only one thing.

He spoke with a lowered voice. "Am I to thank you for that speech? Or for your pity?"

That made her dark blue eyes widen and glitter in the firelight. "It isn't pity. It's the truth."

"And did Lady Fox advise you to say those same words? I somehow cannot imagine her encouraging such an indelicate phrasing." Myles stood and walked to the hearth, glaring into the embers while he put both hands through his hair.

"Of course not. Any fault in my words are my own." Pippa remained in the chair, as still as stone. "I did not mean to offend you. I

felt it important for me to tell you that I find nothing lacking in your person or character."

"It feels as though the opposite must be true," he muttered, glaring at the embers in the hearth. They grew dimmer, the fire smaller. His hope followed suit. "Why are you telling me this?" He turned slowly to face her.

Pippa looked away from him. "Lady Fox said—she made me concerned for you. That you might think yourself broken. That you might need convincing that you are a whole man, worthy of affection and friendship."

"Affection and friendship." Those words were inadequate for what he wanted from her. Perhaps she meant to tell him that was all he would ever receive. He had more to say. So much more. But he settled for proving her thoughtless words wrong. "I *am* broken, Pippa. I am scarred. I am half-blind. My memories are washed in blood and smoke. When the palace celebrated the king's birthday with fireworks—do you remember?—I cowered in the corner of my room when the first went off near my apartments. I didn't even know I possessed such a weakness until that moment."

She stared at him as he spoke, her eyes growing larger. "I didn't know. But that doesn't mean you're—"

Myles laughed quietly. Darkly. Interrupting her. "It does. A clang of pots on the street. Fireworks during a celebration. Sudden noises. Someone sneaking up behind me. All those things send me backward in time, to the killing fields. To the groans of men dying all around me. To the explosion that took several of my regiment—my friends—away from this earth. And you want to tell me you think I am *capable*?"

Friendship. Affection. Watered-down words, flavorless as thinned wine.

"I hate for you to feel that you do not belong." Pippa stood at last, her whole frame trembling in her agitation. "That you cannot be part of something that matters. Because that isn't the truth."

There it was. He knew well enough what mattered to her. She'd told him, since the beginning. "That I cannot be part of Society, you mean?" She stared at him blankly, confirming his suspicion. His shoul-

ders fell. "I hate London. I only live there because I can afford the rent. I can eat at a club. I can *pretend* to be a gentleman, when in reality I have nothing except my pension to my name. A pension bought with my flesh and my soul."

Her face grew pale. Was it his admission about London or his graphic language that she objected to? And why did he feel the twisted desire to push her to greater discomfort? Likely to ignore the hole opening in his heart.

"That is why we left London, isn't it? You pretended it was for you. To avoid the gossip and rumor. But in reality, we were fleeing from Society's eyes the moment I stumbled into memory on the street."

Her mouth fell open, and her protest stumbled from her lips. "That isn't true at all. Yes, I worried for you. That isn't the entire reason—"

"Ah." His heart fractured. "But it is a large part of the reason."

Though her words were defensive, her tone sounded anxious. "I didn't know what it would do to you, to be surrounded by crowds all the time. You never warned me, except at the ball, with your headache." She approached him, hands outstretched and palms up. "I thought you needed a respite. Time in the country, with your family."

Looking down at her hands, then lower to her bare toes, Myles swallowed back the bitterness of disappointment. "You would have preferred to stay in London for the end of the Season." And the worst of it. "Even with the gossip."

She came closer, her voice soft and pleading. "Myles."

"Tell me, Pippa."

Her answer came out with a deep sigh. "Yes." Her hands lowered, and she spoke woodenly. "I wanted to stay in London until the Season ended. I had never fully enjoyed my time in London before. I am aware of how selfish that sounds."

Myles nodded once. "Thank you for telling me the truth. Now, if you'll excuse me." He walked to the door, his steps quick. He had his hand on the latch when she called his name, and when he looked over his shoulder he read the confusion in her lovely face. "I am sorry I forced you out to the country, Pippa. I am sorry you regret marrying a

man as broken as I am. Because I am *not* whole or capable. But someday, I hope to be worthy of more than just your friendship." It was the nearest thing to a confession of his feelings that he could summon.

Turning away from her, Myles left before she said anything else. He went directly down the stairs and out the door. He needed to walk. And think. Away from Pippa, Winston, his parents, and anyone else trying to convince him that he was as sound in mind and body now as he had ever been. Because they were all wrong. They didn't know anything about him.

His wife had wanted freedom to attend events in London, to explore the city, to come and go as she pleased when she pleased. She needed a husband to give her wings, not shackle her to his reclusive needs. Why had he married Pippa when she had made it clear what she wanted?

Because he hadn't thought it would threaten his heart with breaking when he realized she didn't want *him*.

Could he change her mind? If she could see the broken pieces of him and still admire him, could she love him? He didn't know. He didn't even know how to find out. So he went into the darkness beneath the trees and paced. Marching down one path and then another. Until he grew too tired to walk. Too tired to think. And he fell asleep beneath a tree.

Nineteen

Pippa had hesitated too long to follow after her husband. By the time she opened the door to the hall, he was gone. She heard the front door of the house snap shut. She hadn't had the chance to tell him he was wrong—that she didn't regret marrying him.

She went to bed but did not sleep for hours and hours. What stupidity had compelled her to offer him words too tepid to provide true comfort? She hadn't offered him her compassion or understanding. Because she hadn't spoken from her heart—but from her guilt. From a complete lack of understanding what he needed.

Words offered without her heart's intent behind them had wounded her husband. She had done everything wrong. What made matters worse was her hope that he would return proved ill-founded. When she finally fell asleep, the other half of the bed remained empty.

Pippa overslept, not waking until late morning. She shifted in her bed, rolled over, and stared at the empty pillow next to her own. It remained untouched. Slipping from beneath the covers, Pippa went straight to the bellpull to summon her maid.

When her maid appeared, nearly a quarter of an hour later, she curtsied and held out a folded square of paper before Pippa could ask for assistance dressing. She needed to find Myles. They had to talk—

she had to explain to him what she meant the night before. To tell him how sorry she was.

"What is this?" Pippa took the paper and unfolded it, realizing it was a note. She recognized the strong, swooping handwriting immediately.

The maid ducked her head and spoke quietly. "Mr. Cobbett asked that I give that to you. After I packed a valise for him."

Pippa walked to the window and pulled back the curtains, letting the morning sunlight fall upon the paper.

Lady Philippa,

Forgive me for taking my leave through paper and pen. There is something I must do. I will return in a weeks' time. My family will look after you until then. Please know, despite all I said last evening, that I hold your happiness dearer above all else. There is more I would say, but it must wait.

Your Husband,

Myles

The note was far too short. Too vague. And what was it that Myles had to do? Where was he going?

Folding the paper, Pippa looked up at her maid. "When did he leave?" Or could he still be in the house? Perhaps she could catch him—

"Two hours ago, my lady."

Pippa turned away from her servant and stared out the window, no longer seeing the vibrant flower garden or the trees. She saw nothing. Felt only cold disappointment. "I would like a tray brought to my room, please. I do not feel well."

Not well enough to face the family. To answer questions they might have about where Myles had gone.

But then—what if one of them knew why he had left?

"Wait—I changed my mind." Pippa held her hand out to stay the maid, who was nearly to the door to obey her first order. She swallowed her pride and forced herself to appear calm. "It would be rude to stay away. Please, find something for me to wear so I might spend the day with my mother-in-law."

If anyone knew what Myles was up to, it would likely be his mother or his brother. Myles and Winston spent a lot of time in each other's company. Surely her husband couldn't have disappeared without telling *someone* where he had gone.

Except half an hour later, it seemed he had done just that.

"Myles left with nary a word to me, my dear." Lady Greenwood held a watering can in one hand and a small potted fern in the other. Pippa had found her mother-in-law busy in the greenhouse. "Other than goodbye, of course. He promised he would return soon. I asked where he was going—we have engagements for the two of you to attend. He only said, 'There is something I must do.'" She narrowed her eyes at Pippa. "Most cryptic. I had hoped you knew what he was up to."

Pippa slowly shook her head, then gestured to the fern. She could find Winston later. "Might I help with your work in here? I need something to keep my hands busy."

"Of course, dear. Here. Find a suitable place for this one where it won't be covered over by larger fronds." After that, Pippa helped trim hothouse flowers for the house. Fragrant blossoms were to go in every room. "The roses outside the greenhouse will bloom soon. I have already spied several buds among my whites and pinks. The reds are slow to wake this year. I have a party for my closest friends in the garden, once all the rosebushes are showing color."

"That sounds lovely. I hope I am here to see it." Pippa couldn't bring herself to say much more, but her mother-in-law kept up a comforting stream of words about flowers, gardens, and all things summery and light.

Lady Greenwood didn't seem upset over her son's absence. And she didn't question Pippa closely about why Myles disappeared without a word to either of them. It was only when they left the greenhouse and inspected the outdoor rose bushes that the older of the two gave Pippa a soft smile. "Did you know that Myles was my least adventurous child?"

Startled by the change in conversation, and the knowledge, Pippa had to shake her head. "No," she drew out the word slowly. "I did not.

Given that he became a soldier, I would have thought the opposite to be true."

"Myles never ventured far from home, except when his sisters or brothers asked it of him." Lady Greenwood smiled fondly, her gaze unfocused as she slipped into memory. "And he only went because he thought he needed to look after everyone. That has always been his way. He looks after people." She bent to inhale the scent of a white rosebud. "When he was a very little boy, only two years old, he found me crying. I don't remember why now. Mothers cry a great deal over nothing, sometimes." She shrugged and turned to face Pippa. "But that little boy toddled to where I sat and patted my cheek. 'No cry, Mama. Love you.' And he gave me a kiss. I tell you, I wrapped him in my arms and held him close. I thought it the sweetest thing."

Pippa lowered herself to an iron chair, keeping her eyes on Myles's mother. "That is a sweet story. So protecting others from harm has always been part of his nature."

"Always." Lady Greenwood swept forward and took the match to Pippa's chair. "Which gives me reason to wonder how the two of you met and married so quickly that he did not have time to write me about it until after the deed was done." Nothing in the woman's tone was threatening, or disapproving, but the way she sat like a queen on a throne meant she expected answers.

"Myles hasn't told you anything?" Pippa asked softly.

"Nothing. Except that he is happy."

Pippa's heart fluttered, but then guilt weighed it down again. She folded her hands in her lap. "I think...I think you should know all the circumstances. Because I wonder if maybe Myles isn't happy at all." Pippa swallowed, then had to look away from the woman whose eyes were so like her son's. "He was looking after me. Protecting me, and by extension, helping his sisters."

"What do you mean?" Lady Greenwood spoke steadily, and her expression softened. "Were you in danger?"

Though Pippa had no desire to tell their story without Myles, the peace of the garden wrapped around her heart and soul. Lady Greenwood's gentle presence made it easier to confide in her, too. Haltingly

at first, and then more steadily, Pippa told her mother-in-law their story. From the moment she first met Myles in the ballroom, up until the day they arrived at Ambleside. She tried not to speak much about Myles's struggles in London, focusing instead on his readiness to do whatever necessary to please *her*.

"I never thought myself spoiled, or selfish," Pippa admitted, unable to look her mother-in-law in the eye. "I wanted to be better than that. Better than my mother and my elder sister. They are horribly vain. They accept nothing less than what they think the best, in everything. I thought I was different. But lately, I think I have been just as terrible as them. Your son has sacrificed his future for mine, when he might've been happier to marry someone else. Someone who didn't demand so much from him."

Lady Greenwood said nothing. Pippa couldn't bring herself to look at the other woman's expression, certain as she was that it would hold disappointment. Or disgust. The silence lay heavily on her heart, the only sounds penetrating her guilt the soft rustle of the leaves. Far away, a bird called, and another answered.

"Pippa." Lady Greenwood spoke firmly. "Look at me, child."

She inhaled deeply, bolstering herself with what little confidence remained to her. Pippa lifted her gaze to her mother-in-law. Lady Greenwood's countenance, soft and maternal as ever, didn't waver as she studied Pippa. "My son isn't one to make important decisions lightly. That he married you doesn't surprise me in the slightest. He saw a way to help people outside of himself. Whatever sacrifice you think he made for that opportunity, you ought to honor it rather than bemoan your own motives."

Leaning closer, Pippa asked, "What do you mean?"

"I mean, dear Pippa, that we all have weaknesses. You. Me. Myles. But I would not declare that his giving heart is one of his. And it does not sound to me as though you came to the conclusion that you must marry with selfishness so much as self-preservation. You needed someone. You found Myles. If you feel you have since been more concerned with yourself than him, that is a weakness that can be corrected. Isn't it?"

That thought made Pippa's head hang lower and her shoulders bunch up toward her ears. "I tried," she admitted quietly. "When I spoke to Myles last night. I tried to correct how I'd behaved—"

"In order to make yourself feel better, dear." Lady Greenwood's voice remained gentle, and Pippa winced again. The baroness had a perceptive mind. "You weren't thinking of Myles so much as you were thinking about you. Were you?"

Pippa released a trembly breath. "No. You are right, of course. I wanted to soothe my conscience more than I thought on what he needed from me." Pippa rose from her chair and walked to one of the rose bushes, not seeing the buds so clearly as the thorns. "What do I do? He must think me such a foolish, childish thing."

Lady Greenwood came to stand beside her, brushing Pippa's cheek as gently as she might a rosebud. Pippa's attention stayed on the greenery, knowing if she saw the way Myles's mother looked at her she would most certainly cry. No one had looked after Pippa in so long. But that was exactly what this felt like. Lady Greenwood mothered Pippa as she would one of her own children.

"I doubt my son would ever think less of you for your mistakes. As I said. We all have them. And Myles—well." Here the woman's voice changed, sounding more amused than comforting. She drew Pippa's gaze up again as she spoke. "Myles has always been a protector, it is true. He has always been kind. But I have never seen him look at a woman as he looks at you."

That afternoon, Lady Greenwood and her daughters Margaret and Elenor, invited Pippa to call on Dr. and Mrs. Johnson with them. "You must come see the Clock House," Elenor, the youngest, said with a bright grin. "It is absolutely charming."

Though Pippa had hoped to visit the doctor with Myles, she had no intention of passing up the opportunity now presented. Myles thought highly of the doctor and his wife. She wanted to get to know them, for his sake. Thus she rode in an open carriage with her new in-laws. Lady Greenwood drove, rather than have a servant accompany them.

They passed through a beautiful wood to emerge in a sun-

drenched lane surrounded on either side by rolling hills of green. "This is Highdale land," Lady Greenwood told Pippa. "The same gentleman owns it that leases the Clock House to the Johnsons. He used to raise cattle, but recently sold most of his herds." She pursed her lips. "He is being quite close-mouthed as to why. Though the baron and I think he means to sell."

"He hasn't any family," Margaret said, speaking in a soft voice as though the gentleman himself might hear her. "And he must be seventy if he is a day."

"It would be interesting, would it not? To have new neighbors at such a time in my life." Lady Greenwood shook her head and then pointed. "Ah, there it is. The Clock House."

An ordinary brick house, with slate roof, sat back not twenty feet from the road. Pippa studied it carefully, from its green-painted shutters to the pleasant yellow door, and the ivy creeping up one side. "Why is it called the Clock House?"

"Look at the barn," Elenor said, pointing to a brick building set near the house.

At the top of the barn, several feet in diameter, was a bright white clockface. Two long hands pointed out the hour and minutes. The clock faced the house, and anyone coming toward it on the road.

"Dear me. Why would anyone put a clock on the barn?" Pippa laughed. "Do the animals keep to a strict schedule?"

"The first owner of the house—when it was a gatehouse to Highdale House many years ago—thought it important that anyone coming or going knew the time. The main bedroom at Clock House looks directly at the clock, too. Some say the old gatekeeper put the clock in for himself, so he might never be tardy to work."

Lady Greenwood drove the carriage up to the door, which opened immediately by a male servant. The man came out to tie up the horses. The doctor himself emerged next, and he helped the ladies step down.

"Lady Philippa, Lady Greenwood, Miss Greenwood, Miss Elenor. How wonderful to have you all here. Do come inside. Mrs. Johnson and I were just speaking of the pleasant time we had at the picnic."

They passed nearly an hour in the company of the Johnsons, and

by the time they took their leave, Pippa wished very much to make Mrs. Johnson a particular friend. The woman was kind and gracious, and quite proud of her husband's work as a physician. Pippa secured a promise from Mrs. Johnson of a visit the following day. Given the sly smile of her mother-in-law, Pippa wondered if that had been the aim all along. Not to make Pippa feel better, but to give her a friend whose values were quite different from the ladies in London's highest society.

As they stood in the garden, the horses ready, another thought occurred to Pippa. "Do you know your landlord very well?" she asked Mrs. Johnson. "I have only heard of him this afternoon. What is his name?"

"Mr. Young." The doctor's wife appeared suddenly quite solemn. "My husband visits him often." She did not say whether it was as a doctor or tenant but given the line of worry appearing between her eyebrows, Pippa guessed the former was the case. "Would you like to meet him? He is a talkative gentleman, to be sure, and has the most diverting stories of local history."

"I would like that very much." Thus they planned yet another time to see one another and call upon Mr. Young.

On the ride back to Ambleside, Lady Greenwood gave Pippa a knowing glance. Her dark eyebrows raised as she said, seemingly to all three younger women, "Mrs. Johnson is one of the most compassionate women of my acquaintance. I do hope we all might learn from her, for as long as she and her husband may be persuaded to live in our neighborhood." While Margaret and Elenor murmured their agreement, Pippa leaned back and lifted her face to the sun.

With the warmth of the late-spring sun upon her face, Pippa's thoughts shifted. She planted new ideas in the garden of her mind as one would seedlings—delicately, and with great hope for the future.

Twenty

It took more time than Myles liked to reach Pippa's childhood home. The groom who rode with him never once complained, and indeed the lad seemed to think the whole thing an adventure. When they rode up the long white lane to the Earl of Montecliff's house, the young man let out a low whistle. When Myles turned to look at the boy, eyebrow raised, the groom hastily apologized.

"Sorry, sir. It's just—cor—I didn't know they built houses so large." The lad bowed his head, but whether it was in respect for Myles or the house, Myles didn't know.

"It is only a house, Garrett. Made of brick and mortar." Myles looked up at the large house, noting the number of windows and the way the sun reflected off several glazed surfaces. The landscaping of the home was immaculate, in the old style, with hedges trimmed into cubes and spheres with mathematical precision.

This was the Earl of Montecliff's home. Where Pippa had been born and grew up. The building was palatial, and Myles wondered anew how he would ever be enough for a woman of Lady Philippa's standing.

When they rode up to the door, a servant already waited for Myles

to approach. The livery the man wore was tailored to fit him as perfectly as any lord's coat.

"I am Mr. Myles Cobbett," Myles said, holding out one of his new cards. Pippa had ordered them for him in London, but he had not seen them until the day they departed Town. The cards were on thick, expensive paper, his name rendered with exquisite calligraphy. It was a small thing, yet Myles was grateful for the quality when the butler took the card.

From the doorway, another servant appeared, this one older and dressed in finer clothing. "John, allow me. Lady Philippa's husband must be treated with all courtesy."

A story Pippa had told him came back, one in which she admitted she thought the family butler often looked the other way when she sneaked away from her lessons or disappeared to visit her great-uncle. The man's name came to Myles, and he blurted it without thought. "Rigby?"

The servant, posture already perfect, somehow appeared more alert than before. "The same, sir." He waved away the footman, then led Myles into the house. "While it is not my place, Mr. Cobbett, I feel Lady Philippa would wish me to warn you—his lordship is at home and not in good humor."

Myles stopped walking, and the butler did, too. Myles tried to get the man's measure, staring the servant in the eye in a way no nobleman would ever permit himself. "Pippa speaks highly of you, Rigby."

Rigby's eyes brightened somewhat, and he bowed his head. "I am honored to learn it, Mr. Cobbett."

Sensing a possible ally in the servant, Myles lowered his voice as though speaking to a coconspirator. "I am going to confide in you, Rigby. I am here to liberate Lady Philippa's mare. Bunny." How any grown man could call a horse by that name without smiling, Myles couldn't say. "I trust, given that a bill of sale on the horse bears her name as the purchaser, I will not have any difficulty leaving with my wife's property."

The butler stared at him before giving one long, slow blink. "That sounds sensible, sir. Allow me to show you to his lordship at once. He

is in the library. As you are family, it will not be necessary to announce you."

When Myles had ridden into battle during the war, he'd always been afraid. But he took courage in the fact that the men around him experienced the same fear, the same determination to look after one another. The fellowship between him and his regiment had gotten them through everything from near-starvation to long marches into enemy territory.

Though he had just met Rigby, Myles's instincts gave him that same feeling of assurance when it came to the butler.

The massive scale of the house, though it may have cowed men of humbler origins, did nothing to intimidate Myles, though he admired Pippa all the more for giving up a connection, a marriage, that would've kept her amid such splendor. When they went up the stairs and down two different corridors, the butler paused before a pair of large, oak doors. Two footmen stood on either side of them, looking ahead, like soldiers at attention.

"Good luck, Mr. Cobbett," the butler said, and with a slight gesture of his hand, signaled the footmen to open the library doors. True to his word, the butler did not follow. The doors closed behind Myles.

The library, paneled in dark wood, impressed the wealth of its owner on Myles. The dark green, velvet curtains along the many windows hung on gold rods. The bookcases stretched from floor to ceiling, most with glass doors protecting the volumes inside. A globe the size of a man stood at the center of the room, flanked on either side by maps stretched atop tables and protected by yet more glass.

Myles approached one of the maps, curious despite himself, and saw it was a Dutch masterpiece from the seventeenth century. Fireplaces were on either wall, tall enough that Myles could have stepped inside of them if he wished. Chairs and tables were scattered throughout the room. And in one of those chairs sat the earl, staring at Myles the way a kitchen maid might stare at a rat in the pantry.

"You." The earl did not even bother closing the book in his lap.

"What are *you* doing here? Had enough of my sister? Come to see if I will buy her back from you?"

That crass idea made Myles recoil a step from the earl, disgusted. "You have peculiar ideas, your lordship, of how to speak of a lady."

"Is that a no?" Lord Montecliff smirked. "Perhaps you are here to ask for funds. Have you already tired of living beneath her thumb? I will save you the trouble, now and in the future. Neither of you will ever get a penny from me."

Myles walked toward the earl, slowly, pretending to study the map as he went. "I would never dream of asking you for anything, except that which already belongs to my wife. I am here for her property." And he had the feeling it would not be easy to get that horse off the earl's land.

Finally, the earl closed his book with a deliberate snap. "I cannot think what you imagine belongs to her in my house. She practically moved in at that cursed Tertium Park before going to London, where her belongings from my townhouse were delivered to my younger brother." He spoke with one lip curled in a sneer. "My sister cannot demand anything else of me."

"She demands nothing," Myles said, tucking his hands behind his back. He moved without hurry to the hearth, his gaze on a painting that depicted a horse and gentleman, the likenesses as large as the actual creature and man had been. "I am here for her mare."

The earl stood abruptly, tossing down his book. "Here for a horse? You traveled all this way—you are a fool, Cobbett."

Myles turned to fully face the earl. "I am here to collect my wife's property," he repeated, voice low and calm. "Then I will be on my way."

With a baleful glare, Lord Montecliff folded his arms across his chest, which had puffed out like an overstuffed pheasant. "I have a better idea. You leave, empty-handed. Then you apply for an annulment with my sister. Once it is granted, I will compensate you handsomely and see to it you live in comfort the rest of your days. Without my sister as your keeper."

"That is the second time you have implied the relationship between

Lady Philippa and myself is unequal." Myles considered that information, his eyebrows raising. "You have obtained a copy of our marital agreement."

The lord's eyes glittered, his smirk grew. "It explicitly states that my sister has full financial control, other than a small allowance granted to you." He rocked back on his heels. "Surely, a man of action like yourself must feel stifled at such a thing."

Myles wondered how England would ever progress with men like Montecliff in control of laws and politics. "I fail to understand how an annulment would give you any satisfaction. The scandal of a broken marriage would hardly add to your sister's reputation or your own."

"Scandal." The earl scoffed. "I control what is and isn't a scandal. And Lord Walter does not care if he must hide the chit away in some far-flung house. He wants the connection and the money." A twitch to Montecliff's eye gave Myles pause.

"And what do you want?" Myles asked, studying the other man's slightest change in expression. A crease appeared on the earl's forehead but smoothed again. His nostrils flared. Then he tipped his chin up.

"That is none of your affair."

"And yet," Myles said, narrowing his eye, "I am the only man who can give you what you want. So perhaps you ought to confide in me, brother-in-law."

The disgusted sneer appeared on the earl's face again, this time not directed at Myles. "I owe funds to Lord Walter's father. He will forgive the debt if his idiot son marries Philippa. There. Does that satisfy you?"

The debt had to be large if a man living in such opulence was willing to give his sister away to pay off his creditor. Myles couldn't countenance the idea. "There must be another way for you to settle the matter with the man. A way that doesn't require sacrificing Philippa."

"Selling my property and land is out of the question," the earl snapped. "I have a reputation to maintain. A duty to my heirs."

Thinking of his own sisters, Myles's estimation of the earl dropped even further. The items in the library alone were worth several fortunes. But rather than give up anything that might make him appear

less, the earl had decided on sacrificing Philippa's future and her happiness.

Myles met the other man's gaze squarely. "You, sir, are a disgrace to your title. That a nobleman of our country would so willingly sacrifice an innocent to pay your own debts is a shame. I stood shoulder to shoulder with men of lower birth who stood ready to give their lives up for another. To provide peace and safety to strangers. To people like you, sitting comfortably in your opulence. You are a dragon with its hoard, taking pleasure in nothing but your own self-importance. Greedily guarding what ought to be used to help others."

The earl went purple as Myles spoke, then spluttered, "How dare you give such insult. Get out of my house. Now."

"With pleasure. I will collect my wife's mare." Myles strode directly past the irate earl, seething inside.

"You will not step one foot in my stables," the earl shouted at Myles's back. "You will remove yourself from my property at once, or I will have you shot!"

The earl could likely get away with it, too. But Myles wouldn't leave without that horse. Bunny—the silly thing—meant too much to Pippa. The mare was part of her long-desired freedom from her family's expectations and machinations. He would walk out the front door, mount his own horse, and ride directly to the stables. Avoiding gunfire, if necessary.

The earl came out the library doors behind Myles and started barking orders to his footmen. "See him off the property. Loose the dogs and bring me my rifle."

Myles didn't run. He had too much dignity for that. But he did cast a dangerous look at the footmen—both of whom wisely refrained from laying hands on him as they walked at his side until he made it to the door.

If the earl hoped to humiliate him, he had chosen the wrong method.

Rigby, the butler, stood at the front door. Which he opened himself, expression staid and posture correct. Myles gave the butler a curious glance as he stepped outside—and found his groom waiting

with three horses. The two they had traveled with, and a white mare wearing a lady's side-saddle.

Myles spun on his heel to look at the butler, whose proper mask broke just long enough for him to smile. Then he said, "Give Lady Philippa my best, if you would, Mr. Cobbett." Then the butler closed the door.

Myles grinned at the closed door, then jumped down the steps several at a time before mounting. "Come, Garrett. We are leaving under fire."

The lad's eyes widened comically, but he wasted no time in following Myles, leading Bunny behind him.

No shots chased them out of the earl's lands, but that did nothing to diminish the victorious hope in Myles's heart. He had done something for his wife. Something she hadn't done for herself, and that others might not think important to do for her at all. This would be the first step in showing Pippa his true feelings for her.

Proving that he loved her.

Twenty-One

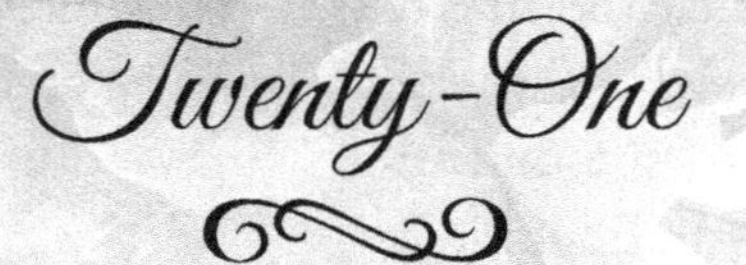

While some might say Philippa *paced* in the rose garden, she much preferred to describe her aimless wandering as a pleasant exercise. Even if she moved too sedately to gain any healthful benefits. And despite being so lost in her own thoughts, she did not notice the roses finally in bloom.

In her hands she held two letters. The Greenwood butler had delivered them to her while she read a book in the sitting room. One was addressed to her husband, sealed with the Earl of Inglewood's crest. She debated opening it, as her natural curiosity wanted to know what sort of impression they had made on a man known for his political work. A man of stone, they had called him in the papers.

The other letter she had opened. Mr. Young had written to lay out his terms for a most exciting proposition she had given him the day before.

If only Myles would return. She wanted him to read Mr. Young's letter. She needed him to approve her idea before she sent on her proposal to Adam and Elaine. But since he had disappeared a week before, without word to anyone of when he might return or how they could contact him, she had to exercise patience.

Which wasn't a simple matter when she was fairly bursting to discuss her ideas with someone who understood them. Someone who had invested more energy and thought in that particular topic than she had.

Philippa held up the expensive, well-folded ivory paper with the earl's seal. She studied the fine hand with which he'd written Myles's name. Then she sighed and tucked it into the band of her gown. "I will wait for you, Myles," she murmured to a nodding pink bloom. Then bent to inhale its sweet fragrance.

She missed him.

Pippa took up the basket and garden shears she had brought outside with her. Lady Greenwood planned to send a single bloom to her friends, along with an invitation to take tea in the garden the following week. In need of a distraction, Pippa had volunteered to clip the flowers herself.

Myles's family treated her well. Better than her own mother and eldest brother. They felt as much like family to her as Adam and Elaine. Each day she spent with them taught her more about the man she married, whether they shared stories with her about Myles's childhood or Lady Greenwood performed some kindness for another member of the family. They were thoughtful of one another, yet that did not lessen their ability to tease or laugh.

Lord Greenwood had proven an exceptional conversationalist, and she found his dry humor a match for his son's. He treated her with respect, and a fatherly manner she could not recall her own father showing toward her. She quite adored him.

With another snip of the shears, Pippa laid the pink blossom in her basket. She walked from bush to bush, mindful of the thorns each time she took hold of a flower. A dozen perfect blooms. That's what she needed to fulfill her mother-in-law's request.

Snip.

When would Myles return?

Snip.

Why had he left without speaking to her?

Snip.

Though they had argued, and she had said all the wrong things, never did she think he would disappear without taking his leave.

Snip.

Then she sniffled. Her eyes burned with tears, though she refused to so much as acknowledge them. Tears. How silly. Myles would return. And when he did, he would tell her where he had gone.

Snip.

And she would tell him...what? How she spent her days waiting for him? Rising every time she thought a horse or carriage approached, looking out the window? She had hoped for his return every day.

Snip.

But he might not even be halfway finished with his journey. Errand. Whatever it was he had undertaken to accomplish without telling her.

Snip.

It bothered her less that he had left than that she did not know when to expect his return. Left in a state of constant anticipation, her heart and mind had run away with her. She dreamed about Myles. She woke missing his presence at her side. She struggled to sleep at night without him near.

Snip.

The tears dared fall at last, but she dashed them away too quickly for them to leave a trail upon her cheeks. When Myles returned, she wouldn't cry. Even if her heart constricted every time she went to bed alone. And warmed when she thought on his smile, or the touch of his hand upon her skin.

Snip.

She wouldn't cry. She would wait patiently for him to tell her where he went. Then, she would calmly tell him how concerned she felt for his welfare. How he ought to be more sensible when he left and tell at least one person where he intended to go and when he planned to return.

Snip.

She sneezed. Then grumbled and went searching for her handker-

chief where she had tucked it in her bodice. Crying nearly always made her nose swell and itch. She sneezed again as she put the scrap of lace and linen to her nose.

"God bless you, Pippa."

A ripple of excitement went through Pippa's body, followed by a wave of blissful relief. She whirled around fast enough that the basket on her arm swung precariously.

"Myles." She gripped the shears tighter.

Dust covered his clothes. He held his hat in both hands, exposing his hair sticking up this way and that, like a thicket of neglected shrubbery. And he hadn't shaved in a few days, given the dark shadow along his cheeks and jaw. He looked a complete mess. Yet she wanted to throw herself into his arms—an urge she had never before experienced.

Because she loved him.

Her heart happily confirmed this sudden knowledge, skipping in her chest like a child in a meadow. She caught her breath. Then expelled it in a single, strangled question. "Where have you been?"

~

WHEN MYLES HAD WALKED THROUGH THE FRONT DOOR OF his childhood home, he'd met Elenor in the hall. She had looked him up and down before exclaiming, "You look absolutely terrible."

Margaret had peeked through the open doorway of the front sitting room. "What was that? Oh! Myles, you're home. Pippa will be so relieved. She's in the rose garden."

Pippa didn't look relieved. Her blue eyes had darkened with what could only be anger, her eyebrows drawn together, her whole body trembling as she looked at him.

"Where have I been?" he repeated her question, shifting his weight from one foot to another. When her eyes narrowed, he adjusted his stance to the same military-posture he would use when addressing a commanding officer. "I had an important errand, Pippa."

He noticed when the hand gripping the gardening shears tight-

ened, and Myles wondered how well his wife might wield such a weapon.

"An errand," she said, voice bland. "You left, without a word, for an errand? What could be so important that you would leave before I woke? Before telling me when you planned to return? Myles—no one knew where you had gone." She went to the table and dropped the basket on it, scattering a few roses from within. She leaned forward, steadying herself with both hands on the table's surface. "I was so worried," she whispered. "And you look ghastly."

That caused a prick of hurt before he realized she meant the dust coating him from heel to head. Maybe he ought to have cleaned up first. But when he'd learned where Pippa was, he had needed to find her at once.

"I am here, and unharmed. I did not think my absence would cause such concern." And now that he realized it had, guilt lodged itself in his gut. "I wanted—that is, I needed to prove something to you. I didn't know how else to do it."

Pippa turned to face him, now leaning back against the table. "What in heaven did you feel you needed to prove?" She gripped the edge of the table. The familiar scent of his mother's roses kept him steady, soothing him and keeping his mind and heart calm.

Had she forgotten their argument the night before he left? Doubtful. Myles approached slowly until he stood directly in front of her, only an arm's length from touch. He turned his hat round and round in his hands, then tossed it to the table. Her gaze never wavered from studying his face.

He really ought to have washed. Or at least shaved. He already wasn't much to look at. Perhaps that was the place to begin. "I know my scarring is unsightly. Especially when it comes to moving about in London Society."

She blinked at him.

"And my difficulty with nightmares, my unsteady nerves, are inconvenient at best, but more often they are...well." She didn't say anything, but a softness stole across her features. "It is frightening, at times. Not knowing when an episode like the one in Town will occur."

"I cannot imagine what you have been through, Myles." Pippa's shoulders relaxed, and her body swayed slightly toward him before she settled more firmly on her heels. "Because I could not understand, I said all the wrong things before." Her cheeks turned a shade of pink that made his heart flip backward. "Will you forgive me?"

"There is nothing to forgive." He shook his head and nearly reached for her. He had to clench his hand at his side to remind himself not to touch her—if he touched her, he would immediately forget everything he meant to say. "I am broken, Pippa. My body is scarred, but so are my mind and my heart. I am not a whole man—I never will be. The war took too much of me. But if you will have me, broken as I am, I swear I will spend the rest of my days working to be worthy of you. Because I love you."

Pippa moved with unpredictable speed. One moment she stood before him, trembling, and the next she had wrapped her arms around his waist and buried her face in his road-dusted cravat. She held him tightly, as though afraid he would slip away again.

Carefully, he put his arms around her. His surprise grew to elation. Myles bent his head to lay his cheek upon the soft curls of dark brown hair. Her honey-sweet scent mingled with the roses around them, creating an entirely new memory he predicted would offer him comfort for years to come. And when she at last tilted her head back enough to look at him, Myles didn't bother to wipe the tears from his good eye.

"I love *you*, Myles. And I intended to say it first." She smiled and put her palm against his cheek. "And if you are broken, so am I. You were raised in a home of such love and acceptance. My father's house was the opposite. You must help me learn to be as you are. Compassionate, honorable, and selfless." She studied him, her lips curving into a gentle smile. "If we are both broken, perhaps we can help one another to fill in the missing pieces. And be whole again someday."

Myles rested his forehead against hers and closed his eye. "I'm not sure when, or if, that will happen for me, Pippa."

She ran her thumb gently across his lips, and a shudder went through his body. "If it takes our whole lives to heal, my love, I don't mind. So long as I am with you."

At last, Myles kissed his bride. He couldn't keep himself from it another moment. Not when she tipped her head back with that inviting warmth in her gaze and the gentle way her lips parted. She kissed him, too. Quite thoroughly. Her hands went up his shoulders, then her fingers found their way to the back of his neck where they entangled themselves in his hair. His hands had a mind of their own, too. Though he began with holding her shoulders, they found the dip of her waist and pulled her closer.

One kiss wasn't enough. They needed more. And they forgot about everything for a time. Myles was far too busy exploring his wife's lips, sharing each breath and kiss with her, to remember that the upstairs sitting room faced the garden. Nor did he know, until later, that much of his family watched the display between the two of them with great satisfaction.

He only cared about that moment. About holding Pippa against his heart and feeling hers beating as hard and fast as his own.

When at last they rested, Pippa still in the circle of his arms, Myles relaxed his stance and tipped his head to one side. Studying her flushed cheeks and swollen lips with an awed pride he couldn't explain, he realized he still hadn't told her where he'd gone.

"I retrieved Bunny for you," he murmured, his words barely louder than the bees visiting his mother's roses. "That was my errand."

Pippa put her hands on his forearms and pushed back, her eyes widening to twice their normal size. "You brought Bunny here? And Richard *let* you?"

"He wasn't keen on the idea, actually. But your old friend, Mr. Rigby, made certain I did not leave empty handed."

"That wonderful butler." Pippa released his hand. "May I see her? Right now?" Pippa asked, bouncing on her toes. She didn't wait for an answer. She took Myles's hand and led him toward the stables while he laughed at her excitement. Then she stopped abruptly and went back to pick up her shears. "I promised your mother—"

He snatched them up first. "How many more does she need?" He'd helped her clip her roses for her annual teas more than once.

"A dozen, she said. I have..." Pippa counted up the stems quickly. "Eleven."

Myles snipped a pink rose, then a red. He placed the pink in her basket and held the red out to her. "For you, my lady."

Pippa twirled the rose between her fingers, staring up at him with open admiration. "I love you, Myles."

"And I you, Pippa." Together, they walked hand-in-hand to the stables where Pippa greeted her horse the way others would a favorite pet. "Sweet Bunny. Oh, my darling, I missed you so."

And all was right, at last.

PIPPA DIDN'T REMEMBER MYLES'S LETTER UNTIL SHE changed for dinner. It fell out of her dress, along with her own. "Botheration." She laid them on her dressing table, determined to give them to him that evening. Which meant waiting a few more hours, as his family had missed him, and everyone insisted he recount his adventurous horse-retrieval to them.

Watching her husband with his family, Pippa felt quite content. Apparently, spending days in the saddle agreed with him. When he told her how much he loved the country, though he avoided visiting his family so they would not feel the need to look after him, Pippa hadn't realized what that truly meant. Here, surrounded by the familiar, Myles was at ease. He appeared more relaxed than she had ever seen him—so much so, she could almost forget he had once been a soldier.

After dinner, when the men rejoined the women for the evening, Pippa waited for her husband to sit next to her near the fire. He took his place happily, one arm stretched along the back of the couch along her shoulders. "My love." He kissed her temple, right there where anyone might see.

"Myles." She studied his profile, wondering at her luck at finding such a handsome man to be her husband. Eyepatch or no eyepatch, Myles had too many attractive qualities to go unnoticed. "I have letters you must read. They are in our room. One is from the Earl of Ingle-

wood. The other…is difficult to explain. Would you come upstairs with me, so we may speak in private?"

"Of course. I think—that is, I hope I know why Lord Inglewood wrote. We spoke at length about the soldiers' hospital." He stood and held his hand out to her, assisting Pippa to her feet. Then he turned to his family to see all eyes upon them. Pippa's cheeks went hot.

"If you will excuse us," Pippa said, giving Myles's hand a squeeze. "I have remembered an important letter for Myles."

"By all means," Lord Greenwood said, his affable smile in place. "I am certain you are both tired from a long day of excitement. We won't expect to see you again until tomorrow."

"Not at breakfast, I'd wager," Winston whispered to his wife, barely loud enough for Pippa to hear him and wonder at his meaning. Myles's glare toward his older brother made the implication clearer to her.

Blushing, Pippa tugged her husband out of the room behind her as quickly as she could go. Did the whole room think—? But then, they didn't all know about their marriage. Only Lady Greenwood, and perhaps Lord Greenwood, knew. Still. A husband and wife retiring to bed together shouldn't raise quite so many eyebrows. Should it?

When they entered their shared bedroom, Pippa couldn't bring herself to look at Myles. Instead, she rushed to the table where she had left the letters. "Here they are." She turned, and her stomach jumped when she realized Myles stood close. So close she hardly needed to extend her hand to give him both his sealed note from the Earl of Inglewood and her open letter from Mr. Young.

Myles stripped off his gloves and tossed them to the dressing table before taking the papers from her. He went to the hearth to read by the light of a lamp resting on its mantel. Pippa had to turn away to compose herself.

Slowly, she removed her gloves. Undoing the buttons at the wrist, then sliding the silken cloth down first one hand and the other. She focused all her attention there, and on her breathing. In and out. Perfectly calm. Composed.

She laid both gloves on the table, next to the shorter, wider pair of

men's gloves Myles had tossed amid her hairbrush and combs without a thought, as though they had freely mingled their personal belongings always. She let her hand linger on the table's surface, then touched his glove. The left one, with the two smallest fingers missing. In Town, he had always worn a stuffed glove. She hadn't even paused to think on it—but here, in his family's home, he didn't bother with the pretense.

Who made his gloves? Had they offered him a glove without fingers, or had he requested it?

Myles broke into her thoughts with a cheery laugh. "Lord Inglewood and Sir Isaac wish to take an active role in the building of our hospital. The earl is offering funds—the largest sum of any patron yet. And Sir Isaac has included a list of political associates to approach. Some of these men are not yet on your brother's lists. This is marvelous."

He looked up at her, his good eye bright with hope. "I hoped the earl might provide introductions, I never thought he would offer so much of his fortune to our cause."

Pippa didn't hide her pleasure at the news. "That is wonderful. Adam and Elaine will be so pleased." She stepped closer, and he held the letter out to her. Rather than take it, she stood at his side, resting a hand on his arm to read the paper he held. Her eyes skimmed the fine handwriting, then she looked up at her husband, proud of him. "This is lovely news. Better than what is in my letter, I should think."

"Ah, yes." Myles put the earl's letter and baron's list upon the mantel. Pippa released his arm but did not step away. She chewed her lip, somewhat anxiously, as he unfolded the letter from Mr. Young. "What did our old reclusive neighbor have to say to my young, beautiful wife?" he asked, narrowing his good eye at the paper.

His pretended suspicion drew a grin from her, and Pippa leaned her head against his shoulder.

"Come now. I couldn't possibly entertain a flirtation with any man—not even the Regent himself—when I have you, my love."

"That is most reassuring." Myles put his left arm around her, holding the paper in his right hand toward the lamp. He read silently,

and Pippa stayed tucked up beside him. Content in a way she had never felt before.

After enough time passed for Myles to have read the letter twice, he peered down at her. His good eye narrowed. "This is a proposed price, which feels quite well negotiated, to purchase all of Mr. Young's property. Including the house he lives in, tenant cottages, and the Clock House."

Pippa nodded slowly. "With the understanding that the cleared land in his western fields will be used to build a hospital for the soldiers." Pippa couldn't quite read her husband's expression. "He has great admiration for military men."

"Pippa. This is incredible." Myles looked down at the letter again. "Have you written your brother and sister-in-law yet?"

She shook her head. "I wanted to be certain you approved. If you thought it a poor idea, or too high a price—"

"No. It's wonderful." He put the paper next to his own letter, then turned so he could hold Pippa in both his arms, the embrace comforting. "My wonderful, intelligent, incredible wife. To have the hospital here would be perfect. The country air, the neighborhood itself, would soothe many a battered man's heart."

"Oh, I am so glad you think it is right. I didn't know if I should even speak to Mr. Young without you, but it would have been so disappointing if he had said no." Pippa laid her cheek against his chest. Myles kissed the top of her forehead.

"You did well, love." He kissed her temple. Her cheek. She tilted her chin up. "I am in awe of you."

Her heart skipped with elation. Feeling mischievous, Pippa leaned away from him, the better to glare up at him. "If that is true, husband, then there ought to be less talking and a great deal more kissing."

His smile turned into a wicked grin. "Is that so? I suppose if my lady demands it—"

"She does." Pippa stood on her toes and kissed him before he could utter another word. They had gone too long married without opening their hearts to one another. She was done waiting. From that moment

forward, she intended to enjoy her husband. His embraces, his laughter, his conversation, his kisses. All of it. All of *him*.

Much later that evening, the fire hardly more than embers, Pippa lay in her husband's arms with her cheek against his chest. Her fingers traced the scars on his left side, marveling at what he had gone through. Grateful that she held him now, safe in her embrace.

Epilogue

The young man's hands trembled as he lowered the rose-bush cuttings into the soft earth of the hospital garden. Myles knelt next to him, holding his own spade and preparing the earth for another cutting from his mother's garden. He remained quiet, though he watched the soldier with a gentle eye.

The soldier leaned back, eyeing his work critically. He gazed down the row of the plants, all newly settled into the earth, then looked at Myles. "It's a good sight. Knowing these here bushes will be part of the hospital makes me proud. I didn't think I'd ever work a garden again." The young man expertly pushed himself up with the use of a cane. The lower half of his right leg, just below the knee, was gone.

He'd lost it in a battle halfway around the world. He'd come home to find the estate where his father worked as head-gardener had no use for him. And Myles had found the lad in London, sitting in an alley, an empty bottle of whiskey in his hand.

"You can stay here as long as you like, Smythe," Myles reassured him, voice gentle. Smythe didn't like loud voices or noises. He'd flinched at loud laughter in the dining hall of the hospital the first night he'd been present, then started taking scraps of food to the gardens rather than eat with the other men.

Patients—or wards, as Myles preferred to call them—of the hospital often arrived distrusting and nervous. Some thought they would be put to work until they were sick and useless. Others worried they'd be treated like madmen. But the Gillensfords had hired only sympathetic staff and doctors, most of whom had seen active duty themselves, or lost loved ones to battle. The atmosphere was one of compassion and hope.

They couldn't help everyone. Some men left not long after arriving, too lost in their minds or hearts to accept assistance. Others, thankfully, stayed until they were well enough to return to families or seek employment. Thanks to the patronage of the Gillensfords and people like the Earl of Inglewood and Sir Isaac, those men left with excellent references.

"Papa?"

Myles brushed off his hands and turned around, looking to where his youngest son walked along the brick wall that circled the future rose garden. The little scamp had snuck up on them. Smythe didn't seem to mind. "Yes, Pip?"

Philip, all of five years old, jumped down from the wall. "Mama said to remind you that we have dinner at Ambleside tonight."

"I haven't forgotten. Mr. Smythe, this is my son Philip."

Philip bowed at the waist. "Pleased to meet you, Mr. Smythe."

"And you, Master Philip." Smythe's grin widened. "You best take your father in hand. I think he likes gardening near as much as I do."

Philip didn't hesitate to take Myles's hand in his. "Yes, sir. Come along, Papa. Mama is waiting for us."

Myles chuckled, and he let his son lead him through the growing garden. The walls were new, built of the same brick as the hospital. They passed a fountain with water spilling down its tiers, and two men sitting on its edge quietly talking. One was a doctor, trained at the naval hospital, and the other, their newest patient. A man who had lost his brother, as both served in the same regiment.

Though normally a spirited child, taking after his mother, Philip walked with quiet respect through hedgerows and down the paths of the gardens to the hospital. Near the front doors, a carriage waited.

Two children already inside peered out the windows and waved. A beautiful woman stood on the drive, speaking to the housekeeper of the hospital.

Philip released Myles's hand to run up to his mother. "I found Papa," he said, then darted up into the carriage to sit with his elder sister and brother.

The hospital housekeeper curtsied to Pippa, then to Myles, before going back inside to her duties. Pippa, meanwhile, fixed her gaze on her husband. She raised both eyebrows elegantly, her deep-blue eyes fixed upon him.

"There you are, my wayward husband." She waited for him to bend to kiss her cheek, then she took his hand and gave it a firm squeeze. "We cannot be late to dinner this evening. Your mother has something special planned."

"In honor of our wedding anniversary. I know." Myles handed her up into the carriage. He did not immediately climb inside to join her. Standing there, looking into the carriage, he looked from one side where his three children sat talking excitedly about seeing their cousins to the other, where Pippa fluffed the skirts of her gown. Then she looked up, catching him staring, and a smile crept onto her lovely face. Ten years had passed since their wedding day in London, yet Myles found her more beautiful than ever.

"What are you staring at so intently, sir?" she asked, her lips curving into a smile he found both charming and attractive.

Myles shook his head, then climbed into the carriage to take his seat beside her. He threaded his fingers with hers, holding onto her tightly. Though there were still moments when he could feel the fissures of his heart and soul, scarred as they were, they were not nearly so frequent as the feeling of wholeness he had when he thought of his wife. His children. The hospital he had assisted in building and managing.

Mr. Young's house and tenant buildings had become theirs, purchased by Pippa. The surrounding lands belonged to the Peter Gillensford Hospital for Wounded Men. Doctor Johnson still lived at the Clock House, working closely with Myles to manage the hospital and the needs of its wards.

"I cannot imagine a happier life," Myles murmured at last, looking from his three giggling children to his wife. "And it is all due to you, Pippa."

She shook her head, her gaze softening. "No, darling. It is you we have to thank for this. I thought I would find my happiness in London, at parties and in ballrooms. Not here, in the country."

They still visited London during the Season. But they stayed with Adam and Elaine, or the Earl of Inglewood, and spent more time visiting those who wanted to know about their work at the hospital than they did going about in Society. Of course, Myles always took Pippa to the plays and museums that most suited her fancy.

"Thank you, Pippa." Myles kissed her forehead. "For loving me."

"Always, Myles." She leaned against his shoulder, her head nestled against him and fitting perfectly.

Their daughter, Beth, watched them with a wide grin. "Mama and Papa are going to kiss again." The boys groaned, though he caught the mischief in their gazes as they watched their parents, ready to giggle and protest their parents' displays of affection.

And what could Myles do but oblige them? He kissed his wife, the keeper of his heart. His children, Peter, Beth, and Philip, would grow up as he had. Knowing that their parents loved one another and their children, and would, forever and ever.

IF YOU ENJOYED THIS ROMANCE, MAKE CERTAIN YOU CHECK out Sally Britton's other titles! Never miss Sally's new books by signing up for her newsletter on her website. Or join the fun on Facebook at Sally's Sweet Romance Fans group.

Notes & Acknowledgements

This is the part where I get to explain myself - and thank everyone who helped with this story.

The Royal Hospital Chelsea is an incredible institution, founded in the seventeenth century as a place for British veterans to be cared for from the time their service ended until the end of their lives. It was meant mostly for officers or for those who didn't have jobs, homes, or families to return to after battle. However, the hospital wasn't meant to hold large numbers of pensioners. There was also a naval hospital that performed the same services for members of the Royal Navy—but that also wasn't built for the numbers of men coming in after the war with France.

By 1815, there were 36,757 men collecting military pensions. The hospital could only hold the smallest fraction of this number: 476 residents, plus staff.

There were many private donors who offered military veterans work and places to live, but there were more homeless soldiers standing on street corners in the large towns than we can possibly number. Because most of them were lost, forgotten, and buried in paupers' graves.

The government of England was quite forward thinking, in terms of caring for its veterans, but I wanted to do more for the soldiers in my fictional world. Thus, the Gillensfords came into play with their enormous fortune, inherited by Mrs. Gillensford in my book *His Unexpected Heiress*. What better way to bring back my characters from that story than to show how they used that fortune to help others?

PTSD isn't a modern problem. It's only a modern name. Soldiers

throughout history have returned home from war scarred in more than physical ways. I encourage my readers to look into ways you can thank the soldiers of your country—wherever you may be—for their willingness to sacrifice themselves for others. Write letters. Donate to legitimately helpful organizations. Be kind. Just because the men and women of our military come home, doesn't mean they are finished with the battle for their health and hearts.

Now, to thank those who helped in this latest endeavor! As always, many thanks goes to my editor, the fabulous Jenny Proctor (go read her books, she's an excellent author). Jenny helped me polish this story so you could enjoy it.

I must thank my Regency author friends, though I cannot possibly mention them all. They put up with a lot of questions, late-night writing rants, and me pulling my hair out. But then, that's just what we do for each other.

Thank you to Ashtyn Newbold for designing a gorgeous cover for this story. Her talents are many. Her books are awesome.

And the most gratitude of all goes to my family, for their love, support, and patience. Every book I write is for them. For my husband who inspires the strength and compassion of my heroes, and for my children who remind me what joy and love look like in their purest forms. Thank you, darlings. I love you all.

Also by Sally Britton

CASTLE CLAIRVOIR ROMANCES

Mr. Gardiner and the Governess | *A Companion for the Count* | *Sir Andrew and the Authoress*

HEARTS OF ARIZONA SERIES:

Silver Dollar Duke | *Copper for the Countess*

THE INGLEWOOD SERIES:

Rescuing Lord Inglewood | *Discovering Grace*

Saving Miss Everly | *Engaging Sir Isaac*

Reforming Lord Neil

THE BRANCHES OF LOVE SERIES:

Martha's Patience | *The Social Tutor*

The Gentleman Physician | *His Bluestocking Bride*

The Earl and His Lady | *Miss Devon's Choice*

Courting the Vicar's Daughter | *Penny's Yuletide Wish*

STAND ALONE ROMANCES:

The Captain and Miss Winter | *His Unexpected Heiress*

A Haunting at Havenwood | *Her Unsuitable Match* | *An Unsuitable Suitor*

About the Author

Sally Britton, along with her husband, their four incredible children, their tabby Willow, and their dog named Izzie, live in Oklahoma. So far, they really like it there, even if the family will always consider Texas home.

Sally started writing her first story on her mother's electric typewriter when she was fourteen years old. Reading her way through Jane Austen, Louisa May Alcott, and Lucy Maud Montgomery, Sally decided to write about the complex world of centuries past.

Sally graduated from Brigham Young University in 2007 with a bachelor's in English. She met and married her husband not long after and started working on their happily ever after.

Vincent Van Gogh is attributed with the quote, "What is done in love is done well." Sally has taken that as her motto, writing stories where love is a choice.

All of Sally's published works are available on Amazon.com and you can connect with Sally and sign up for her newsletter on her website, AuthorSallyBritton.com.

Made in the USA
Monee, IL
07 September 2022

13519017R00151